The Black March

Visit the on-line world of The Black March at
www.soldierofthelegion.com

Booklocker.com, Inc.
2007

The Black March

by

Marshall S. Thomas

To Kim Lien

Black March: "Black March" originally referred to the Diaspora of Outworlder and Assidic refugees fleeing System slavery and oppression by seeking new worlds and a new life in the unexplored reaches of the Outvac frontier. Here they discovered and settled scores of uninhabited but primeval virgin worlds in the Crista Cluster. When System forces threatened to intrude, they declared their independence, forming the Confederation of Free Worlds in Year One, CGS. The successful but costly efforts of Fleetcom and the ConFree Legion to drive System DefCorps units from the Outers were also referred to as the "Black March" because of the terrible casualties suffered by our forces during the campaign.

Veltros Training Command—Basic—Intro—History.
  Date: 312 CGS.

PART I

THE FORGE

"I have burnt the book of laws
To serve the Deadman's Cause
As a Soldier of the Legion."

Chant of the Legion

She cares nothing for politics, and knows nothing of history. She makes dinner for her children, and kisses them good night. And she is why we fight.

Why We Fight, Duties of a Legion Trooper

Chapter 1

The Kitchen of the Gods

I awoke to a great light shining directly into my eyes. My body ached, but it was beyond pain, just as I was beyond pain. I propped myself up on my elbows and looked around. I was stunned.

I was clad in my A–suit on a black beach on the shore of a vast, luminous white lava sea that glowed under dark skies. Little volcanic islands rose here and there in the sea, smoking. On the lake's distant shores, great steaming slabs of tortured rock rose almost straight up to an opaque sky. Overhead, evil clouds streaked the sky, clouds with glittering edges of fire, a volcano sky.

The lava lake, this was the lava lake. The surface moved in a slow, relentless flow towards a thunderous roar where the lake dropped over its edge to some hellish conclusion.

The river had spit us out, right into the lake.

All of the 12th had dropped on to Andrion 3, but for us that only meant Squad Beta, CAT 24, Second of the Ship. One under–strength squad, that's all we were; and to us it didn't matter who else was out there. It was only us, against the O's. The mission was clear. The Second had clarified it for us, back on the *Spawn*: "Our mission is to die for the Legion." Well, we were almost there, already. It was a bad drop, the aircar took a horrific hit and we crash–landed in one piece on an island in the middle of a fast–flowing river of molten lava. We quickly cannibalized the aircar, built a cenite raft, and launched ourselves into the river. All of Beta drifted along helplessly as a giant Omni shuttle passed overhead, attacked by Legion fighters. Then our pitiful, brave little raft, the *Beyond*, pitched over the lava falls, and right into Hell.

The squad! I struggled to my feet, dizzy and weak.

There was no sign of the *Beyond*. The earth shuddered and a flight of leathery birds shot past me, screeching. Lightning arced down into the lake. Thunder reverberated. It was a wide lake of bubbling lava, several K across, the far walls misty and indistinct. I was alone, horribly alone, on a beach of black pumice, at the end of the Magic Road. My E was still strapped to my chest, but I knew that would be no

help if the O's found me. With every passing instant, the danger grew—
movement, heat, metal, energy—even in this hellhole, the O's would
find me. I knew it.

Stunned and despairing, I staggered along the beach; the pumice
crackled underneath my boots. Thunder rattled my bones. Lava rain
hissed down from the skies—fire in the heavens, rolling overhead. A
distant volcano was erupting. A geyser of lava boomed out of the lake
near the far shore, lighting up the scene. There was no life except for
the deathbirds wheeling and croaking in the sky. Even the exosegs did
not venture this far—this was a planetary graveyard, fit only for
deathbirds and Legionnaires.

Past a steep rock wall, I found the falls—a golden, glittering torrent
of molten lava shooting over the caldera's face, falling almost straight
down to the lake, awesomely beautiful, hitting the surface with a
continual thunder. How could anyone survive such a fall? How had I?

"Thinker." It was a whisper. I stopped, confused. I could see
nothing, only tortured rocks, black sands and a white-hot lava lake.

"Thinker." Were the Gods mocking me? My faceplate filled with
information and Sweety, my Persist, blinked the designation—Beta
Nine. A form stepped forward from the rocks, an A–suited
Legionnaire—Priestess! She ran into my arms and we met in a clash of
armor, two prehistoric warbeasts in the kitchen of the Gods. She smiled
behind the faceplate, but her cheeks were streaked with tears.

"Priestess! I can hardly believe it!" She was so real that my legs
weakened. A lovely, enchanting girl with black, silky hair and hypnotic
dark eyes.

"Thinker! God, I'm so glad! I'm so glad!" We stood there together,
swaying in each other's arms. "Hold me, Thinker! Hold me! Deadman,
I thank you! I'll never leave the Legion, Thinker—never! I promised
Deadman."

Movement in the rocks. My adrenalin exploded. "Beta Ten,"
Sweety informed me immediately. My heart was in my throat. Priestess
pulled away from me.

"It's Redhawk," she informed me. "He's all right, Thinker—he
saved me! He pulled me from the lake. He saved my life, Thinker!"

We approached Beta Ten—Redhawk. He was lying on his back in
the rocks, almost invisible in his camfax. I leaned over him. He grinned
at me weakly. Sweat covered his forehead, but there was still fire in his

eyes. Strands of sticky long hair were plastered over a pale splotchy face with a scraggly red beard.

"You earthers can't even pilot a raft," he declared. "Should have let me do it—you'd have had a soft landing."

"How ya doin', Redhawk!" I could scarcely contain my joy. We had tangled with the O's air defense units near the ground, and Redhawk, our pilot, had taken one burst right in the cockpit. He had serious multiple injuries—but he was alive.

"The doll took good care of me—think I'll keep her."

"She says you saved her, Redhawk."

"Ha! Funny. I was just hanging on 'cause I didn't want to lose my mag supply."

"We'll get you out of here, man, don't you worry—nothing's going to stop us!"

"Where's the rest of the guys?"

I did not answer him. I stole a glance over to Priestess, and she shook her head glumly. I looked around. Primeval chaos—lightning flickered in the distance. Fire in the sky.

"I suggest you get under cover quickly, Thinker," Sweety said. "This is an extremely dangerous area."

"Where do you suggest we go?" Sweety usually had good ideas. She had been programmed to do my thinking for me.

"We are in the vicinity of the starport. Search the shoreline and the cliffs for an entrance."

"It's good advice. Priestess?" I turned to her.

"What about Redhawk?" she asked me.

"Can you walk, Redhawk?"

"I can fly, Thinker. As high as the sky. But I can't walk. Not any more." He sighed, and looked up at the dark sky.

"I have to stay with him, Thinker," Priestess informed me.

"Tenners, Nine," I replied. "I'm going to recon the shore. Sweety's right, we've got to get under cover. Stay there in the rocks and don't move. I'll be back, I promise—I'll be back!" I reached out and touched her, hand to hand, one last time, and then I turned and crunched away along the pumice shoreline. It was hard to leave her behind like that.

* * *

I could see it from the beach and it turned my blood cold. I waded out into the molten lava and got a grip on a jagged shard of metal and pulled it to shore. There was no mistaking it—it was cenite planking from the deck of the *Beyond*. I had found a tiny fragment of our raft. It had been ripped and torn by tremendous forces. I released my grip and let it fall to the black sands. It was an evil omen, I knew.

"Alert! Lifeform! Muffled signals! Legion camfax! Beta One and Five ahead!" Sweety was on top of it this time. She highlighted their location on my faceplate.

"One! It's Three," I whispered. "Hold your fire!" I scrambled off the narrow beach and up a steep slope of loose rocks. Snow Leopard and Psycho were barely visible, two lumpy volcanic rocks, blending in perfectly with their surroundings. The A–suit camfax is excellent. A lightning flash lit up their faceplates. There was lunacy in Psycho's eyes and a raging fire in Snow Leopard's.

"Go to ground, Trooper," Snow Leopard ordered. "Don't move." I dropped, and froze.

"Good to see you, guys!" I ventured.

"Likewise," Snow Leopard replied. "Report!"

"Nine and Ten survived. They're hiding on the shore, waiting for my return. Ten can't walk."

"What about Six?" Snow Leopard demanded. I could see his face behind the faceplate—deathly pale flesh, a lock of white–blond hair, and hot pink eyes that glowed like coals.

"I haven't seen him."

"Damn. Neither have we. Any equipment saved from the boat?"

"I found a torn–up piece of the deck—that's all."

"We've located a way out. It may be an entrance to the base," Snow Leopard said. "It may be undefended. We've got to get in there quick."

"You have! What about Six?"

"Yeah. What direction did you come from?"

"Uhh...Northeast from here, along the shoreline; the lavafall is back there."

"No sign of Warhound?"

"Nothing from the falls to here."

"I'm not leaving Warhound." It was Psycho. He had been silent up to that point. I don't know why, but his voice brought a chill to my flesh. Psycho was a little guy, but he carried a great big gun. He had short blond hair and pale blue eyes that never seemed to be quite with us.

"You'll do what you're told," Snow Leopard replied. "Nobody's leaving anybody. Three, we've been two K up the shore to the southwest—he's not there."

"Deadman." I tried to deal with the thought. Beta Six—Warhound—was dead. I could hardly comprehend it. He had been with us so long, he was a part of us.

"I'm not leaving Warhound." Psycho just sat there, a child of chaos, clutching his Manlink. I was glad I did not have to deal with Psycho—he was Beta One's headache. A sharp triple explosion boomed overhead. Dark volcanic skies, blotting out the sun.

"Aircraft," Sweety informed me. "Readings unclear."

"Death," Psycho commented. It was so instinctive he probably did not even realize he had said it.

"All right, Thinker," Snow Leopard said. "Let's get Priestess and Redhawk over here."

"I'll need some help with Redhawk."

"We go together. Psycho, get off your ass. Maybe we can spot Warhound on the way. Let's go."

Chapter 2

In the Camp of the O's

Lunchtime on Andrion 3. Try it sometime; you're not likely to forget it. Somebody said it's always lunchtime on Andrion 3, and the trick is to be the diner, and not the dinner. That was Psycho, of course. He was having a good time, on Andrion 3. But he was a homicidal maniac. Frankly, the place bothered me. Psycho said it was because I was a pussy.

Lunchtime! No, you won't find this place in any Galactic Guide to Fine Dining. It was bitterly cold and as black as the back of my soul. The only light was what we brought along, and we were not advertising. We were in the O's unholy world, so close I thought I could hear them breathing, all around us. We were freezing, but not from the cold. I was having a lot of trouble with my body parts. We were all terrified and exhausted. I really believe even Psycho was scared.

Priestess and I lay close together, blocking one end of the corridor. The Omnis had made this place; it was part of their starport, burrowed into the heart of a massive volcano in the tortured primeval terrain of Andrion 3. We had said our initial hello with a barrage of antimats, right on the starport, and it upset the O's. I can tell you the O's get very cranky when they're upset.

Snow Leopard ordered a food break. We hadn't eaten since the drop. I didn't care much for food, but my body did. We were in armor, eating cold comrats from the rat tubes in the helmets. It was an awkward procedure. I saw Nine through her faceplate by the cold muted Iolite of my flash. She was a pale angel, stricken with some terrible, mortal malady. She trembled in the cold and the dark, eyes glazed, lips wet from the food. The Iolite glimmered dully off her black armor. We were all in bad shape. I felt we were inside the beast that was the O. Its metal coils wrapped around us like cenite intestines; dark wet alien metal, a corridor for fools, our own death's road, and I thought it was everything we deserved.

"Deadman!" A hoarse whisper from Psycho. "This is the second best thing I've ever tasted!"

"Blackout!" Snow Leopard whispered back. We were all a little tense. One did not want any noise, so nobody asked Beta Five the obvious question. I already knew the answer—"Your sister!"

Deadman, it was cold! The base was in the heart of a volcano—how could it be so damned cold? My faceplate kept melting the frost. This corridor had once been pressurized and breathable, for both the O's and us, but we had vaporized a good deal of the base, and Andrion 3's poisonous atmosphere was seeping into what was left through shattered walls and airlocks. The corridor we were following burrowed into the rim of the lava lake that sheltered the Omni starport.

A faint light flickered to one side. Black armor, a red faceplate, a pale ghostly face, piercing red eyes, a loose lock of white–blond hair. It was Beta One—Snow Leopard.

"How's the food?" he whispered.

I paused briefly. "It's fine! Haven't you eaten?"

"Not yet. Somebody's got to stay on guard." He cradled his E in his arms, and his helmet continued to track from side to side as he spoke. His faceplate was pitted with scars; we had caught it good when we decarred. I swear, our One was so good he was hardly human.

"I'll take the watch," I said. "Get some eats!"

"Appreciate it," Snow Leopard responded. "Keep scanning, all over. We won't have much warning if it's the O's."

I snapped on max alert, and the screens glowed to life on my faceplate. I knew we would not have much warning if it was the O's. I knew that, for sure. There wouldn't even be time to say our prayers. I cradled my E and slipped off the safeties and set it to xmax. My mouth was all wet and sticky from the food. My body, inside the A–suit, stunk like a corpse. I sipped some water from the helmet tube and focused on Priestess.

She had stopped eating. Her E lay across her legs, and she was using her fieldpak as a cushion for her head. I was exhausted and stunned; and the whole world seemed to focus in on Priestess at that moment. I was overwhelmed with longing and gratitude and regrets when I thought of Priestess. She didn't have to be here at all; she didn't even have to be in the Legion. She had told me about her world, Korkush, a Legion world; it was hard to believe she had ever left such a place. Now she was here, at the very end of Atom's Road, a child of the

Legion, clutching an E instead of a doll, worrying about casualties instead of boyfriends.

Crawling, cold and frightened and hungry, into the domain of the dead, awaiting the evil embrace of the O's. Hopeless—surely it was hopeless. We did not know what had happened to the mission; deceptors were so heavy, we couldn't even hear command overrides. We were on blackout, dead to the world, cowering like dogs, burrowing like worms, twitching at every sound, every movement.

Priestess deserved better, I knew. We would die together, at least. Together. My eyes roamed over the corridor walls. A slimy, gritty, dark cenite metal. Centuries of filth encrusted the deck. I did not like it. It reminded me of the exos. This was an exoseg world, and this corridor stank of exos. Perhaps the Omnis didn't use it any more—well, that was fine with me.

"How ya doin', Redhawk?" A quiet whisper from Psycho, down the corridor.

"Flying...I'm flying, Psycho. Pink clouds, it's really beautiful. I'm all right, earther, big ten on that." Redhawk was completely out of his head. He was our worst casualty. Priestess had kept him alive and stabilized the wounds and patched his armor. Now he was in Neverland, Nineland, courtesy of Priestess's tender armored fingers. Priestess kept us all alive, in Death's Holy Land. Redhawk could not even walk, now. But Priestess would keep him alive, until we all died. Redhawk, Beta Ten—a certified lunatic. He had gotten us almost there, almost down, when it happened.

Psycho was trying to get Redhawk to swallow his rats. I saw them as shadows in cold muted light. Psycho was having trouble—Redhawk's face was flushed and beaded with sweat, and he was hallucinating and didn't want to eat. Priestess had been struggling with him when Psycho pushed her aside and told her to get something to eat herself.

"Priestess—how you doing?" I whispered it.

She stirred slowly and came to life, looking my way. "Thinker...I'm all right. Psycho, how's Redhawk? Is he eating?"

"Yeah, he's eating now," Psycho responded. "He's not all here, though. You sure you didn't give him too much of that stuff?"

"I gave him the correct dosage. His injuries are extensive—we must spare him the pain." Priestess raised her eyes, looking up into the dark.

What was there for her to see? Nothing—there was only nothing, for us all.

Spare him the pain, I thought. Why not the rest of us as well? There was probably a regulation against it somewhere. Pain is good for you— that's what we believed, that was Legion doctrine. Pain is good for you.

The earth trembled, a faint, distant shudder, and suddenly it was as if the corridor was made of jelly and we were moving. We could feel the vibrations in our bones, a deep deep lava heartbeat. Specks of dirt floated down from the roof, and we all froze, in the grip of the Gods, awaiting our fate.

It slowed, and stopped. Once again it was solid rock, all around us. Adrenalin, still flooding my veins. Terror, cold and exhausted. How much more? Deadman, how much more?

"Earthquake. Scut." Five sounded disappointed.

"It's the lake," One informed us. "The whole starport is floating under the lava, and the lava is moving all around it—and through it. The lava must be busting up their starport. We dropped two antis right into the lake—it's got to be an unholy mess by now."

"Nice job," Psycho responded. "How come the O can build a starport like that, when we can't?" Psycho was short and wiry, pale blue eyes and a smooth, child's face. But if you looked closely into his eyes, you could see there was something wrong.

"I'm sure Merlin could explain it," One replied wearily, "but I can't." Merlin was Beta Four, our science wizard.

"Well, let's go back to Atom and ask him." Psycho was an incurable little smart–ass.

"Fine idea," Snow Leopard said. "You got an ops plan that will accomplish that, you let me know." It was indeed a fine idea. Beta Four had all the answers, but he had lost his legs in the Coldmark raid, and he was growing a new pair back on Atom. Atom was all we wanted, just to see Atom, again. Atom's Road was a holy place to us, our only home in a hostile galaxy. Atom held Beta Four; and Beta Eight, Dragon; another casualty from Coldmark. Deadman, I missed them! Merlin was a genius—we could sure use his insight here! And Dragon—he was like a force of nature, he was simply unstoppable. I'd rather have Dragon covering my back than anyone I knew, but Dragon was not with us either. Serious internal injuries, and a clenched fist, to show he'd pull through. There was not much left of Beta now—Two

and Seven—Coolhand and Ironman—were also back on Atom, in the
Body Shop. Coolhand was my blood brother, from Providence and
Hell. It was not the same without his calm, faint smile. I wondered how
Ironman was. We all had a soft spot for Ironman, the Kid. But he was
long gone now—Two and Four and Seven and Eight were only
memories, here in the guts of the beast. Whatever was to happen here
would depend entirely on us: our leader Beta One, warname Snow
Leopard; our Manlink Beta Five, warname Psycho; our medic Beta
Nine, warname Priestess; our pilot Beta Ten, warname Redhawk; and
yours truly Beta Three, warname Thinker, the Fool, the Fatalist. Lastly
was Beta Six, Warhound, now missing in action. Six soldiers, out for a
walk in the dark. We were still on Atom's Road; believe me, we all
knew that.

Priestess sat up, her hands moving against the corridor wall. A faint
reflection from a cold knife. Now what?

"What're you doing, Priestess?" She did not answer. I moved
closer. Her pale face held no emotion. She was scratching something
into the dark cenite metal of the corridor wall with her cold knife. I
moved the lolite closer. It was a Legion cross, spidery silver lines cut
into the black grime of the centuries. She wrote her lover's name under
the cross: 12/22.

She put away the knife, and contemplated her handiwork calmly. I
wondered if Beta Nine was going over the edge. I pondered the cross.
12/22, the 12th of the 22nd, the 12th Colonial Expeditionary Regiment of
the 22nd Legion. The Black 12th, we called it, and the 22nd was the
Black Legion, the Rimguard. The Legion was Priestess's lover, and my
rival.

She always had a Legion cross on the wall in her quarters. I
wondered about that, but I thought it a harmless eccentricity. Priestess
was a believer, I knew. And here, in the cold jaws of death, she still
believed. I took a deep breath.

"You planning to be here long, Priestess?" I whispered.

She slowly turned her head and focused on me with a sad little
smile. "No, Thinker...no, I hope not. I just wanted to show we had been
here."

"Who do you think is going to see it?"

She sighed wearily, and let her eyes stray back to the cross. "It
doesn't matter, Thinker—it doesn't matter. Probably nobody. But it

means we were here. It shows we came this far. This far, at least, into the camp of the O's."

Into the camp of the O's. Lord, that we were! The Twenty-second's motto was "Deliver us from Evil," only in the Legion chant, it was "I will deliver us from Evil." Well, this was it, all right; the O's were all the Evil you could ever want, and it was up to us to do the delivering. It was all up to us—one under–strength squad, Beta of CAT 24, Second of the Ship, Atom's Road, 12th CER, 22nd Legion. And maybe Beta Nine was right; why shouldn't we mark this place with our sign? It might be our epitaph. But even if we were never heard of again, at least we knew we had done it. Perhaps a million stellar years in the future, an intrepid band of brave archaeologists would come probing into a cold, dead world; full of extinct volcanoes and dead lava seas; and billions of bizarre, petrified, monstrous fossils; and come across our Legion cross and the notation: 12/22. What would they think? What sort of lunacy, they would wonder, could have drawn intelligent life to such a violent, savage, primeval world?

What sort of lunacy, indeed? The Second had stated it clearly, back on the *Spawn*. He had put it in terms we could easily understand. The mission was to die, for the Legion. What else did we need? It was as good an explanation as any.

My faceplate lit up. "Alert! Movement!" It was Sweety's clear, metallic voice, right in my ears. My adrenalin exploded.

"Don't move," I hissed. The visible lights vanished, but to me, it was as clear as daylight, a cold green invisible light, my faceplate's darksight illuminating the corridor with its magical glow.

"Life form!" Sweety whispered in my ear. A red glow on my faceplate, outlining the target somewhere down tunnel. "Exoseg Gigantic, species unknown. Advancing as marked."

"Nobody move!" I repeated. "It's an exo—I've got it on scope."

"Scut!" Psycho cursed. "Scut!"

"No movement!" Snow Leopard ordered. "Not a muscle! Thinker, try biobloc. If that doesn't work, go to flame. No energy weapons! The rest of you, as soon as Thinker fires, attack, but until then don't move a frac!" Exos could see in the dark and they could spot the slightest movement. If nobody moved, they would not detect us. I was positively relieved it was only an exoseg. Only an exoseg! The creature could tear us all to shreds and have us for breakfast, armor and all, but they were a lot more fun than the O's—that was a definite ten.

"Species unknown! Exoseg advancing! Recommend no movement!" Sweety was absolutely right. The O had already demonstrated their mastery over these nasty exoseg buggers, and we had no way of knowing what kind of exo this was; we could not let it escape. I was frozen inside my suit, on my knees, the E in my arms. Priestess was on the deck before me.

"One, can we forget the biobloc?" I asked. "Let me go to flame right away." We all know the biobloc would probably not work, and it might spark the creature into fleeing. We did not dare try laser, or xmax. We were afraid the O would detect it—we did not know their capabilities.

"Negative, Three. Do biobloc, then flame." One knows best, kiddies!

"Exoseg Gigantic approaching, species unknown!" Sweety had it on scope. I could see it vaguely now, a green blur twitching on my faceplate.

"Thinker, you earther, don't screw this up!" Psycho was angry, probably because he wanted the exo himself. I ignored him.

"Blackout, Five," One ordered. One put up with Psycho only because the little lunatic was totally fearless in combat and a genius with his Manlink. He had saved us on Andrion 2, even I had to admit.

"Exoseg within range! Biobloc is set!" Sweety had it under control. I could see the exoseg clearly now, magnified on my faceplate. A grotesque bulbous head, glistening with compound eyes, topped with a mass of spiky, coarse bristles. Gaping, pincered jaws; long antennae, trembling, probing. Flashing black forelegs, snapping out in front of it. Exoseg Gigantic, species unknown. These were the natives of Andrion 3, and this one had probably found its way in from the outside after we did the starport. On the other hand, it could be a watchdog.

I was frozen with terror, but it did not matter. By this time, we could all deal with terror. I watched the creature twitch, coming closer and closer. I could hear it now, clicking and snapping. I raised the E and fired on biobloc. Biobloc was soundless. The creature stopped, stunned.

"Firing biobloc!" I informed the squad through clenched teeth. "No effect!"

"Thinker, give it a few more fracs!" A frantic scrambling, all around me, armor clashing against armor. I stood up and stepped over Priestess and walked forward, into the green, and that mindless horror filled the tunnel ahead of me—Deadman, it was big! I watched myself as if from far away, ice cold and paralyzed. My body functioned perfectly. I leaned into the biobloc, the E at my shoulder, aiming right at the exo's massive head. The creature twitched once, then the antennae cracked forward and the forelegs snapped to life. It came straight at me, berserk. My very own death, my image glowing in every facet of those dead compound eyes; multiman, microman, a whole squad of Thinkers, cold black armor and winking red faceplates.

I fired and the corridor exploded in a thunderous boom and a great rolling ball of fire hit the exo with a mighty fist of flame, enveloping it immediately in spitting, blue–hot sheets of sticky, burning gas. The exoseg exploded in flames, stopped in its tracks; now burning brightly, an obscene, fiery monstrosity, doing a dance of death. I took a few more steps, hypnotized. I had the E on autoflame and I directed the stream right at its awful head. It melted like wax right before my eyes. The corridor walls glowed white–hot; the filth spitting and burning; my black armor now glowing white in waves of superheated air, a great roar in my ears; the exoseg's massive legs curling and melting, burnt black, the entire exoskeleton one great sheet of flame.

I stopped. I released the trigger, and raised the E. I stood in a river of fire. Flames licked up my A–suit; and the corridor walls were afire and the massive exo burned like paper, crackling and spitting sparks, its insides popping open, its head all burnt and melted, evil greasy smoke rolling over me. I was frozen, hypnotized. I felt nothing except a cold, mute terror. Psycho appeared beside me, the barrel of his Manlink probing ahead of him. "Well, scut," he said. "You didn't leave much, did you?"

I did not answer. I watched the exoseg die. Why in the world had I advanced on it like that? Lunacy. Sheer lunacy. I was losing it. We were all losing it, in the Camp of the O's.

"Good work, Thinker," Snow Leopard said.

"Override encoded transmission from Command," Sweety interrupted. "I have recorded, amplified, filtered, and repeated." At last! We were all getting the same report, each from our own Tacmods.

The burst was almost inaudible in the howling roar of the deceptors. I strained to hear it, closing my eyes for better concentration. "...obtain

objectives..." a piercing shriek drowned it out, then it warbled back in.
"...by the magma. All units..." Another ear–shattering screech. Then a
few more words, very faint. "...the lower levels. Maintain blackout
but..." inaudible, drowned out in a rushing blast of static.

"What does it mean, Snow Leopard?" I asked.

"Hard to tell, Thinker. Something's happening in the lower levels of
the base, or the starport, or whatever is down there. Sounds like it
involves magma. Maybe the base is being torn apart. But whether we're
supposed to go further in, or get out, it's not clear."

"So what do we do?"

"We continue the mission. This corridor leads somewhere, and
that's where we're going. We're inside the rim of the caldera and not
far from the edge. I want that starport. That's our mission. Priestess,
you're in charge of Redhawk. Let's go." Snow Leopard was right next
to me. I saw him clearly through his faceplate—his square cut, chunky
face was deathly pale, and blue veins were throbbing faintly at his
temples. His pink eyes glowed, eyes from another world. I had been
close to him once, but now he was lost to us all. Our One was always
decisive. I'm glad he was, because I sure as hell wasn't.

We set off, Priestess pulling Redhawk in a jury–rigged trav we had
fashioned as a stretcher. Redhawk was mercifully unconscious. The
dead exoseg glowed as we passed it, still faintly burning. Dying flames
licked here and there on the walls, and wisps of dirty smoke drifted past
us. It was dead quiet. There had been no reaction to our killing of the
exoseg.

It appeared the Omnis did not know we were there.

Chapter 3

The Souls of the Dead

"All right, Beta—you know the drill," Snow Leopard said quietly. "I'm in first, left—Three next, right. Cover, advance; cover, advance. Five next, Manlink, left. Nine is backup." He looked back at us. We were all in position, sprawled motionless among the rocks behind our weapons, clinging to the near–vertical cliff like lizards. The entrance was just ahead and above, on a steep slope. It was a black, gaping hole in the cliff face. Warped cenite beams and a tangle of cables dangled from the hole. An anti had touched the caldera here, sheering off megatons of rock and exposing a hardsited, camfaxed entryway leading from the shore of the lava lake. Our corridor had been split in two, ending in a sheer drop, but it had led right to the entryway. The lake glowed off to one side and a fiery sky rolled overhead. We were exposed to whoever—or whatever—might be looking.

"E's on flame," Snow Leopard added. "I want to avoid laser, vac or x—and biobloc won't help us if they're O's. Five, give us smoke."

Psycho aimed carefully, and a smoker exploded with a faint pop off to the left of the entrance. My adrenalin count went up. The wind whipped the smoke over the entrance, obscuring it from view. My faceplate switched to darksight, and I could see it again. The earth rumbled. Snow Leopard scrambled to his feet and up the slope, then picked his way through a tangled mass of wreckage and was suddenly gone, into the dark. I exploded to my feet and charged up the slope and into a nightmare tangle of shattered bulkheads, melted cenite beams, and shredded decking. Snow Leopard lay motionless on his belly near the left wall. I went to ground on the right behind a massive chunk of metal, my E pointed down tunnel. It was dark and quiet.

"One advancing." Snow Leopard was off; I covered him. Psycho stepped into the tunnel in a puff of smoke. I was sweating. There was no sign of life. Snow Leopard stopped, again in position on the left. I advanced, a low rush, passing Snow Leopard by, breathing hard, my E at the ready. I slid to a stop by a pile of wreckage. My tacmod was silent. A power strip ran overhead on one wall, and dead light panels lined the ceiling. There was an airlock ahead on the left. It was partially open, a dead black hole. I suddenly realized this was not an Omni installation—it was human. Systies!

"Open airlock," I hissed. "This is a Systie base!" There was Inter lettering on the power strip: DANGER NUKEFLOW 22TVF, and smaller letters: ERIDOS POWER SYSTEMS. I could make out something on the airlock too: EMERGENCY LOCK—1T AT—DANGER AUTOACT—KEEP DOOR CLEAR.

"Five, up," Snow Leopard ordered.

"What's it look like, Sweety?" I asked my tacmod.

"No life, Thinker. I detect organic matter. Bodies—humans."

"Nothing alive?"

"Negative life."

"You got that, One?"

"Smoke, Five." Normally it would have been deceptors, but normality did not apply to this place. Deceptors were too damned noisy.

Psycho fired right into the doorway and the smoke exploded violently out into our corridor. Snow Leopard and I burst in through an airlock partially blocked with wreckage, our fingers twitching on flame. We skidded to a stop in a room swirling with thick black smoke. It didn't bother us at all. There were bodies everywhere. Nothing moved. Psycho popped in the door, Manlink at the ready. We froze. It was dead quiet but for the hissing of the smoke. There were plenty of rooms and corridors ahead of us. We moved forward, scanning every room. My heart pounded, adrenalin surged, sweat trickled down my temples. We found only bodies, dead Systies, not even in armor. They had been caught completely off guard.

* * *

"Let's get these stiffs out of here." As the smoke slowly drifted out the airlock, it became clear what had happened. The outer airlock, at the end of the corridor closest to the lava lake, had been shattered in microfracs by our antimat. An explosion of wreckage had shot down the corridor at supersonic speed; one jagged chunk of cenite planking had lodged in the doorway of the second airlock, two emergency doors which should have autoacted instantly to save the installation. But the doors slammed up against cenite metal that blocked the doorway, and all within had died instantly as Andrion 3's poisonous atmosphere rushed in. The twisted slice of cenite, still lodged in the airlock, put a chill to my blood. What a stupid way to die.

Corpses were sprawled across the deck, faces swollen purple in death, limbs already stiff. They were all in litesuits, DefCorps duty uniforms. Some of them had been seated before a large control panel, monitoring the instruments. The first room was the duty station; the living quarters were beyond. There were dead in there, too—in the cubicles and the mess hall and the ex room and the store room. It looked like a neat little world the Systies had made for themselves here, in the Camp of the O's, but it had certainly ended abruptly.

"Move it, Thinker. Get that one." We dragged them outside, into the corridor. I reached down for the corpse.

A female, her swollen face contorted in horror, frozen hands clawing at nothing. A sudden end to her life. I got ahold of her tunic and dragged her through the airlock.

"Give me a hand here." Psycho was helping Priestess carry Redhawk into the room. There was a growing line of dead out in the corridor. A grisly, obscene spectacle. There must have been twenty of them, but I did not have the heart to count.

"Redhawk, can you sit up?" Snow Leopard stood by the control panel, puzzling it out. There were several huge, dead screens and an elaborate series of modules.

"Yeah...Priestess, honey, can you get me in that seat?" I helped Priestess ease Redhawk into the seat. We were all fully suited up, and still jumpy. Redhawk was the closest thing we had to Merlin. He was a tech's tech, and he would understand the panel.

"Nothing outside, Priestess?"

"Negative." She sounded tired.

"We're not leaving without Warhound."

"I know."

"So what is it, Redhawk?" Snow Leopard asked.

Psycho had stationed himself by the open airlock with his Manlink. All the bodies we could find were now outside. Our smoke still hung in the air and the atmosphere of violence and death was palpable. Somebody's dox mug lay on the floor in a blizzard of flimsy printouts and plastic manuals, a pitiful reminder of the lives that had so suddenly ended here.

"Aircars. Damn, this is an aircar control center!" Redhawk was astounded.

"Good," Snow Leopard said calmly. "That's good! Where are the aircars?"

"Don't know—we've got to activate power. Everything's down."

"How do we do that?"

"Give me a little time."

"We've got to do it very, very quietly. We can't tap into any outside power—you understand?"

"Sure, sure—they'll have emergency power. Deadman!" Redhawk gripped the edge of the console with his armored fingers. "Priestess, I need a bit more of your magic." Priestess gave him a biotic charge, slipping the tip into an access port on his A–suit.

"Thinker, Psyco—get that wreckage out of the airlock," Snow Leopard ordered. "I want to seal the lock and blow the at, and get us something we can breathe in here."

I had been lost in dreams, thinking of the Systies who had lived and worked here. It was almost unbelievable, knowing what we knew of the Omnis. How had the Systies coexisted with them? Even as allies, it was hard to believe.

Five and I removed the wreckage and dumped it in the corridor. The doors remained stuck in place. Everything here was dead, dead and frozen in one catastrophic instant of time.

"I want the absolute minimum power we need to breathe, and run these systems."

"That's a ten."

"How about that airlock?"

"I can close it manually," I replied. "The control's right here." I opened the access port and unfolded the manual crank. We were certainly back to basics, but it turned easily and the airlock doors began to move. As I cranked away, I closed my eyes and prayed for the souls of all who had died here. I was not certain to whom I was praying, and I had no sympathy for Systies and certainly none for Systies who had betrayed humanity by aligning themselves with the O's. But I prayed for them anyway. What could they have been doing here? How could they have lived with the O's? Were they willingly betraying their own race, their own species? Did they realize the enormity of what they were doing?

* * *

"Airlock doors secure."

"Power on. Emergency ventilation activated. Stand by."

The dead air within the installation stirred. The papers on the floor suddenly fluttered. The ceiling panels flickered and flashed on, illuminating us with a cold white light. The control panel came to life, reds and blues and greens glowing calmly, as if all was well—but all was not well, not at all.

"Confirm we're on blackout systems," Redhawk said. "No link to outside power sources. Commo all down..."

"Keep it that way," Snow Leopard ordered. "Tenners. Confirm the installation is airtight. Pressure building..."

The deck was filthy underfoot, sticky and gritty. We had dragged the dead through here. I bent down and picked up the dox mug. It bore the insignia of the 15th DefCorps—the same bunch we had run into on Andrion 2. I put it aside and recovered a manual from the deck— OPERATING INSTRUCTIONS—2200 LOCKON—MODE COMMANDS— fascinating stuff. I dropped it back onto the deck.

"Redhawk, can you bring the screens up? Will it attract any attention?" Snow Leopard was looking over the controls carefully.

"I can and it shouldn't. This installation is designed to function effectively on full blackout. And we're on emergency power. Just a frac." Redhawk turned to the task.

"According to the panel, the main screen should give us an overall view of the lake—can you confirm that?"

"Tenners," Redhawk responded. "Port visuals—that should be the starport. External, internal—Deadman!"

"Don't touch the internal! Not yet, anyway."

"Deadman! We'll be able to see everything!"

"Go slow! Nice and easy, or they'll be on us in a flash!"

"That's a big ten! Deadman!"

A dull explosion thundered through the walls. The lights flickered and the deck trembled. Sharp vibrations echoed up through our boots. We looked around, but there was nothing to see.

"What was that?"

"Antimat," Sweety replied calmly.

"Deadman. Somebody's still out there."

Psycho squatted by the airlock, checking his Manlink. Priestess appeared in the doorway to the living quarters. She had a pocket–sized datapak in one hand. She passed it to me, wordlessly. OPSKED, it was entitled—15 DefCorps—Starfleet Commandos—Property of United System Alliance—Responsible Officer—Lt. Jeffleigh Karmion.

"Fifty percent pressure," Redhawk noted. "Atmix confirmed."

Priestess sat down, exhausted, and leaned against a wall. I ran through the contents of the datapak. The entire opsked was classified— SECRET SYSRES NOCIV DEFOR DEFCON. The first few docs were mission orders for Karmion's unit—Hqs Company, Aircar Squadron 303, 4th Commandos, 15 DefCorps. I glanced through the memos; there were several references to an Oplan Gold.

"I've got the external screen psyched. I think," Redhawk said.

"Don't do anything until you're sure," Snow Leopard replied.

The miscellaneous data was a lot more extensive than it should have been, I noted. I went into it. It wanted a password.

"Priestess, did you get into the miscellaneous?"

"Yes. That's the interesting part. The password is 'Jenny'."

"Now how did you do that?"

"There's a solid of his girl on his desk. And her name. It was just a guess—he was not very imaginative."

I punched in Jenny and the data came up on the screen.

It was a journal—the personal journal of Jeffleigh Karmion.

"Main screen coming on," Redhawk reported.

I raised my eyes. It glowed to life suddenly, taking our breath away.

The entire lake was there, massive black slopes glittering with pumice, cloaked in smoke, the great incandescent, golden lake of lava bubbling and hissing, grinding along slowly, black smoky clouds close overhead, the wind tracing eerie patterns on the surface of the lava. Lightning arced down from the clouds, striking the lake. A spidery complex of nav lines overlay the image, invisible highways in the sky, and a status box revealed there were no aircars in sight.

"Where are the aircars?" Redhawk asked himself.

"Never mind the aircars," Snow Leopard replied. "We use this screen to find Warhound. Tell me what it can do."

"Go to it, One," Psycho said dreamily. "Go to it. We find

Warhound! That's our mission." He looked over his Manlink, holding it up to the light. Sometimes I thought Psycho was just as dangerous to us as to the enemy. But he had held together so far, I had to admit.

I turned my attention back to the datapak, browsing through the entries. It quickly became apparent that Karmion had some problems with the mission.

> '1444/02/01 SS. They awarded us a unit citation
> today. What reeking hypocrisy. A unit citation, for
> Vulcan Station. Conspicuous prudence, above and
> beyond. A unit citation awarded to slaves by
> cowards, from a very safe distance away. A
> justification for their own crimes. Why don't our
> leaders present the citation in person? It's for them,
> not for us. It's a unit citation for the System. This
> makes us physically sick. We'd rather die with
> what's left of our honor than live like this.'

"Full pressure," Redhawk announced. "Air is pure, full normal. Take a bite!"

Snow Leopard straightened up before the control panel. "I'll try it." He cracked the visor of his faceplate open and took a breath. We all watched him silently.

"Tastes fine to me," Snow Leopard concluded. "I'll take first watch—the rest of you can off helmets, but keep them within reach. Have we got water in the lines?"

"That's a ten."

"All right, one at a time can wash up in the heads. One at a time. Get it all done, 'cause we're not staying long." Snow Leopard closed his visor again and turned back to the control panel.

"Redhawk," Priestess said, "I want you naked. I've got to work on your wounds. You should be first in the shower." We all laughed at Priestess's comment. When it came to her medical duties, Nine was so serious she sometimes did not seem quite real.

"A tempting offer, Priestess," Redhawk responded. "But I'm too damned busy right now. Why don't you go first, and call me when you finish. Oh, and, uh...I want you naked, too."

We popped our helmets, still laughing at Priestess's remark. The air stunk, a strange heady perfume, but we knew it was really us who stunk. I removed my helmet and hooked it on my u–belt. The air lanced through my nostrils and mouth like fire. My eyes stung and watered. We were all gasping, taking deep breaths. I looked at the others and grinned.

Psycho was a mutant werewolf with yellow fangs and glittering lunatic eyes. Redhawk was a savage hairy gargoyle, bleeding and covered with slime. Priestess was a vaguely female zombie, dead pale splotchy skin and cold glazed eyes and dirty matted hair. Snow Leopard was still in helmet so we could not see him. I did not want to know what I looked like but judging by the others, I imagined I had lost my dashing good looks.

"Psycho, stay here," Snow Leopard ordered. "We're going to use this screen to search for Warhound. Thinker, accompany Priestess and secure the area while she cleans up. Redhawk, you're next after Priestess. Now, tell me how you work the zoom. I want to search every fraction of this crater for Warhound."

I accompanied Priestess into the living quarters. The lights were on and the floor was sticky. Priestess chose a cube at random. The door was open, as we had thoroughly searched the area. It was even smaller than a Legion cube—there was barely room to turn around. The head was a tiny closet with a toilet, sink, and shower. Priestess tossed her helmet and E on the bed. She reached into the head and hit the shower tab. The line coughed once and then a needle spray of water hissed steadily from the nozzle. It was so lovely a thrill ran over my skin.

"Help me out of this A–suit, Thinker. Lord, I stink like a cesspool. Look at that—soap! Towels! Oh, save me!" I helped her unlink. She was sticky with sweat and trembling with anticipation.

"Wait for me, Thinker—don't go. I may be awhile," she said.

"I'll be right here," I replied, taking a position in the doorway to the cube. Priestess flashed me a weary smile and stepped into the head and the door slid shut.

I expected a long wait. Fortunately I had some good reading material. I sat in the doorway, my E strapped to my chest, and read through the next entry in the datapak.

"1444/02/07 SS—Frantic activity, and all of it
correct, all by the regs. We are doing terrific work,
but we keep asking ourself how this benefits the
System. We have concluded that the System wants
the status quo maintained in this sector. And it is

willing to sacrifice us for the status quo. But surely
STRATCOM realizes that our activities here are not
maintaining the status quo—to the contrary, as soon
as these creatures are ready, the System will have to
deal with its monstrous creation.
"So what is our mission? It is to strengthen the V
until we are no further threat to them. It is to betray
our own, in the name of galactic peace. We are
Peacemakers, they tell us, holding the Dogs of War
at bay. But the dogs are growing stronger, for we
feed them with our flesh and blood.
Soon they will tear out our throats. Why are we
here? We must be cursed by the Gods!"

"Well, I don't see a thing." It was Redhawk, muttering to himself.
"Not a sign of life!" Snow Leopard, in awe. "This is really strange."
"He's out there," Psycho declared. "He's out there somewhere."
They were searching for Warhound on the screen. I felt sick inside.
How could he have survived? It was a miracle that any of us did. How
could we hope for more?

We'd have spotted him by now if he had survived. No, Warhound
was gone—at the bottom of the lava. A black depression settled over
me. Beta Six, Warhound—he was as faithful as a dog. He was young
and trusting, always did what he was told, a good and dependable
soldier of the Legion. How could it end like this? He had his whole
immortal life ahead of him. He had a crush on Gamma Five, Scrapper,
but she didn't like him. He'd tell me his troubles, and I'd give him
advice. And now he was gone. He was a friend; I should have told him
how I felt, but we never did that in the Legion. Now I regretted it. I
gazed blankly at the datapak. I had been reading it without thought.

"...death, death, death! Every day, hovering right
outside. Black ships, and black skies. Lunacy! To
think we have any control over events, or that we are
accomplishing anything at all, except for the V.
Lunacy! We are slaves, trapped and terrified.
Abandoned, by STRATCOM, by the System itself.
We are still useful, we know, to the V, but the
instant that ends, we will all die like bacteria. The
Old Man is already gone. It called a meeting—fool!

We told it not to do so, but it insisted, and now it's
gone. A troublesome bacteria. That was five full
days ago, and we just huddle here, terrified. We
don't even dare ask about it. The V can have us for
lunch, whenever they want."

The V—that was Systie slang for the O. We called them the Omnis.
The System called them the Variants. It would never have occurred to
the Legion to try and communicate with the O—except with antimats.
But then we had a lot more experience fighting the Omnis than the
System did. It was becoming increasingly clear why that was—the
Systies had done a deal with the O's, a dirty, secret deal, right here on
Andrion 3. And the unitium mines on Andrion 2 were part of it.
Genetic suicide, for our species—death to the children! I got dizzy just
thinking about it.

"Thinker." The door to the head slid open. Priestess posed in the
doorway, completely naked, soapsuds glistening all over her heavenly
body, long dark hair clean and wet, her skin glowing with life,
sparkling angel eyes and a pink tongue teasing me behind even white
teeth. Her breasts were perfect, rosy pink nipples, long slim lovely legs
knocking my eyes out. The shower was still on behind her. She
pirouetted once, showing me her petite, tender rear, smiling back over
her shoulder. I dropped the datacase and scrambled violently to my
feet, armor ringing against the door frame.

Nine giggled once and disappeared as the door to the head slid shut
abruptly. I hurled myself against it.

"Priestess! Open up! Open up!" I pounded on the door with my
armored fists, leaving dents in the metal.

"What's wrong, Thinker? Answer up!" It was Snow Leopard,
alerted by my shouts.

"Uhh...nothing!" I answered quickly. "Nothing at all! It's all right—
uh, it's nothing."

"Well, keep it down! And let us know when Priestess is through."

"Right! Right." I leaned against the door to the head, breathing
hard. On the other side was the most lovely creature in the galaxy.

"Priestess..." I whispered feverishly. "Open up. Please?"

"No! You're all smelly. I just cleaned up!" She giggled again.

"Are you trying to torture me, Priestess?" My blood raced. "What
did you do that for?"

"Didn't you like it?" She sounded disappointed.

"Yes! Yes, oh yes, I liked it! It's just, uh, well—let me in. All right?"

"Don't be silly! We don't have time to play! Besides, I have a date already—with Redhawk. Remember?"

"Priestess, why are you doing this to me?" I was so frustrated I trembled.

"I just wanted to remind you what you're missing," she replied through the door. "If we survive this place, I'm yours, Three. I hope you appreciate me."

* * *

"All right, listen up." Beta One never had to raise his voice to get our attention. We gathered around the main panel of the aircar control center. We had all cleaned up, and Priestess had prepped Redhawk's wounds. Now we were all back in our stinking A–suits helmets still off, E's within easy reach. We had turned the place upside down looking for clues to what the Systies were doing there, and we'd found plenty, stacks of datapaks and datacards and minicards full of info for the analysts to ponder, should we ever return. We were stuffing our faces with Systie rats, hot food and cold drinks, and loving every frac. We had raided their kitchen, and the working surfaces of the control panel were littered with steaming meal trays and icy cans of soft drinks.

I felt almost human.

The chilling spectacle of the lava lake stretched out before us on the main screen. A brilliant explosion of lava boomed out of the luminous golden lake even as we watched. A faint shudder rattled the walls. The skies were dark and smoky, and fires burned on black mountain ranges in the hazy distance. We could hear a faint howling.

"We've used the screen to search the entire area for Warhound," One informed us bleakly. "We haven't found him." We greeted the news in silence. One appeared calm and rational, in icy control. His white–blond hair was clean and wet, and blue veins throbbed on his pale flesh. His pink eyes were cold and distant. "The screen gave us the best possible chance at finding him. It appears that he's not there. I believe we have to conclude it is likely he's at the bottom of the lake."

"We're not there, either," Psycho pointed out quietly. "But that doesn't mean we're at the bottom of the lake."

"That's right, Snow Leopard," I added. "He could be under cover somewhere. Our camfax is damned good, and there are plenty of nooks and crannies out there. It would be only natural for him to get under cover."

"Nevertheless," he said, "We have to proceed on the assumption that he's gone. Unless we go to full power, there's nothing further we can do to find him. And if we go to full power, we're dead. Now, I can promise you we are going to go to full power, as our final effort to locate Beta Six. But the time for that has not yet arrived. First, we have a mission to accomplish. And we can't do that if we're dead."

We pondered that without comment. One was right—what else could we do? Chances were high that Six was dead. And if we stayed in the neighborhood much longer, we would be, too.

"We have to move out," One concluded, "as rapidly as possible. This is an extremely dangerous area. I consider it a miracle that we're still alive. Our antis fell right here. This was our primary target. Now, I've been getting fragments of info on the command channel, but it's so throughly shot by deceptors that I can't tell exactly what's happening. One thing I can tell, though—the assault is still underway. There are Legion units fighting their way through the Omni base, and that means they are inside the base, and under the lava. That's where we should be. Ten, report."

"Right," Redhawk responded. "The aircar station is located about sixty mikes below us. There are two personnel elevators and a freight elevator that should get us there. All still functional. Air and pressure full normal as well." His wild eyes flickered over the readings, shaggy red hair hanging over one eye. "There are two aircars on–site, but neither is in ready status."

"Why not?" Snow Leopard asked.

"Don't know," Redhawk replied. "I can probably get a status report if you give me a little more time."

"There's only two aircars?"

"The other bays are all empty."

Aircars! My blood stirred; we could all feel it. Priestess put down her drink. Psycho raised his head and blinked expressionless eyes.

"Can you get us a visual?"

"Affirmative."

"Not yet! Is this aircar garage a part of the starport?"

"That's a twelve. The launching ports open in the side of the caldera, right into the air, slightly above the level of the lake. The actual starport—or what's left of it—is below the lake, and launches of major spacecraft are probably made through a central launch tube that breaks surface when necessary. Landings would be the same routine. That's my conjecture." He scratched at his scruffy beard.

"And the starport—you can get me an internal visual of that, as well?"

"Ten high, Beta. Sure looks like it."

That one would knock us on our asses, I knew. An internal visual, on an Omni starport! The aircar control center was a Systie installation, but nobody—nobody—had ever seen the inside of an O starport, and lived to tell about it. My adrenalin was going again. I picked up a cold juice, and tried to get it to my lips without spilling any. It felt as if my muscles were just barely connected.

The datapak was on the console before me. My eyes strayed to the next entry.

> "1444/03/11 SS—We are doomed. We share it with no one, but we know it. Death stares us in the face, every morning. Our rotation times have come and gone, and still STRATCOM is on the screen making promises. The others believe. They have to believe, for the sake of sanity. But we no longer believe. Show your faces here, STRATCOM, and we'll believe you.
>
> "Soldiers of Peace. We are slaves. We saw the V only once, and that was enough. Our whole body stopped functioning. At first we thought they were trying to kill us, but later we decided they were just saying hello. We will never recover."

Chapter 4

Under Strange Stars

Every once in awhile, I get so much adrenalin in my system that I just kind of freeze up and have a lot of difficulty moving my body. This was one of those times.

"You girls ready?" Snow Leopard asked.

"Oh, yeah." Psycho and I were both dangling in a darkened elevator shaft like a couple of black robot spiders, rapelling silently down our lifelines to the aircar hanger far below. Snow Leopard did not want to risk using the elevator until we knew the hanger was secure. We needed the elevator because Redhawk could not walk.

"Race ya," Psycho said, dropping like a stone.

"Scut! Slow Down!" I triggered the catch and the cable sang through the mounts. I dropped, slowing gently, boots glancing off the walls. The shaft was dark and cold and full of thick oily cables. My A–suit whispered to me, and green readouts glowed on my faceplate.

"Negative life. Proceed."

I hissed past Psycho, and he was a deadly camfax shadow, just another shadow, all the power of the Legion, coiled like a snake. We were nearing the entrance to the hanger. I slowed and stopped.

"All right, Psycho—go. Deadman!" I was breathing heavily, leaning off the wall, my E at the ready.

"Come on, Thinker, admit it—you love it, don't you?" Psycho giggled, and I could see him coming at me from above, an obscene black beast armored for war. My E was set on flame. Psycho flashed past me, dropping, his cable whistling eerily.

We had seen the hanger on the screen, cold and still, undamaged, fully lighted, two aircars in the repair bays. Not a sign of life. Then we tried the internal view of the Omni starport, but the screen was dead. Perhaps the starport was crushed flat, popped open by our antis, then torn apart by the lake of molten lava. I wondered how many O's had died in the disaster. It made me feel good, thinking about all those dead O's, knowing that we had contributed.

"I'm just above the elevator door," Psycho reported.

"Coming," I responded. I was there in fracs. I slid down a bit further. I could see the door activator. I eased my way down until it was between my legs. "I'm at the activator."

"Can you see the emergency lever?" Redhawk spoke from the aircar control center.

"I've got it." I looked up at Psycho. "You ready?"

"Mother's on barbecue," he replied. "Do it."

I pulled down on the control and pushed away from the wall, still dangling from the line. The double doors to the elevator shaft slid open smoothly. Psycho went hurtling in with a sharp crack, his Manlink suddenly spitting raw flame.

I followed him, swinging in like a great alien ape, firing my E on flame. A brilliant, dazzling ball of flame exploded violently before us where our streams met, a dull boom, the world erupting, white–hot streaks shooting past us, hissing and spitting. Anyone waiting for us was going to have a very hot welcome. We landed in the center of the holocaust and dropped to our knees in the heart of our own hell, weapons at the ready, sheets of eerie blue and yellow and white–hot gas dancing all over my A–suit, Psycho right beside me. We kneeled there as the flames slowly died.

"Negative life," Sweety assured me. The hanger was full of black smoke. Flames licked all over the floor.

Negative life. My armor glowed. My heart was thumping. "Scut," I observed.

"You love it, Thinker. You don't fool me." Psycho was high, snapping his head around in his helmet, looking for something to cook with his Manlink.

* * *

The elevator hissed open, and Snow Leopard and Priestess dragged Redhawk in on a camfax poncho. Psycho and I were standing by with weapons balanced on our hips. It was a large, well–stocked aircar hanger. There were only two aircars left, still in the repair bays. The launching bays were all sealed and empty. Green lights glowed everywhere—the installation was intact and functioning, but completely deserted.

"Let me at 'em," Redhawk said throatily. He was fighting off the pain. Priestess helped him to his feet.

"Which is the one you wanted?" Priestess asked.

"Bay Three—right over there. Get me in the cockpit."

"Three, Five—" Beta One looked around the installation, his E in one hand. "Cover all the exits—see the tacmap. It looks like this site connects directly with the starport. See that corridor? The O's could kick in the door in a frac. I want silence. Ten, what's the sit?"

"Let me get in the cockpit first, will you?" Priestess was helping him hobble up the service stairs to the aircar cabin.

"Do it!" Snow Leopard was uncharacteristically nervous.

"Ten sir! Deadman!" I wasn't worried. If the aircar could be fixed, Redhawk would do it. Psycho and I found our places. We were each covering two doorways. Snow Leopard craned his neck, inspecting the ceiling and the launching locks.

"Three, Five—if it's the O's, we go all out. Five, use tacstars. The rest of us go to xmax and laser."

"Mother is pleased," Psycho replied. Snow Leopard ignored him. Mother was Five's Manlink—the Mother of Destruction. She'd saved our asses more than once.

"These bastards shouldn't be here," Snow Leopard said, kicking a door open into what looked like a mini office. "I'll be in here looking for info." He ripped a file drawer open and scattered the contents.

"Ohhh, that's good." Redhawk was off his feet, in the pilot's seat, right where he belonged. "Now let's see what's ailing this old gal." It was a DefCorps aircar, an older model, but still a highly dangerous beast.

My blood stirred just looking at it. I couldn't help it—I had been bound for the Legion ever since my birth. It had just taken a little time for me to realize it. But all it took nowadays was an aircar, sitting in the repair bay. On Andrion 2, we had seen Legion fighters, booming over the burning ruins of the Systie base, flashing past and wheeling in the night sky; and they were so beautiful, I had almost cried. On Coldmark, the *Spawn* had dropped in the whole fighter force to rescue us and the System had met us, face to face; and we had smashed them to bits. No, I was with the Legion, for life or death, for good or evil, in sickness or in health, for better or for worse, no looking back. And every once in awhile I realized it. It was scary. I tore my eyes away from the aircar and clutched my E tighter. My fate was to die, under strange stars, for the Legion.

"Ten, report." Snow Leopard did not like it here, I could tell.

"I can fix this girl, One. But I'm going to need some new internal power packs. I'm giving Priestess instructions on what I'll need right now."

"Is it all here?"

"Sure, we'll find it."

"So you can fix the aircar?"

"That's a big ten!" Salvation, for us all! Redhawk was a genius— how could we survive without him? We were going to get out of this madhouse!

"Alert! Movement! Life! Human! Target approaching, as marked!" Sweety's icy metal voice hissed in my ears, the tacmap glowing red, pinpointing the target, a flashing red dot approaching us in the corridor to the starport. We ran to cover the door. It was a personnel door, closed and locked. Snow Leopard and Psycho and I skidded to a stop, bracketing the door, ready to fire. My E was at my shoulder.

"Three, E on v–max auto," Snow Leopard ordered. "Fire when the target appears. Five, stand by on laser. Fire only if the target's in armor. This one's human. I want it alive." Priestess dropped to the deck from the aircar, running to us, shouldering her E. "Nine, cover the other entrances. If anything else shows up, be prepared to go to energy systems."

Priestess whirled around to cover the other doors.

I could taste the fear. E on v–max auto, sights centered on the door. I watched the target on the tacmap. As it came closer, Sweety got a faint energy image.

"Target not in armor," she informed me. "Confirm it's human. No weapons."

"Thinker, v–min auto," Snow Leopard hissed. I made the adjustment.

"This is crap!" Psycho objected. "I don't believe this!"

"Stick to your orders!" Snow Leopard snapped.

"Target approaching door!"

I was ready, ready, ready, ready. The locks snapping open, he's got access, the door hissing open, a frozen instant of time, a male, pale face, my autovac cracking wildly, white–hot flashes erupting all over his body, the crack of doom echoing around the hanger; and suddenly he was down.

"Cease fire!" I ran up to the open door.

He lay sprawled in the corridor, litesuit smoking. His eyes were open, his mouth was open. The barrel of my E was right at his face. Then Snow Leopard was there, and Psycho leaped over the body and took up a position in the corridor with his Manlink.

I touched the Systie's throat with my armored fingers. "He's not breathing!"

"Priestess, up!" Snow Leopard commanded. She was there in a frac, tearing open her medkit.

"Save him, Priestess!"

"Biotic charge!" she responded, slamming the instrument on to his chest. His litesuit was still smoking. Vacmin is not normally lethal, but autovac is a bit heavy.

He jerked, and took a breath. His eyelids fluttered.

"You got him, Priestess!"

"Corridor is secure," Sweety informed me.

"Back to the hanger," Snow Leopard said. "Give me a hand." He had the Systie by one foot. I grabbed the other foot and Priestess took an arm. We dragged him through the door and Psycho backed in, waving his Manlink back and forth, giggling to himself. Psycho was getting stranger and stranger. He hit the control and the door hissed shut silently, sealing us off again from the corridor.

Chapter 5
Oplan Gold

The Systie trembled. We had secured his hands behind his back and when Priestess brought him back to full consciousness, he found himself surrounded by Legion soldiers in black A–suits and darkened red faceplates. He could see no human faces, only his own reflection flashing off the faceplates of the enemy. I stood to one side, my E pointed right at his chest. He was indeed a weird bird, still young, unarmed and unarmored, pale and sickly, thin and wiry, cold blue eyes and shaven head, dressed in a rumpled civilian litesuit. He did not look like a soldier.

Snow Leopard cracked open his helmet and removed it. He was a pale horror, white hair and hot pink eyes glaring at the Systie. The Systie stared at him, wide–eyed.

"Systie, this is a combat tactical interrogation," Snow Leopard recited coldly. "You are a combatant, and you are being interrogated by field elements of the Twenty-second Legion of the Confederation of Free Worlds. We are now in a combat situation, and your cooperation is essential to our tactical success. If you refuse interrogation or attempt to deceive us, you will be shot dead immediately as a combatant. If you cease resistance..."

"Just a moment," the Systie squeaked. "Just a moment—Legion's mistaken. We're not a combatant."

"Silence!" Snow Leopard barked. "The decision is ours to make. You will speak only when responding to our questions! All Systies here are combatants. You have been designated a combatant by us, based on your presence here. If you cease resistance, and cooperate to our satisfaction, you will be granted official ConFree prisoner of war status and will come under the protection of the laws of the Confederation and of the interstellar code on prisoners of war. Do you understand the situation?"

"No! It's Legion who doesn't understand! We're not a combatant! We're a diplomat! We're a diplomat of the Galactic Service of the Government of the United System Alliance. Our status is protected by interstellar law. We are not a combatant!" The Systie was twitching.

Snow Leopard paused, staring silently at the Systie. Then he turned to me. "Set your E to flame, Three," he said calmly. "I don't want to alert the O's." I made the adjustment. Snow Leopard focused on the Systie again.

"A diplomat, huh? What's a Systie diplomat doing in ConFree vac? Or—better yet—what's a Systie diplomat doing in an Omni starport? Would you care to answer either of those questions?"

The Systie froze, blinking his eyes nervously. He appeared very uneasy. Understandable, considering the circumstances. "We are on a diplomatic mission for the United System Alliance," he answered carefully. "We're afraid that's all we can tell it. We can discuss no further details of our instructions. We must remind it that we have diplomatic immunity from arrest or detention, under solemn interstellar agreements signed by both our governments." For a skinny, bald little creep he certainly had a way with words.

"You haven't been keeping on top of current events, Systie!" Snow Leopard snarled. "The System and the Confederation are at war! Or hadn't you noticed? You seem kind of slow, for a diplomat! As a matter of fact I don't think you are a diplomat—but it doesn't matter now—not in the slightest. You have been officially designated as a combatant by the Legion. Your choice is to cooperate fully, or die! Do you understand?"

"We are not a combatant! We are a..."

"Talk or die! Choose!"

"We object! We object! We're not a combatant! We are a diplomat!" He was wild–eyed and frantic.

"Kill him." Snow Leopard turned on his heel and walked away. "Ten, is the aircar ready yet?"

I shouldered my E and centered it on the Systie's chest.

His eyes widened and focused on my faceplate. I knew he could not see my face. I was Death, cold and merciless and totally impersonal. I had never before killed an unarmed, helpless prisoner. I reflected briefly on this as my finger tightened on the trigger, but I could feel no emotion. His death would be mercifully brief, for the flames were quick and powerful.

"Wait! Wait! Wait! All right, all right, we'll tell it! All right!" The Systie was bathed in sweat. He was shaking violently. I raised my E and turned to Snow Leopard. He impatiently returned to the Systie and stood there looking down at him.

"Last chance, Systie. No more games. Complete cooperation, or you die. Do you understand? Yes or no."

"Yes."

"Will you cooperate?"

"Yes."

"One lie and you die. Understand?"

"We understand." He sat there on the floor sweating, hands secured behind his back.

For the first time, Snow Leopard squatted down before the prisoner. "Three," he said. "Join me. Five, you're on guard."

"Ten."

"Ten." I cracked open my helmet and secured it to my U–belt. The Systie stared at me. I glared back at him.

"Would it really have killed us?" he asked me quietly.

"Silence!" Snow Leopard barked. "It's you who'll answer the questions. Now—what is a Systie diplomat doing in an Omni starport?"

"We've never really been in the starport proper. We have always been restricted to our own installations."

"Answer the question."

"STRATCOM called it Oplan Gold," he said quietly. "It was Cosmic Secret—it was our greatest achievement. It's been almost a hundred stellar years we've held the secret. And it's meant a hundred years of peace in the Galaxy. Generations, without the curse of war. And the System was responsible! Yes, we brought it about. Do you expect us to apologize? We're proud of what we've done—proud! We are peacemakers. Peacemakers! Billions of our citizens have lived in peace, without ever knowing the sacrifices made for them by the System. Does Legion think it was easy? So many of us have given our lives, quietly, willingly, for the cause. But now the Legion is here, and it has all changed—it doesn't know what it's done. It hasn't the slightest idea. Billions will die, now. Billions!"

"My patience is limited," Snow Leopard stated. "I am getting tired of repeating myself, and I will add that we do not have much time."

The Systie licked his lips. "Is it that difficult to comprehend? We made contact with them, almost a hundred years ago. Contact with the Variants—we communicated with them! They communicated with us! It's a wonderful story, a heroic story—so many sacrifices, so many dead! And yet reason prevailed, and we refused to give up on our efforts. Some day there will be monuments to all those who died, for peace!

"The result we see before us—a Variant starport, a System base, two different species cooperating, for a common goal—peace in the galaxy, peace in our time, peace for all, peace for the Variants, peace for us. But now the Legion is here, and it's all going to end!"

"You're damned right on that! What were you giving the Variants?"

"Unitium. Unitium from the mines of Andrion Two."

"Why didn't the Variants set up their base right there?"

"They never revealed that. We believe they were concerned about the Legion. It was easier to camouflage the starport on Andrion Three. If the mines were discovered, there would still be no reason to suspect the Variants."

"Do you know what they do with the unitium?"

"Well, no—that was never clear, although we're fairly certain it's vital to their star drives."

"This has been going on for almost a hundred years, you say."

"Yes, that's right—a hundred years of peace!"

"In exchange for a hundred years of unitium."

"Yes. That's one way of putting it. But what's important is what we gained from the exchange, in terms of peace, and in terms of understanding."

"So the Variants understand you?"

"Well...no. That was never clear, either. There are many problems. But we understand them, much more than we did. We've learned so much!"

"Have you learned how to kill them?" I could not resist interrupting. The Systie looked at me as if I had slapped him.

"We are not authorized to conduct research in such subjects! And we don't want to. Our mission is understanding. The Variants are very powerful psychics—very powerful! We can hide nothing from them."

"Redhawk," One broke in. "Progress report."

"We're getting there, One! Not much longer! Priestess, will you hold the light steady, please?"

Snow Leopard had his hand on his forehead. I knew he was weary. "Release him, Thinker." I touched the release and the Systie's bonds fell away. He moved his hands gingerly around to his front and began massaging his wrists. From time to time, he stole little glances at me. My face was a stony mask.

"Give him water, Thinker." I unhooked a canteen and handed it to him. He took a sip, carefully, then a deep swig. He looked into my eyes when he finished.

"Do we think we can fight them?" he asked. "Do us a favor— surrender now! Legion has no chance. It will not leave this planet alive."

"Systie," One said patiently. "This is the last time I'm going to ask this question. If you don't answer it, we're going to kill you. Why are you here?"

"We were negotiating with the Variants. We were communicating—deciding on a joint response to counter the Legion aggression on Andrion Two. Legion has no idea what tragic consequences its interference will have, for everyone."

"A joint response. How do you do that—compromise?" Snow Leopard asked.

"Well...no. We respect their wishes. We have no choice, if we wish to preserve the peace."

"I see. Describe what happened here when we attacked."

"It doesn't know? We're sorry, we can't help it. We were right here in the aircar base when its antimats hit. We had just returned from a visit to our science station when the alert went up, and they announced a full–scale attack against the starport. They launched all the aircars— except these two—and then its antimats went off. Incredible! We were talking with them—communicating! And it attacks with antimats. It's hard to accept."

"It was just our way of getting their attention," I responded. I was beginning to dislike this Systie dip. He gave me a poisonous look.

"It was simply barbaric. It certainly confirmed their worst suspicions about us."

"What happened!" Snow Leopard was impatient.

"It was very confusing. We lost commo with everyone. We had reports of Legion troopers landing. The starport seemed to be gone. The aircar control center didn't answer.

"The duty crew at the hanger split up and left, to investigate the situation. They only left one unit to cover the hanger—and us. Finally it left, too."

"Where did he go?"

"We think the V called it. We thought perhaps the Variants didn't understand, about the attack—about the difference between the System and the Legion."

"It's you who don't understand," Snow Leopard said. "The O—the V—understand us perfectly."

"All our work is for nothing now. A hundred years." The Systie gazed blankly into space. "We were alone after that. Just us. It has no idea what a tragedy this is."

"I find it amazing," Snow Leopard remarked, "that a person of your obvious intelligence is so totally blind to the true consequences of what the System has done here. Don't you have any doubts at all about the morality of your mission?"

"Doubts? Doubts? None! No! We are soldiers of peace, giving our lives for peace, for understanding between two worlds, two species, two entirely different forms of life. And the result has been clear— generations of peace!"

"And the cost?"

"What cost? Unitium? Something we don't need? Yes, some of our people have died—too many! But it's a small sacrifice, for galactic peace!"

"How many billions of humans were exterminated by the Omnis— the V—in the Plague War?"

"Our point exactly! How many billions have lived since our successful contact?"

"We defeated the Omnis in the Plague War. We shattered their fleets, and drove them back."

"We have no argument with that."

"And the unitium? You don't wonder about the unitium?"

"Well, of course, we wonder."

"You don't wonder why they're willing to communicate with the enemy—to suspend their advance for a hundred years—to gain an endless supply of unitium?"

"Does Legion have the answer?"

"You don't wonder how many billions are going to die, because of your stupid, short–sighted policies? You don't wonder about your children? You don't wonder about the future of our own species? Don't you think it worth defending? How about the next generation? What are you willing to them? Slavery? How about your own children? Do you have children?"

"We...we have no children."

"I'm sorry. I forgot. Diplomats don't have children. Such emotions might confuse you." We knew Outworlder diplomats serving the System were castrated upon entry into the service.

"We are not ashamed of our condition. It was completely voluntary. A diplomat cannot afford to have a biased viewpoint. We deal with important questions."

"Important questions? Do you believe slavery is preferable to death? Do you believe freedom from slavery is worth risking your life? No, let's change the question—is your life more important than your children's? What's the logical response to that? How about a choice of life—this generation or the next. One gets to live, one gets to die. What's your choice?"

"Legion doesn't understand."

"No, it's you who don't understand! You despise the Legion because our objectives are different. You're focused on the present. We look at the future. We're not fighting for us—we knew we're all doomed, every last one of us. We're fighting for our descendants, for the unborn. I don't want children of mine living as slaves to the Omnis. If it was up to you and the System, they would."

"It's making assumptions about the Variants without evidence."

"Two billion dead. Is that enough evidence? My proven assumption is that they want us all dead."

"We've learned so much about them! They're learning about us, too! With understanding comes tolerance."

"The only thing they want to learn about us is how to kill us most efficiently. And I'm sure you've been a great help to them."

"It's too bad Legion's government does not agree with that."

"What do you mean by that?"

"We mean its self–righteous braying arises from ignorance. It's easy to criticize the System, isn't it? Blame it all on the Systies! Does it think its own govenment was ignorant of what we were doing?"

"You're lying!" Snow Leopard appeared genuinely shocked.

"Oh, yes—this would be a good time to lie, wouldn't it, one lie and you die. No, we're not lying."

"Explain!"

"The highest levels of ConFree have known about our efforts for at least a decade. We were briefed on that when they gave us the mission. A delegate from ConFree even visited STRATCOM for a briefing—we briefed it ourself!"

"That's insane! We knew nothing of this!"

"Of course not! It was a sensitive matter. Why should ConFree brief the Legion? They probably don't trust the Legion—would it brief a soldier about a sensitive diplomatic and political secret such as this? Of course not! So don't be so damned self–righteous! Its own people knew about this, and approved, and kept the secret—otherwise the entire inhabited galaxy would know about it! The Legion has a very efficient proprop apparatus."

"I don't believe it, One," I said. I was stunned by the Systie's claim. "ConFree wouldn't do that. Why would they do that?" Even as I spoke, I knew the Systie was telling the truth. I was horrified—my whole world was falling apart.

We fought for ConFree—we died for ConFree. Why would they do that?

"I don't believe it either," Snow Leopard replied quietly.

"One!" It was Redhawk. The assault doors to the aircar were wide open. Redhawk was in the pilot's seat; Priestess was leaning over him. The instrument panel was aglow with green lights. A faint, eerie whine grew in intensity to a dull, throaty hum. The aircar was alive! A chill ran over my flesh.

"Aircar functional," Redhawk reported. "Fully charged, fully armed. All combat systems report ready status. We are prepped for launch. Awaiting your orders."

Snow Leopard stood up. The Systie cautiously got up as well, hypnotized by the aircar. "It isn't going out there in that thing, is it? They'll swat it in a frac. It won't last an instant!"

"Shut down!" Snow Leopard snapped. "Three, escort the prisoner into the aircar and board. Five, board. We're going to go out there and attack whatever we find." I pointed the barrel of my E at the Systie's face and he moved in slow motion to the aircar. Now it was clear— Snow Leopard had made up his mind. We were going to die, just as the Second had said, for the Legion. A whirlwind of conflicting emotions shot through my heart. But I knew, no matter what, I would do exactly as Beta One said.

"We can't oppose them," the Systie said. "It's not possible! Believe us! We know them better than it!"

"Shut up or I'll kill you," I threatened him. I was angry. I didn't want this Systie worm to witness our deaths.

"His opinions are just what you'd expect," Psycho commented acidly, "from somebody who has no balls." We boarded the aircar. Psycho took the left door, I took the right. Priestess found a seat behind Redhawk. The Systie sat near me, sweating. We were waiting for Snow Leopard.

Snow Leopard stood several mikes away from the car, his back to us. His helmet was still hooked to his U–belt. He held his E in one hand. He appeared to be looking around. His gaze wandered up to the ceiling, then around the walls. We waited. Redhawk looked back at us from the pilot's seat, gave us his craziest grin, and locked on his helmet. The car was purring like a cat. I snapped my helmet on and the screens came up on my faceplate. I checked my E—all set. A & A, armored and armed—Beta was ready for its last mission. I felt fear and sorrow and a dull, aching regret. All I really wanted was to live with Priestess, forever and ever and ever, someplace where nobody could find us. But it was not to be. We were both soldiers of the Legion, and the Legion needed us.

What was Snow Leopard up to? He looked back at us once, his face cold and troubled. Then he turned and took a step away from us, switching his E to the other hand.

"What's the story with One?" Psycho asked me on private.

"Three, what's Snow Leopard doing?" Priestess was also on private to me, one arm over her seatback, staring fixedly at Snow Leopard.

"Don't know, guys," I responded.

"Ask him," Priestess urged me. She knew I was closer to Snow Leopard than anyone else. He was still standing there, helmetless, motionless, facing away from us. It was not like him. I slipped out of my seat and jumped out of the aircar to the deck. One did not stir. I walked over to him.

"Snow Leopard," I whispered on private. "What's up?" He snapped his head around to face me. He was pale as death and his eyes were wet. Cold sweat beaded his forehead. He was breathing hard. He gasped something that I did not catch.

"What?"

"We're not going," he hissed.

"We're not going?" I echoed in disbelief.

He snapped his head away from me, looking wildly around the hanger again. "We're not going," he repeated. "Warhound is out there. I know he is. We're not going." He was gripping his E tightly.

"Warhound? Warhound is out there? How do you know?"

"Warhound is out there. I know it. I know it! We're not going! We're going to find Warhound. Everybody out of the car!" He whipped around, facing the aircar. "Everybody out! We're not going! No! No! Redhawk, you stay with the aircar. Priestess, you stay with Redhawk. Psycho, secure the prisoner, then join us. Priestess, kill the Systie if necessary. The three of you in the aircar—Redhawk, Priestess, Systie— wait for us. Psycho, Thinker, come with me. We're going to find Warhound! We're not coming back without him! Priestess, you're in command here. If you're discovered, launch the aircar and escape. Otherwise, wait for our return."

Psycho jumped off the aircar, his Manlink ready for action. "Creep secured, sir!" He sounded perfectly content.

Snow Leopard took his helmet off his U–belt and slipped it over his head and locked it on.

"Beta," he said, "On me." He grasped his E and moved toward the door where we had bagged the Systie. I turned to look back at the aircar. Priestess raised a hand in farewell. I raised my fist.

"Goodbye, Priestess," I said on private. "Wait for me."

"I'll wait," she promised. "You hurry back, Thinker." I hastened to catch up to Snow Leopard and Psycho. Snow Leopard had the door open already. We were off—three fools, back on Atom's Road. It doesn't matter, I told myself. It doesn't matter. A million years from now nobody will care what we did, or what we didn't do. But for us there was really no choice, no choice at all. Warhound was out there, One said, and we were going to find him. That was all that mattered to us.

* * *

"Energy," Sweety whispered to me. Icy futures, in my veins. The whole world was mine, mine to shoot. I could feel it on my skin, inside the Λ-suit. I was magman—cruising, cold and free. We were in the O starport, ready to die. It was dark, and we waded through water up to our chests, hot steaming water covered with a luminous scum. The rad count was off the scale—we swam in Death's hot breath. It was ob the installation had been crushed by our antimats and by the lava lake. So far we had not had to deal with the lava. We were crawling through megatons of tangled wreckage, Psycho and I following Snow Leopard as he cut a way through the mess, silent and grim, explaining nothing, just slashing his way through twisted alien metal with his torch, a man with a mission known only to him and maybe God.

Energy. Deadman! Something stirred up ahead in the flickering green of our darksight. Something to swat us, and maybe laugh. I almost laughed myself, I was so charged. I could taste the adrenalin in my mouth. We had crawled down into this mess. There was no way of telling what it had been. Whatever function it had served, the place we were wading through had been very large—a tremendous hall of some sort, full of massive black cylindrical columns that glittered like charcoal. Now the great, coiled roof was flattened down onto the columns, crushing them, and a flood of boiling radioactive water had rushed in from somewhere; bubbling, slimy water full of unidentifiable floating debris. The radioactivity was the least of our worries—if we survived, the Body Shop would fix us up. If we didn't survive, it wouldn't matter. We kept stumbling against large, angular objects under the water. Snow Leopard was highlighted on my faceplate right up ahead. I turned to the rear. Psycho was right there, almost neck–deep, his Manlink at his shoulder. I could see his face. He was smiling.

"Mommy's with us, kiddies. Don't be scared!" Psycho was having the time of his life. But if it got any deeper the little runt was going to be underwater.

"Prepare to fire, gang," Snow Leopard ordered calmly. "Laser or xmax. Psycho, up to you. It's coming, and we can't hide any more." Snow Leopard stopped moving and shouldered his E. I did the same, and set it to auto xmax. I was right next to a huge black cenite column. A twisted coil of ceiling was right overhead. The water was up to my armpits. Whatever it was would come in fast and low. Psycho sloshed forward to get in position to cover us both. My heart was pounding. I wanted nothing better than to let loose with a long burst of xmax. It was all a ghastly green glow, all around us.

"Energy point approaching," Sweety called out, "as marked." A white–hot dot on my faceplate. Another. Another! "Multiple targets," Sweety corrected, "approaching. Four, six targets—fire xmax auto!" I squeezed the trigger and held it down.

We ripped open the world. Shrieking, awful catastrophe, auto xmax shattering our ears, dazzling our eyes, exploding wildly, flashing off the columns and the roof, filling the air with supersonic slivers of glowing shrapnel, white phospo starbursts, the flowers of the Legion. My blood froze in awe. Psycho's Manlink spoke once, Tacstar Goddess, and reality parted briefly with a terrible ripping crack as a micronuke sun erupted before us, crackling and spitting, our own sun, right on my darkened faceplate, melting the ceiling, evaporating tons of water. My flesh crawled. Psycho whimpered in ecstasy. Something large and dark flashed past me. I whipped around to fire after it. An explosion of water. Psycho fired laser with his Manlink, right into the water. A black delta–shaped wing popped up steaming from underwater. I hit laser and joined Psycho in zapping it. The laser shrieked and popped and the device shuddered and burst open, spitting sparks.

"More of them!" Snow Leopard fired his E on auto xmax. "Keep firing!" I caught a fleeting glimpse of a dart–shaped probe flashing past the columns, circling around for another go at us, a ghostly track flickering on my faceplate. I fired auto xmax, filling the air with death. Sweety was shrieking at me—another! The world exploded in my face, red phospho starburst, the shock hammering me underwater. I rose with my head ringing, tracks all over my faceplate, my vision all blurry. Snow Leopard was chest–deep in the water, his back against a column, firing auto xmax nonstop. The probes flashed past us like birds and the water erupted in their wake, hissing and steaming. The columns rang with hits, white–hot holes, suddenly there. The laser flickered like lightning all around us. One of the probes exploded in the air, rolling along the ceiling in a fiery trail of destruction, showering us with wreckage. I spotted another one and nailed it with a laser burst. It kept on going, then exploded with a brilliant flash against one of the columns. Psycho let loose with a long burst of xmax. Sweety was filling my ears with data, but it was not getting through to my brain. I crouched almost neck–deep in the water, my head whirling.

"Enemy probes eliminated," Sweety remarked calmly. There was no more movement on the tacmap. A cold darkness enveloped us again. I slowly straightened up out of my crouch, my E at the ready.

"Everybody all right?"

"Tenners."

"Ten." I could hardly believe I was still in one piece.

"Nasty little critters, huh?" Psycho commented.

"Those weren't Systie probes—they were from the Omnis," Snow Leopard informed us. "Firing laser."

"Nice to see we could kill them," Psycho replied.

"Move it, gang—we're gone." Snow Leopard wasn't wasting any time. He began sloshing vigorously through the scummy water. We followed, quickly. We passed a downed probe, a large wing jutting out of the water, riddled with xmax and laser, glowing pale green in my darksight.

"Look at that—nobody's ever seen anything like that before," Snow Leopard remarked. One was a student of history, and he always felt he was a direct participant in momentous events.

"I'd just as soon have passed on the honor, thanks," I responded.

"They're not unbeatable, Thinker—we shot down their probes!" Psycho insisted. "I'll bet some O probe jockey is catching hell right now from his One."

"Look at this." Snow Leopard paused before an open doorway. It was a very odd doorway, narrow and high—about twice the height of a man. A corridor, flooded with filthy water, the walls glistening with slime. One had one hand out, almost as if he was feeling the air.

"We go in." No explanation. Never an explanation, from Beta One. Just an order, and we move. In, we go in. He was just as crazy as Psycho.

Into the unknown, again. A cold sweating corridor as black as death, sloshing through chest–deep water, our shoulders almost touching the walls. Into the Camp of the O's. I knew we were crazy— all of us, totally insane.

We were so far gone there was simply no reason left.

A terrible grinding noise shook the walls, and the starport trembled. We stopped as the walls moved around us and the water shivered. Vibrations, in our bones. The base was tearing itself apart.

* * *

Nobody said a word. I think we were all stunned into silence by the sight. We were in a tall, lightless, ice–cold room, the walls covered with slime. The room was full of corpses, pale blue naked human corpses lying on slabs, rubbery plastic tubing glistening with black blood running from cold pale arms up to an overhead rack.

"Life, life, life!" Sweety's reaction was more human than our own. "They are alive, Thinker. All of them—still alive!"

We followed the tubing to an auto device where the tubing spit the blood into a mechanism which eventually squirted it into an endless line of pale plastic bottles.

Bottles of blood, for the O's. Strange. I picked up one of the bottles and slipped it into a pouch on my U–belt.

Snow Leopard turned back to the living dead. It was pitch black to the Systies. They glowed green in our darksight. Sightless open eyes, glazed dead eyes. One of them blinked. A female, hovering before the gates of death, cold and skeletal and wasted. She could see nothing. Perhaps she sensed movement. Her mouth opened, a silent scream before the gates. She could feel the cold. She thought we were the O.

I gently pulled the tubing from her arm—it was attached with a regulator of some sort. I slapped on a patch. She began trembling violently. What could we do? They were only alive because the air in this section of the base was still breathable. How could we take them with us? It would be a procession of the dead and the doomed, sleepwalking through the Realm of the Ghouls. I did not even dare to voice my questions.

"Come on you, slimy subs! Mommy's ready!" Psycho was going berserk. "I'll roast you alive! Crawl out of your holes, subs! Try Legion blood, you worms! I'll stick this link right up your ass!" Psycho was whirling his Manlink around wildly, ready to fire, his eyes flashing behind his faceplate.

"Calm down, Five!" Snow Leopard ordered. "I have some news for you."

"News? News? Scut! I got news for you—we're not leaving here until every last, stinking O is dead!"

"Warhound is here," Snow Leopard said calmly.

"What? Where?"

"Close. He's close. He's getting closer. Follow me."

We were shocked into silence by Snow Leopard's statement. And now he was moving again, into another open, dark doorway.

Follow me. No explanations, from our One. How could he know where Warhound was, when even Sweety did not know? What would happen to the Systies? We followed. What the hell else could we do?

We followed.

* * *

"Six on scope," Sweety announced calmly. A chill shot through my veins. This was not a good place. It was a seemingly endless series of tall cubicles, cloaked in total darkness, strange grilled glassy walls, a mushroom–shaped column rising from the center of each cubicle, as tall as a man. Alien devices hung from the ceiling, and many of them had fallen to the floor, blocking the cubicles. Each cubicle was open where the walls would have met, four separate exits leading to eight adjoining cubicles. It was a twisted maze, and it was buckling and breaking up.

The dying starport shuddered and groaned. Tortured metal shrieked and moaned. Vibrations rattled our bones.

The floor shifted under me. A dull boom echoed in my ears.

The roof cracked and rippled. The lava was getting closer. I checked out the tacmap. Snow Leopard was in an adjoining cubicle just ahead of me. Psycho was in a cubicle just behind me.

Warhound was up ahead—clearly marked on my scope, a glowing point of light: B6. There was no doubt about it. One had been right all along—it was Warhound!

"Six, One. Report." Silence, only the hissing of the tacnet in our ears.

"Six, One. Report." Silence. Silence, silence. Warhound was moving.

"Six approaching," Sweety informed me.

"Warhound, it's Snow Leopard. Report! Have you got us on scope?" Snow Leopard was moving forward, toward Warhound. I followed, threading my way past massive, downed instruments, in and out of cubicles. This was not good. I did not like this at all.

"Warhound, we're approaching you. Is your commo out?"

Silence. Only silence, from Beta Six. Snow Leopard was almost on him.

"Six on xmax, safety off!" A warning, from Sweety.

"Six, it's One. Don't..."

A shattering explosion, brilliant white–hot shrapnel ricocheting everywhere, burning white tracks on my darksight. Again, again! Warhound was firing auto xmax at Snow Leopard!

"Cease fire! Cease fire! It's One!" I shouted.

"Warhound, it's Snow Leopard! Cease fire!" One ordered. I charged forward, dodging around massive chunks of metal, in and out of cubicles, snatching glances at Warhound and Snow Leopard on the tacmap. Warhound was only a few cubicles away now.

"Warhound, it's Thinker! Cease fire!" The wall exploded, glowing with laser tracks.

"Six firing at you with laser!" Sweety informed me briskly.

"Psycho, Warhound is firing at us!"

"Scut!"

"Beta, retreat! Six is firing at us!" Xmax auto, ripping away, a long, wild burst, flashes of lightning dancing on my faceplate. A tremendous explosion split the darkness. My tacmap flickered and faded. A deceptor was banging away, scrambling everything.

"I've fired deceptor," I heard Psycho in a wave of crackling static. "Get out..."

"Six advancing on you!" Sweety was still with me!

"Don't shoot him, Thinker!" Snow Leopard ordered—I could barely hear him. I was scrambling to get away, darting in and out of cubicles at random, heading away from Warhound, a glowing dot on my tacmap.

"Six pursuing!" Xmax, supersonic slivers of steel whistling all around me, my suit suddenly ringing with hits, rocking me off my feet.

"Multiple hits!" I landed up against one of the metal mushrooms, my ears ringing, my faceplate a flashing mass of red lights, alarms ringing in my ears. Warhound stepped into the cubicle.

Warhound, armored and armed, black armor smoking, red faceplate dark and dead, raising his E calmly, the stock sliding easily into his shoulder, the barrel pointed right at me, brilliant laser sight flooding my faceplate, as cold as death. I snapped my E to V–max auto and fired. The world exploded in my face. I winked out in a flash of atoms.

Chapter 6

Death's Cold Road

"Get up! Get up! Get up! Deadman, get up, Three!"

Urgent commands in my ears. It was One, it was Sweety, it was Five. I was burning—burning to ashes. My blood was on fire, my bones all shattered, my muscles shredded, my brain split wide open.

"Get up, Thinker! Alert! Alert! Situation Violet! Enemy approaching! Alert! Alert!" Shot in the heart, I came back to life, crawling up out of the dark. It was pitch black—I could see nothing! No, a glimmer of light—a lolite! My helmet was off, someone leaning over me. It was Snow Leopard, a quick glance at me, his E flashing past my face.

"Three's back. Get up, Thinker, they're coming." Snow Leopard was maddeningly calm. The lolite was suddenly gone and darkness rushed over me. I tried to get up. Pain shot through my body. My helmet was slammed into place and locked on—darksight, green phospho magic with me, Sweety in my ears, chill futures, the tacmap flashing to life.

"Prep for tacstar, Five."

"It's a ten, One. They're dead—the walking dead." Psycho was cold as ice.

"Unidentified life form approaching! Probable Omni! Life form masked by mag field!"

Adrenalin shot through my system. I struggled to my feet, raising my E. Unidentified life form—Deadman, save us! It was the O, coming right at us.

"Unidentified energy probe—high mags—off the scale."

Sweety's words were like daggers. Warhound was lying on the deck in a pile of smashed–up O equipment, his helmet off, his armored wrists tied together in front of him. He was staring sightlessly into the dark, sweat beading his forehead.

"Deadman! What happened?" I blurted out, setting my E to xmax.

"Warhound tried to kill us," Snow Leopard responded quietly. "Don't know why. Psycho got you both with a stunstar."

"God! Is Warhound all right?"

"Beta...Beta!" Warhound gasped, words from a dark pit of terror. "Fight them! Fight them! Fight them!"

"Unidentified life form on screen! Single target now in range. Probable O—recommend multiple tacstars." A phospho red dot pulsed on my faceplate, readouts flashing over the screen.

"Blast 'em, Five!"

Five leaped forward to Snow Leopard's command, an obscene black metal spider, faceplate glowing red, Manlink up to his shoulder. The universe split wide open in a lightning flash, ripping audibly like a hot knife in rotten silk, screeching like wounded metal, rising in intensity, freezing my flesh. Tacstars, flashing straight to the target; multiple cenite walls disintegrating like jelly, again, again, again, lighting us up, bursting, a nuclear flash; my faceplate dead black; sudden brilliant holy white glare; glittering flowers of death. The shock wave hit us, knocking me flat. Psycho fired full auto tacstar, micronukes bursting to life, poison toadstools of power, Legion stars, rocking the entire base. I scrambled to my feet and rushed forward screaming hoarsely, firing full auto xmax. Snow Leopard rose up, his E flashing—full auto x. I held my finger down on the trigger. The noise was shattering; I could hear only a single, high screeching note, overriding everything else. The xmax burst everywhere and hits from our own shrapnel riddled my armor. My faceplate suddenly glowed faintly with a wild white webbing of tracks and I could feel the hits pinging onto my A-suit. I continued firing. Tacstars flashed wildly over my head and micronukes detonated to life again, again, again, burning white–hot in my eyes. The walls disintegrated, riddled, melted, ripped and torn and shot full of holes, supersonic slivers of death—my finger was frozen on the trigger. Xmax, xmax, xmax, ripping forth from my E, my holy E, death to all our foes. We stood in a wilderness of smoking metal, a shredded, twisted ceiling overhead, a junkyard of glowing metal all around us.

"Unidentified life form approaching!"

"Ahhh, scut!"

"Five, tacstars! Three, lasers!" Snow Leopard was on it.

I switched to lasers. More tacstars flashed overhead with that horrible ripping as micronukes exploded right on top of the O, brilliant flashes, shock waves rocking us back on our boot–heels. I could see the O on my tacmap—still there!

What the hell! One and I fired lasers simultaneously. Energy from the face of a star at the speed of light, flashing, dancing, lancing through alien metal like an axe through paper, relentless, merciless. We speared the O like a bug on a pin.

"Probable Omni approaching! Extremely high mag readings! Tacstars, xmax, laser no effect! Recommend random auto biobloc!"

Frozen with fear, I went to flame; I had no time to screw around with biobloc. We had no idea of the creature's frequency, and it was almost on us! I fired flame.

It burst out, a raging explosion of burning gas, a firestorm. Walk into that, alien. Breathe that! Burn, O!

A wave of cold rushed over us. My armor glittered with ice. My finger slipped off the trigger. Snow Leopard ceased firing. Psycho raised his Manlink, stunned and spent. Molten metal ran past our feet, smoking in the cold. A skeletal cenite wasteland of our own creation glowed all around us, a ghostly phospho green in my darksight. It burnt in the dark like the heart of Hell.

"Mag overload! Unidentified life form approaching, fire auto biobloc, Thinker!"

Sweety was insistent, but I could not comply. My heart had stopped. Icy fingers of death clutched my chest. I could hardly breathe, and a hot wave of weakness rolled through my body. I fell to my knees, dizzy and helpless, a cold knot of terror burning in my chest.

"It's here..." a strangled whisper from Warhound.

Snow Leopard was on his feet, weaving, clutching a silent E. Psycho buckled and fell to one knee, his Manlink clutched protectively to his chest, his eyes wild.

The O stepped out of smoke and fire, a towering black shadow, its image shimmering and wavering, glowing violet, not quite real. My muscles short–circuited, trembling violently. I had no control over them—no control. I gasped for breath. It had taken my breath away, my lungs burned. The O was like a mirage in superhot air, its image blurry and changing, tall and black and leathery, a deformed head, all wrong, split in two, dead wet eyes winking. Is it in armor? Terror shot through my veins; my hands trembled. I lost my grip on the E!

The O reached down for Snow Leopard in slow motion. A long twisted arm cloaked in darkness, shimmering, the O moving dreamily in a force field of glowing violet air. Snow Leopard stood paralyzed, motionless. The O's arm brushed past him lightly. Snow Leopard crashed to the deck violently, one hand clawing at the air. The O called out, a blood–chilling, reptilian croak; it was laughing at us!

"Fire full auto biobloc, Thinker!" Sweety urged me.

I could not breathe! Someone gurgled in my ears. My hands slapped at my E, but it was secured to my chest. I could not control my arms. The O moved. It came toward me, shimmering, hazy, relentless. The eyes—freezing me in place; dead alien eyes blinking slowly; my death, here like a dream; an obscene maw, rows of sharp wet needle teeth. The skeletal arm reached out to me, a leathery, slithering, scratching on the deck. Metallic fingers snapped onto my chest plate and the O jerked me off the ground like a rag doll. My body convulsed, twitching, out of control.

A flicker of movement behind me. Warhound hurled himself at the O, howling. His wrists were still tied but his armored fists clutched a cold knife. He struck. The blade slashed into the O.

Sweety shot a mag right into my heart and my fingers closed reflexively over the trigger of my plasmapak torch and squeezed. A sudden flash of energy burst from my chest, lancing straight into the O. Plasma, gas from the heart of a star. A hair–raising shriek and the O thrashed loose like a whirling demon, a cyclone, a tornado, shooting past me. I fell to the deck, helpless. I caught a glimpse of Psycho moving like a puppet, still on one knee, his Manlink suddenly functional. The air cracked and snapped—biobloc!

Sweety had never stopped talking, almost frantic now, what was she saying..."pulse firing random auto biobloc, Thinker! Get your E up! Aim it! I am firing it! Another mag! Get up, soldier! Get up! Get up!"

An explosion, shot in the heart! I screamed. I jerked to my feet, fingers still on the torch. Blue–hot plasma danced before me. The O was an icy tornado backing away from me, bouncing off Snow Leopard, who was on his knees. Snow Leopard raised his E and fired laser, right into the O. The laser ricocheted off wildly, dancing along the ceiling. The O shrieked, freezing my blood. It twirled madly, long limbs whirling, a cyclone of icy air, thrashing back through the wreckage, suddenly gone.

Gone! A whirlwind of air swirled around us in its wake—gone! And I could breathe again, gasping, great gasps of air, my lungs still burning.

"Deadman! I dropped those nukes right on its head!" Psycho gulped, exhausted.

"The damned laser bounced right off it," Snow Leopard panted. "That's a first!"

"Enemy still retreating," Sweety informed me.

"Sweety saved us," I said hoarsely.

The O was gone. All the cubicles around us were also gone, vaporized, blown to bits, now eerie metal skeletons crackling in a sea of fire, black smoke swirling all around us. Shot–up equipment dangled from the tortured ceiling in a writhing mass of snake–like cables. Warhound lay face–down on the deck, his wrists still tied, the cold knife still clutched in his armored hands.

"Warhound! Are you all right? Deadman, who tied his wrists?"

"Water. Water!" Warhound called. I put my canteen to his lips and he drank greedily. His eyes were wild.

"Get his helmet on."

"What happened, Six?"

"It was the O," Warhound explained slowly. "The O. I had to kill you. I had to!"

"Explain, Six!" Snow Leopard was right beside me.

Warhound was in agony; the thoughts rushing through his mind reflected on the harsh angular features of his tortured face. "I got out of the lake—the lava. They...called me. I couldn't resist. They took it all. There was a passage, a crack in the cliff. It was dark—I could hardly see them."

"How many O's?"

"I don't know! It was dark...and after awhile I knew the Aliens were coming. And I had to kill you—all of you."

"The Aliens?"

"Yes," Warhound bit his lip. "You were the Aliens. We...we were the Aliens. And the Aliens were evil. I had no doubts. You all had to die."

"Persuasive creeps, aren't they?" Psycho was upset—his beloved Manlink had failed us for the first time.

"Your helmet, Warhound." Snow Leopard handed it to me.

"Can you untie my hands?"

"Yeah, sure." I hit the release.

"Alert! Life! Human! Legion! Beta Nine approaching!"

Adrenalin, again. I could not take much more of this. I raised my E.

"Priestess! I asked you to stay with the aircar!" Snow Leopard was furious.

"I'm sorry, One. I heard you fight with Warhound, and then the O. I couldn't stay there." Priestess approached us through the skeletalized cubes, her E at her shoulder. Black smoke swirled around her; flames still licked along the wreckage. We kept our E's trained on her, set to vacmin.

"Lower your E, Nine!"

"It's all right, Beta—I'm fine," she assured us, lowering the E. "Redhawk is guarding the Systie. Is everyone all right?"

"We're all right," Snow Leopard responded. "Now—Thinker, Psycho, what happened? This is very important. The O retreated. Why?"

"Warhound attacked him with a cold knife," I replied. "And Sweety stung me, and I triggered my torch, and the plasma hit the O, at close range."

"Negative, Thinker," Psycho interrupted. "It was Mother that saved us. My tacmod fired the Manlink by itself—full auto random pulse biobloc. One of the settings must have affected it."

"I fired your E as well, Thinker," Sweety said in my ears. "Auto random biobloc, unaimed. It is possible one of the frequencies upset it."

"Surely it wasn't the knife," Snow Leopard said. "Let me see it."

Warhound handed it over. The blade was wet and sticky.

"Deadman, what's this?"

"I stabbed it, One," Warhound replied. "I stabbed the O."

"How did you do that, Warhound? I thought it had you under mental control. Deadman! How can a knife penetrate the force field?"

"I don't know, One. I don't know."

"One!" I was on my knees, inspecting the deck. "Look at this!" There was some filth on the floor. Dark, slimy filth.

"Priestess," Snow Leopard ordered, "Take a sample of that, and don't lose it. And take the knife, too. Lord, I can hardly believe this! He brushes off tacstars and xmax and laser like gnats, and then we take him out with a cold knife and biobloc."

"Don't forget the plasma!" I reminded him. "I got the O right in the chest with the torch."

"So it might have been the knife..."

"Or the biobloc..."

"Or the plasma."

"Or maybe a combination! Let's get outta here!"

"I've got the samples," Priestess said.

"Get up, Warhound. Helmets—let's go, let's go."

We backed out slowly, back the way we had come, through a spreading fire. The complex shuddered again, and we could hear a tortured grinding. The lava was forcing its way into the starport. It was definitely time to leave.

"NOVA! NOVA! NOVA! ANY LEGION UNIT...WE'RE UNDER ATTACK!"

The alarm almost shattered our ears. It was a full power burst, a wild and desperate appeal for help, a frenzied, suicidal gamble. We froze, our own holocaust burning all around us.

"Full power! They've had it." Snow Leopard declared grimly.

"Who is it?" Psycho whispered.

"Home in! Sweety, did you get that?"

"Ten, Thinker! I have zeroed the site, as marked." It flashed onto my faceplate.

"NOVA! NOVA! GAMMA TWO FOUR..." It turned into a scream, a shriek of agony. It raised the hairs on the back of my neck. Then there was only dead air.

"Gamma!"

"Oh no...Gamma!"

"Do we answer?"

"Move it, Beta! We answer with our feet! Everyone in the area will be moving on that site. But there's a good chance that's only us."

"That's where the O came from!"

"Is anyone going to give me my E back?"

"Somebody give Six his E back." Snow Leopard led the way. We followed him, tracking the O like a pack of wolves. Further into the Camp of the O's. We would never get back to that aircar, I decided. Never. We would follow Snow Leopard to our deaths. We would die with Gamma, face to face with every O on the planet. We would die for the Legion, just as we should. We would die with our E's on auto xmax, we would die in a burst of our own tacstars.

We would die for Gamma.

Dead air. Only dead air from Gamma, hissing in our ears. A full–

power Nova. Suicide—only a truly desperate sit would justify a full–power burst. The tacmap showed Gamma was in the heart of the starport, far far below us.

Deadman only knew how they had got in there. The entire starport was being slowly crushed as the magma forced its way in. I figured we had zero chances of surviving this one.

I tried not to think about Valkyrie—Gamma Two. I had once promised her—in a different life—that she would always have a call on me, no matter what the future brought. I had promised her that she only had to call, and I'd be there, no matter what. No matter what, I had said. Well, she had called. And we were coming—no matter what. It didn't get much clearer than that. You call a Nova and the Legion is going to respond—no matter what. That's the difference between the Legion and the rest of humanity. Try it sometime with your non–Legion friends. It's a very fast method of discovering Truth.

* * *

We cut our way to Gamma with plasma. As we got closer to the heart of the starport, the structural integrity of the base became worse and worse until finally we were just slicing our way through a massive tangle of compressed metal.

"Gamma, Beta. Approaching your position."

Silence.

We slashed away at coils of solid cenite—why so damned thick? And thousands of writhing cables, spitting pale liquid. Only the Gods of Hell knew what that was. We cut straight down; our tacmods showed Gamma was right below us.

"Gamma, Beta! We're on you! Respond!"

Muffled curses, as we cut away at the metal. They were right below us! The deck glowed and melted.

"Fire at will, gang," Snow Leopard ordered. "Take it easy on the tacstars, Psycho—we don't want to hurt Gamma. But I expect the O's will be here. See you all in Hell."

It was One's farewell. How could we not follow our One? Yes, we'd follow him into the heart of Hell and shoot Satan right between the eyes. I wished a quick prayer as the deck collapsed beneath our feet.

"Gamma, Beta! Respond! Damn! Nine, take out that section there."

They had to be right below us, a steep drop. We could see down through several levels, tacstar shafts, spiderweb cables and twisted cenite junk dangling in air, a thunderous fire roaring down below, thick clouds of black smoke rising. Gamma had fought a desperate battle, and had unleashed a hurricane of tacstars.

"Gamma on scope, as marked! All weapons live, tacstar, laser, xmax, flame, biobloc. Recommend extreme caution!"

Good advice from Sweety—good advice.

"Deadman. Gamma, Gamma, Gamma, Beta, Beta! Beta responding to your Nova! Gamma, it's Beta! Answer, Gamma! We're here! Don't fire!"

Silence—only silence.

We cut away another massive slab of metal and it fell in a rush of sparks, trailing a chaotic jumble of cenite cables.

I could see Gamma now on the tacmap, lower left plate, a ragged circle of glowing dots. Why weren't they answering?

"Beta, Gamma." Cold and dead, it was a voice without soul. "Board. Watch out for the spheres—there's no defense." It was Gamma One, I suddenly realized—Boudicca. Her voice was a hoarse, chill whisper.

We had to rappel down to Gamma's position. Everything was burning all around them, a flaming, glowing holocaust.

Gamma was in a fighting circle, but most of them were not moving. Some of the A–suits were glowing cherry–red. There was no sign of the O's. We approached cautiously, E's up. I reached for one of the glowing A–suits.

"Don't touch him!" A stinging rebuke from Boudicca. "Don't touch our dead!" I withdrew my hand quickly.

"Report, Gamma!" Snow Leopard demanded. Some of them were still alive, I could see. I was frantically looking for Valkyrie. It was so smoky, and I was so charged I could not see clearly.

"One hundred percent casualties," Boudicca replied coldly. My adrenalin count jumped.

Snow Leopard knelt before Boudicca and gently moved her E to one side. "Gamma—tell me what happened."

I could see into one of the faceplates of the dead. I looked away quickly. Broiled alive, the inside of the faceplate covered with heat bubbles, a glimpse of what had once been a human face. Deadman, I never want to see it again. My heart pounded frantically.

"Spheres," Boudicca responded. "Glowing spheres of energy. Probes. We tried tacstars, we tried stunstars, we tried xmax, we tried laser, we tried flame, we tried vac. Scut, we even tried biobloc. None of it worked. The spheres hit our A–suits and merged. Five spheres—five dead. They didn't have a chance."

We listened in horror. I was shaking inside my suit.

"Gamma!" Boudicca's voice was like the crack of a whip. "Report!"

"Squad Gamma all present or accounted for, sir!" It was Valkyrie—her voice was shaky, but she was alive!

A body orgasm of sheer joy rushed through my veins. Alive!

"Count off!" Boudicca hissed.

"Gamma Two present!" Valkyrie shot back. I could tell she was just barely in control.

"Gamma Three—mission accomplished!" But the voice was Valkyrie's.

"Gamma Four—mission accomplished!" It was Valkyrie, again, counting off for the dead.

"Gamma Five—present." A hoarse whisper. It was Scrapper—alive! She was Warhound's dream angel, an attractive girl with tawny hair and heavy breasts.

"Gamma Six—mission accomplished." But it was Scrapper's husky voice, again. Gamma Six was dead.

"Gamma Seven—present!" A deep bass voice. Seven was Sassin the Assassin, Gamma's Manlink master, a fierce Cyrillian merc with skin as black as death and cold slit eyes and sharpened teeth.

"Gamma Eight—mission accomplished!" It was Sassin's voice, again.

"Gamma Nine—mission accomplished!" But it was not Gamma Nine—it was Sassin, yet again.

"Squad Gamma all present or accounted for, Beta," Boudicca One reported calmly. "Four effectives, five dead. Please stand back, we're going to vaporize our dead."

We stood there quietly while Boudicca One spoke for the dead in a cold emotionless voice.

"Immortals in blood,
Brothers in arms,
Soldiers of the Legion

Flying black standards,
Gamma Two Four,
Delegates to the stars
"All seasoned recruits
For Heaven's wars
Now recon Death's cold road.
"Gamma Three, Gamma Four, Gamma Six, Gamma Eight, Gamma Nine; you're four effectives short—Remember your brothers–in–arms.
"Missing in action,
We join you soon!"
Sassin then stood forth and fired one final tacstar into the killing ground. It burnt hot as a sun. I cried uncontrollably. I knew we were all going to end up like that—all of us.

* * *

"Let 'em rot!" Boudicca was furious. Through her faceplate I could see the Legion Cross burnt onto her forehead. She was crazier than Psycho. "I'll not risk the rest of my squad for these stinking Systies!" We were back in the blood factory, adrenalin churning. Rows of pale Systies lay naked on slabs, sightless glazed eyes blinking slowly, tubes of blood snaking overhead. They were all dead unless we helped. We popped a flare so the Systies could see. It was a nightmare scene, black armor and cold flesh and leaping, flickering shadows.

"They're all alive," Priestess reported, rising from the last one. "Ten Systies. I've charged them all. This area is still pressurized. If the outside atmosphere leaks in, they die. I need emergency breathers from everyone; you've each got one in your medkits."

"How can we transport them?" Warhound asked. "There's only nine of us."

"I can solve your problem," Boudicca snapped back, "with one tacstar! Or better yet, let's burn 'em! They don't deserve the dignity of a tacstar! These subs were helping the O's. We should kill them!"

"We're not leaving humans behind for the O's," Snow Leopard responded. "We're taking these prisoners to the aircar. We'll do it in shifts, if necessary. Priestess, you decide which Systies go first."

"They're not humans!" Boudicca insisted. "They're Systies! They're traitors! You're risking Legion lives for Mocains! Look at that skin—

those are Mocains!"

"Take the Outworlders first, Nine," Snow Leopard added.

"Tenners." Priestess lifted one of the Systies—a female—from her slab. It was ob she could not stand. "We can carry them easily," Priestess decided, "with our A–suits. Everyone can take one Systie."

"That still leaves one Systie."

"We can't drag anyone—don't forget that radioactive pool."

"Thinker, can you take two of them?"

"Yeah, sure. Tenners. We can strap one on my back." It would be no problem. Systie trash was light.

"All right, do it—so we make only one trip."

"Gamma wasn't planning on making two trips!"

* * *

Doomed, we awaited the end, huddled in the dark. We never even made it back to the flooded hall. The starport was crushed, grinding in on itself, imploding, thousands of megatons of metal crumpling like paper, millions of megatons of lava, rushing in. Our road in had been sheared right off, and we had been carving a new road, with plasma, through a cenite nightmare, a cenite spiderweb. Now we were on our own road, Beta's Road, but it led nowhere. We were lost, pausing, as the base slowly ground itself to pieces all around us. Lolites illuminated the Systies, pale naked bodies sprawled all around us and sinister black A–suits stepping over them, our helmets scraping against the overhead.

We were in a raw, smoking, glowing hole, cut out of the wreckage with our plasma. Now we faced another drop, several levels straight down. No way out for the Systies. They could not even move. We were giving them a break—the Systies were on their backs, twitching. We had each contributed an emergency breather from our medpaks and Priestess had a few extras, so the Systies were still breathing oxygen. The air in the base was no longer breathable, as the lava rushed in with Andrion 3's poisonous air. The temperature was rising. The lava was close.

"Doesn't look good."

"Ten, One. Ten, One." No answer. Only another earthquake, and more shrieking metal. Faint groans from the Systies. "We're still out of range." Snow Leopard considered the options. I knew there was no need for me to think, with Beta One on the job.

"Thinker, do you think we're cut off?" Snow Leopard asked for my opinion. A bad sign. I noted he was on private.

"It could be," I answered carefully. "If not, we soon will be." Once the lava cut off the starport from the aircar station we were done for.

Valkyrie was right next to me, silent. She was my past, my lost love, a stunning blonde with icy emerald eyes. I had asked her how she was, on private, and she had said she was alive. What more could a soldier of the Legion ask?

"All right, Beta, Gamma—" Snow Leopard announced. "I'm going to full power, just for a frac—commo and sensors—just to see if there's still a way out, and to map it. If we're already cut off, we're going to die anyway. If the O's pick up the burst and respond, we die fighting. If not, perhaps we get out—if there's a way. I'm also going to contact Beta Ten. Stand by to die."

Stand by to die. I closed my eyes. I tried breathing deeply. Tangy hot sweat and violent fear—I could taste it.

Beta One would do it, I thought. One would do it.

"Full power," Snow Leopard ordered his tacmod. "Ten, One. Ten, One. Don't respond. Maintain your position. We're on the way. One out. Full power off." My tacmap exploded with data. The entire starport glittered in cool green tracks, all over my faceplate. In microfracs Sweety was listing alternate routes—two, three, five alternates, flashing over the tacmap, the most likely glowing in orange. Bless you, Sweety! Now we had it all—five routes! We were not cut off at all. The only problem was that the O's might have us, as well. Full power was a two–edged sword.

"Let's get out of here!"

"That's a big ten!"

"Deadman! It's the Legion for me!"

"Psycho, can you get that Systie on my back again?"

"Beta, Gamma—on me!" On Beta One we rose, naked Systies lying across our armored arms, our E's live and ready to fire. And we were on our One all the way, into the dark or into the light, to death or life, back on Atom's Road once again. I said a prayer and followed, one Systie on my back, another in my arms. I could hardly see. I was so charged, I think I had convinced myself that I was on a mission for God, and

Snow Leopard was God. I knew damned well that nothing was going to stop us now.

PART II

GHOST RIDERS

"Our mission against the O's is clear—victory or death. Failure means extinction for our species."

Veltros Training Command—Weapons Introduction, 312 CGS

Chapter 7

King of the Dark

Priestess was asleep in my arms when I awoke. It was still and cold, and we were huddled under thick blankets. For a moment, I was unsure where we were. Cold wet air—a partially open window port, a soft grey dawn. A shiver ran over my skin. Planet Two—we were back on the New World, Andrion 2, waiting for a mission.

I did not dare move. Priestess was breathing softly, completely relaxed, one arm draped over my chest. We were naked, and her body was warm against mine. A sleeping angel, fallen from the sky, wounded, right into my arms. She was perfect—a child's face, fine delicate features untouched by cosmetics: long dark eyelashes, a small soft red mouth, pale luminous skin, and a silken cascade of gleaming black hair. Deadman's death, how could I not believe myself in the hands of the Gods, sleeping with an angel? A warm rush, right into my heart—shot between the eyes. How in holy God's name did I deserve such a lovely creature? Who was I, to share her life? I knew Priestess as well as everyone else in Beta—I knew what made her go. She deserved something better than me. But it was not as if we had any choice. I felt like a Peeping Tom. I feared I didn't deserve her. I was cheating someone—the Gods were asleep.

I eased out of bed. It was freezing. A cold, slick floor. I reached the window; why had we left it open? A cold dawn, a soft wet breeze, grey clouds close overhead. A stunning view. We were in a large medmod perched on a rocky hill overlooking a forested valley, a black forest wreathed in grey mist. A dark dawn, for the Legion. This was our S & S, waiting for a mission. I shivered again; I could taste the moisture in the air. Beta would be together again, soon.

I could feel only fear, thinking of tomorrow. Our E's were propped against the wall. I did not know what we would face, but I knew it would be bad.

* * *

Breakfast was on the patio, open to the morning.

Breakfast in the clouds. The forest below was wreathed in mystery, and the jagged rocks of our hill cut through cold grey waves of mist. I felt totally alive, breathing in the new day, setting my tray down gently on the long table we had chosen for the squad. Priestess was beside me, all in black. The patio was filling up with wounded soldiers. The medmod was a recovery facility. A lot of walkers from Andrion 3 were here—survivors. We were survivors, too. Some of us had not even been hit, but we were just as wounded as the rest. The Legion had dropped us here, anxious, perhaps, for a little mental healing before the next ordeal. I suppose we had to wait somewhere, and this was as good as anyplace else.

"Thinker, what do you think?" It was Ironman, Beta Seven, our first casualty. He had missed all the fun on Coldmark and Planet Three. He was clothed in a sleeveless sweater, seated at our table, holding both arms out for my inspection.

"They look the same," I responded. It was the truth; both arms were pale and well muscled. Ironman was a lifter.

He was a little guy, very young, with fine, clean features and a fantastic build. He had always been proud of his body.

Ironman smiled, a flash of white. His long brown hair hung over his eyes. "I've been doing a lot of lifting, trying to get them the same," he said. "Doesn't the right still look bigger?"

"That's a twelve—they're the same, Ironman. Relax—stop worrying, Morning Light won't care. After all, it was only an arm. You're lucky it wasn't something she really cared about."

Ironman grinned shyly and lapsed into silence, picking at his breakfast. He was a good kid, quiet and easily embarrassed. He had been the first one in Beta to pick up a Taka girlfriend. Morning Light adored him.

Ironman's left arm had been blown away in our assault, but the Legion had grown him a new one, and it looked perfectly good to me. Morning Light wouldn't care, that was sure. Ironman had not seen her since arriving here from Atom. It made him a bit more fidgety than norms.

Psycho banged his tray down, grinning foolishly, looking around wildly, taking in the scene. "Another beautiful day! I could get to like it here. The room service is especially good!"

Psycho always annoyed me. I'm not sure why—he was a good soldier, but he just rubbed me the wrong way. He was always shooting his mouth off. He could just walk in the room, and I would start to burn.

"So where is she?" I asked.

"Where is who?"

"Your room service. Didn't she stay the night?"

Psycho laughed, popping the cap on his tray. "The lady has a responsible position in this medical facility. She can't be seen hanging about with an animal like me. Bad for the image, you know—highly unpro. But she is smitten—totally smitten—I assure you." He giggled, and tore into his medrats. I didn't like the part about "highly unpro."

Psycho was a lot sharper than he pretended to be. Priestess and I tried to be discreet, but it would have only taken a call to her cube to ascertain that she had not been there last night. Five had wanted Priestess's body for a long time, but it was a lost cause. Priestess glanced at me. I decided to let it drop. Next time I'd go to Priestess's cube.

"Morning, gang." It was Snow Leopard, fresh and alert, pale blond hair combed carefully back, hot pink eyes darting around the table. Gamma One was right behind him, Boudicca, the Bitch from Hell, short red hair and cold grim face. I wondered if they had spent the night together, but I did not really care. They were a strange pair—I could not imagine what Snow Leopard saw in her.

They sat down at our table. Snow Leopard was quiet. He concentrated on his breakfast, barely looking at Boudicca. Boudicca was brooding, and I could see the ghosts flash over her features. Gamma One was a walker, if anyone was. Her squad had been almost annihilated on Planet Three by the Omnis. But she had been crazy long before Gamma hit Planet Three. Anyone nutty enough to have a Legion cross burnt onto her forehead had a serious death wish. I remembered her on Coldmark, slaughtering a priest just like a pig. Boudicca scared me. I did not know what the O's had done to her mind, but I knew I did not want to be anywhere near her on our next drop.

"It's not bad here." Warhound appeared happy, savoring his dox, taking in the morning, his pale eyes content. He had a rugged face, deep-set eyes, and a short, severe haircut. "Not bad at all. Considerably better than Andrion Three, huh, Thinker?"

"That's a ten, Warhound." We had almost lost Warhound in the Omni base. It was a holy miracle that we got him back. I could still see him, slashing at that Omni with a cold knife. That picture was burnt into my memory circuits for all time. Warhound was a simple kid, but he was a lot more than I had thought, a lot more than a good soldier. He had saved us all, I was convinced.

"Morning." It was Valkyrie, a pale blonde goddess, approaching the table with her tray. Deadman's death! I shot to my feet reflexively, shocked to the heart. Valkyrie, my old flame, had a black Legion cross burnt right onto her lovely forehead. She glanced at me once, vaguely curious, emerald eyes cold. Then she sat down next to Boudicca. Everyone at the table gaped at her, stunned. Boudicca looked her over, and a hard smile slowly appeared. Boudicca raised a fist, wordlessly. Valkyrie returned the gesture and they struck fists. Valkyrie looked into Boudicca's eyes, but her face was cold and distant. She was gone, I knew—gone at last. The girl I had known so well was no longer here. She was out there with Gamma One now, way out on point.

I slowly sat down again, guiltily. Priestess was glaring at me, cold and furious. I had done it again. Valkyrie was my addiction. I'd have to get over her, somehow.

* * *

The sky was falling! I clapped my hands to my ears and opened my mouth. There had been no warning. One instant we were lounging on a pile of dropboxes and the next instant a catastrophic explosion, a thunderous roar, split the sky.

The air shuddered and vibrations ran up through our boots. I cringed. The agonizing shriek continued, full–throttle, shattering the afternoon. Our eyes went to the source—a Legion fighter parked some distance off, a massive slab of blackened metal, raw blue–white flame pulsing out the burners. The pilot eased back on the throttle, and the nuclear thunder faded. We were at Farside Base, awaiting word on our mission, clad in litesuits, comtops at our waists, carrying our E's, our pitiful personal possessions stowed away in our fieldpaks.

The pilot hit the throttle again, and the earth shook.

He wasn't going anywhere—he was probably just testing the engines. Beta and Gamma went crazy. I could hear nothing except the blast, but the troops were shouting and gesturing, clawing at each other in excitement. Psycho silently screamed, a lunatic grin, waving his Manlink above his head.

Ironman had his arms outstretched, his mouth open. Warhound stared at the fighter in rapt fascination, raising his E unconsciously. Priestess gripped my arm strongly, her face fierce and proud, eyes riveted on the fighter. I clenched my teeth as the power filled the air and the vibes ran all over my body. Boudicca stood on top of a stack of metal dropboxes, facing the thunder, her face gleaming. Valkyrie was below her, shrieking something, her lovely features transformed into a frightening mask. Scrapper had her eyes closed, one hand on her chest. Sassin was chanting something, probably a Cyrillian war song, eyes wild, doing a lunatic dance with his Manlink. It was like a fierce troop of apes, answering the thunder of the Gods.

A series of short, sharp explosions. Then the thunder faded, again. I could hear the troops now, hysterical.

"Hit it!"

"Burn 'em up!"

"Git some for me!"

"Louder! Louder!"

"Hit it!"

A banshee howl from Psycho, eyes glazed. He looked like he was set to fire his Manlink for sheer joy. Priestess turned to me, a faint smile. A shiver ran over her body. Ironman laughed, delighted. The thunder faded and stopped. A shocked silence filtered back over the dusty spaceport. We settled back onto the dropboxes, waiting for Beta One. E's and comtops, and my life in a fieldpak. That was the Legion. I could carry everything I owned. I didn't imagine it was ever going to change. I gazed blankly at my E, and wondered where we were going.

"Here's Beta!" An aircar glided up in a cloud of red dust and the doors popped open and Snow Leopard stepped out, his E strapped to his chest. His face was pale and set, expressionless. He paused before us, his cold pink eyes flickering over every trooper.

"Right, we've got a mission. Listen up." Snow Leopard never raised his voice. We strained to catch every word. He paused to take a long sip of water from his canteen. Then he looked up at the sky.

"Say goodbye to Andrion Two," he said. "We lift within the hour. Target will be revealed after we're underway. There's not much more I can say at this point. Except it's not going to be a picnic. And I don't want anyone to have any illusions. We're not coming back unless we accomplish the mission. And I aim to accomplish the mission." He was cold and calm, completely under control. I knew him well enough to understand that he was deeply troubled.

"Are we going in under–strength?" Warhound asked. Snow Leopard had promised that the squad would be reunited.

"That's a twelve," Snow Leopard responded. "We'll be over–strength. Two and Four and Eight and Ten will be with us—they're fully recovered." A muted cheer rippled through the squad. "And in addition, we'll have Gamma attached to us." Silence greeted the last statement. Left unsaid was what function Gamma One would be performing. I no longer trusted her judgement. I remembered a fat, half–naked priest, arms over his head, and Boudicca switching to xmin, cold and calm, and the priest's blood, splattering all over my A–suit.

I had decided she was insane—only in the Legion it was sometimes difficult to tell. I had done the same thing in the same raid, slaughtering an unarmed Coldmarker. The difference was I had been surprised and terrified and acted out of panic and instinct. Boudicca had had plenty of time—and she had not been afraid. Wasn't that the difference?

I had been in a blind panic—how could I blame myself? How could I compare myself with her? She was insane—completely insane. I shuddered. I had never reported Boudicca's crime. I was not sure why—possibly because I thought I was just as guilty as she was.

Snow Leopard finished his speech. We slowly dispersed. Boudicca and the remnants of her squad were silent—they did not seem surprised. Boudicca must have been briefed on this beforehand, otherwise she would have surely exploded. I prayed to the Dead that she would not be in a leadership position over Beta. She had lost most of her squad—nothing could change that. Whether it was her fault or not, the hand of death was on her now.

"Thinker." Ironman said. He settled down beside me, leaning his E against a dropbox. "Got something for you." He was keeping his voice low. "Don't let anybody see it."

He slipped me a tiny, carefully folded square of silky cloth.

"It's from Moontouch," he added. A chill shot through my system. I looked around guiltily. Priestess was lost in dreams, looking up at the sky. Nobody was paying any attention to us.

"How in Heaven's name did you get this?" I asked Ironman quietly as I unfolded the silk. Moontouch was a Taka girl—a sorceress, a princess, and my secret obsession.

"I just received it last night. I got one from Morning Light—Moontouch wrote it for her. Morning Light can't write. That one was enclosed for you." It was covered with spidery, silvery Taka runes.

"Last night?" I gaped at him. We were thousands of K from Sunmarch. Alpha Base was on the opposite side of the planet. We had not seen the girls since we had left on the Coldmark Mission. The Legion had been a tad busy lately, and there was no time for nonsense. "How did they do it?"

"Never mind how they did it. The Taka are very resourceful—as you see." Ironman flashed his innocent little boy smile at me. He was quite a guy.

"Right, how do I read this?" I was so excited I was not thinking. Atom could read Taka by now, but I could only speak it.

"Your Persist can read it, Thinker."

Right. The tacmod, dummy! My comtop was clipped to my waist. I left it there, powered it on and pressed the message up against the visor.

Nobody was paying any attention to me. "You get that, Sweety?" I spoke softly into the shoulder mike.

"Yes, Thinker," my tacmod replied. "This communication is addressed to you. It is written in classical Taka runes from the Age of the Book."

"Translate, please."

"Translation follows: 'For Slayer, my Lord, my King, my Master, my Maker, my Sword, my Heart and my Soul'." Sweety's metallic voice was devoid of emotion. "'Your slave sends her love, from the land of the living dead. You are in my prayers and in my dreams. My nights are yours alone. You walk with me in the halls of the Holy Dead. All of the power of Those Who Went Before is yours now. The Dead be with you, marching before you, in the name of the Book. I bless you, in the name of the Book. My prayers rise in the dark, carried by incense, to the Realm of the Gods.

"'I await you, alone with the dead. I write my Book of Sorrows, for you to read under the Moon upon your return, and burn in the dawn of our new life. I cry, haunted by your ghost. I pray for your return.

"'I knit a cloak of treesilk, for you. When it is finished, you will return to me. When you come, I will kneel before my King and cry grateful tears of joy. I will sing a song of love, for you. I will make warm tea of flowers and herbs, for you. I will bathe your weary limbs in oil and perfume—for you. All this I do for you every night in my dreams and every day in my mind. My days are only a passing mist, not quite real.

"'The past is real and strong. I pray on my knees, in fields of bones, for your glorious return. Tears streak my cheeks, and the chanting of my prayers rises in the halls of the dead.

"'Your child stirs within me. It is strong and active. I pray for a boy. He will be a King, in our bright new world, and King of the Dark as well. I will guard your child with my life, and present him—for you— when you return.

"'I am your slave, and the vessel of your love. She Who Was Moontouch.' End translation."

I sat there stunned, cold rivers running through my veins. Moontouch was pregnant! She was going to have my baby!

* * *

"We're in dock mode." We crowded around a viewport of the assault craft, anxious to see our destination. We were in deep space, unimaginable light years from any inhabited world. Billions of cold silvery stars glowed against a field of velvet black, and glittering phosphorescent nebulae of gas and dust swirled in frozen splendor as far as we could see. This was the Outvac, further from anything than I or anyone else had ever been, or probably ever would be again. It was so far and lonely that the fear was on my skin like a frost, and my heart had slowed. How far can you really go before you die? Surely there must be a limit. And we must be almost there, for there was nothing here—absolutely nothing. Only the Outvac, and billions of strange stars from billions of years ago; some of them not even there any more; ghost stars, the light hitting our retinas, a magical picture of the past, and every star was a lie. I feared maybe there was really nothing there at all, only us, alone in the vac, microbes falling into infinity, a fragile sliver of life.

"There! Look!" A tiny silvery speck, reflecting starlight. Growing.

"Prep for docking. Secure all personnel." We ignored the command

and maintained our post by the viewport. It was growing, glittering, gliding silently through space. A microscopic silver ship, lost in the immensity of the vac. What could it be? They had told us nothing.

Larger. The details coming into view now.

"It's a cruiser!" A magnificent vision, a cruiser of molten mercury, in cold starlight. A Legion cruiser, growing larger and larger. A vision to die for, growing like magic as we approached.

"It's the *Spawn*!" Unmistakable—a ragged cheer. The *Spawn* had carried Beta to Coldmark, then to Andrion 3. She was an old friend.

"Yes, it's the *Spawn*," Snow Leopard said quietly. "Our old friend, the *Spawn*. Come back, to finish the job. She has a surprise for us. A surprise." His pink eyes were far away.

One had been very quiet lately. We did not dare ask him anything. He knew what the mission was, and he didn't like it. I looked around at the others. It did not matter—we were back to the *Spawn*!

* * *

"Permission to board, sir—Beta and Gamma Two Four, Second of the Ship." Beta One gave a smart salute. It was returned by the *Spawn's* docking officer.

"Board, Beta. Welcome back. There's a delegation waiting for you—come on in."

A delegation? We filed through the triple docking lock and four troopers were waiting for us in black dress uniforms, braced, ready for inspection. A thrill of recognition shot through my veins.

"Element reporting for duty, sir!" It was Beta Two, Coolhand, snapping a salute to One. He looked terrific—tall and lean, a mop of curly brown hair, tanned and handsome, in perfect shape.

"Is the element fit for combat, Two?" One paused before Coolhand, looking over the troops.

"Ten sir! We are all cleared for unrestricted duty."

"How's the leg, Coolhand?"

"Excellent, sir! Better than before."

"Good." One paused before Beta Four. "Merlin? How are you feeling?"

"Perfect, sir! Fully recovered." Merlin looked a bit tense, but he always looked nervous. We could certainly use him, wherever we were bound. He was smarter than the rest of us put together.

"They grew you some new legs, did they?"

"Yes sir! Chromite–core Legion legs, sir. They say I can walk through Hell now."

"That's good, Merlin. That's good. Because that's where we're going, and I'm going to need you there. Eight! Did they get your insides patched up?"

"They fixed the plumbing, sir. Added a little armor."

Dragon was strong and confident, a commanding presence. His dark eyes glittered. Tattoos covered his knuckles and scarred his neck and ears. He was a warrior's warrior. It was great to have him back.

"Redhawk, you were pretty dinged up. Sure you're right?"

"Tenners, One! We're ready to lift!" A tight smile. His red hair was long and tangled, his scruffy beard was even scruffier than before, and his hot eyes gleamed with the light of a joyful madness.

"How's the aircar, Redhawk?"

"She's more than an aircar, One. She's a bitch from Hell. And she's dressed to kill. You got any planets you don't like, just let me know."

"We'll do that, Redhawk. Beta, Gamma—mission briefing—now. In the capmod." Snow Leopard wasn't even giving us time to drop our gear. E's and all, we trooped along the narrow halls to the capmod.

* * *

I had never been in the capmod. It was a lot smaller than the wardroom where we had been briefed on the Coldmark mission. The Capmod was for CAT commanders and sometimes squad leaders, depending on the sit. It was not often they'd ask a squad of troopies to sit in.

We filed in, choosing seats around a table covered with green felt, leaning our weapons against the bulkheads. A new doxcup was set before each airchair. A nice touch! I popped the top on mine quietly; hot dox was better than sex.

Psycho grinned, bouncing slightly in his chair. What a fool! He'd make us look like idiots.

The Second, Cubes, sat at one end of the table. Two Four One, Lowdrop, was beside him. One of the ship's officers whispered something to the Second. Cubes nodded, and the man went away. Snow

Leopard found a seat beside Lowdrop. He looked tense and alert. I was very uncomfortable being this close to Cubes, and I simply did not like Lowdrop. Cubes was a scary guy, but I respected him. My own experience with Lowdrop convinced me that his only concern was with the mission, and that all his assets were expendable.

A shrill whistle shot through the ship like a flicker of lightning. "Antimat drive initiating!" The announcement echoed through the room. "Prep for vac run red!" The ship shuddered, and lurched. My stomach swirled within me. We were underway. They were not wasting any time.

"Beta, Gamma, welcome." Cubes spoke, his icy eyes flickering over us all. "Have some dox. This is highly informal. Two Four and I wanted to brief you all personally on your mission. It's an important mission. It's a very important mission. A mission which we believe can best be accomplished by Two Four Beta and Gamma."

The dox was good. Boudicca was sullen, staring into space. Valkyrie was beside her, cold and empty. I could still hardly believe she had burnt that Legion cross into her forehead. It was a sign of insanity. I knew she was lost to us all—not all of Gamma's fatalities died on Andrion 3.

"Beta and Gamma—especially Gamma—gave more than anyone could ever ask on Andrion Three," Cubes said. "Don't think we don't know it. I know every trooper in the Second. I knew all those who died. They weren't numbers to me. I see their faces every night. And a lot of others as well. Hundreds of them..." He faded for a moment, and a cold hush fell over the capmod. Then he resumed.

"The Legion knows you've given enough. But we're asking for more. As you know, the Systie frontier has collapsed under a massive assault from the Omnis. All of the Gassies worlds are falling, one by one. At latest count, nineteen inhabited Systie worlds have been over–run. And it's only the beginning. The Systies are paying for their legacy of treason to humanity. Unfortunately it's not as simple as that. We can't just laugh as the Systies get what's coming to them. Every new planet the O's seize is a direct threat to us. The Confederation has to get involved. The O's are a plague—a galactic disease—fatal to humanity—and we must exterminate them all. We must!" The Second's eyes blazed.

"We must—and so we're asking for more. More from Beta—and

more from Gamma. Beta—are your troops ready for combat?"

"Yes sir," Snow Leopard responded quickly. "We're ready."

"Any problems?"

"No sir!"

"Good. Gamma—how about you?"

She gave him a cold, dead stare. "We're ready."

"Gamma Two—how do you feel?"

"Will we be fighting the Omnis?" Valkyrie asked quietly. She was a pale angel, branded with the Legion cross. It was like a curse.

"That's a ten, trooper."

"Good. I want to fight the O. I'm happy to hear it."

Insane. My lovely girl was quite insane.

"Gamma Five—what do you say?" He was hitting every Gamma trooper. He must have been worried about them.

"It's fine with me," Scrapper said quietly. "I don't like the O's. Fighting them sounds good to me." It was as if she had been asked whether she wanted her dox sweet or bitter. Scrapper had always been eminently sensible. Now even she sounded as if she had lost it.

"Seven? Any comments?"

"Why don't you just tell us the mission?" Sassin growled. "There's nobody from Gamma going to walk out on the mission."

Gamma Seven was more quiet and reserved than most professional assassins. I could hardly believe he had spoken to the Second that way. Cubes stared at him for just a frac, and then a slow, somewhat sad little smile appeared.

"Good." Cubes said. "Good. Lowdrop, you were right. Beta and Gamma can do it. Give them the briefing. Give them whatever they need. Beta—Gamma—may the Gods be with you." Cubes got up and left the room, off to brief another unit.

I felt sorry for him; I'm not sure why. The man had simply seen too much. But I knew it was ourselves for whom I should really feel sorry.

"Right, troopers—listen up." Lowdrop was always all business, harsh and demanding. "This is your target—Mongera." It appeared on a large wall screen, a pale blue world laced with soft white clouds, icy phospho polar caps glowing against the vac.

What a beautiful world, I thought.

"As you all know," Lowdrop continued, "we did a job on the O ships in the Andrion engagement, and we believe this was what prompted their retreat from Confederation vac and their subsequent attack on the Systies. We were pleased to discover that we are still technically superior to the O in ship–to–ship engagements. Otherwise we'd all be dead. Unfortunately we did not do that good on the ground. We took unacceptable casualties on Andrion Three. We have no counter to their psypower. Everywhere we met the O face to face, we lost. With one exception—Beta Two Four. Beta, you managed— somehow—to force an Omni to retreat. You've all been exhaustively debriefed on this, but the hard truth is we still don't understand what it is that caused that behavior on the part of the O. We have some ideas, however. Some good ideas. The purpose of your mission is to test these ideas. We want to duplicate the conditions you were facing on Andrion Three and test our theories."

"Test your theories." Snow Leopard remarked coldly.

"That's correct. You'll be in a better position this time than last. You'll have some new weapons as well, weapons designed specifically to zero in on the O's weak link, and then exploit it. The tissue and blood samples you brought back from Andrion Three were invaluable."

I wondered if they were planning on issuing us new, improved cold knives. Duplicate the conditions! Terrific—as if once wasn't enough, now we're going to have to do it again! Only in the Legion. A wave of despair rolled over me.

"...on Mongera." Lowdrop said. "The sit is total chaos. The planet is heavily populated, the O put down a major expeditionary force, and the Systies have committed major fleet units. The engagement is still underway. However, it appears clear that the O are taking the planet. Most of the population is being slaughtered. The remainder are desperate to escape. The O are running around loose on the ground—no effective opposition. But we estimate it will be some time before they seize the port. It's perfect for our sit. You shouldn't have any trouble zeroing a single O to work on."

We were all silent, listening to Lowdrop without comment. A single O to work on—right. Trouble is, he would probably object strenuously to our working on him.

"Beta One, you are in command of a reinforced squad for this mission, to consist of Beta at full strength and Gamma at current strength. Your call sign will be Badboy. Gamma One, you are to retain command of your element, but take your orders from Beta One. Beta,

I'd suggest Beta Two take command of your second element as usual, but that's up to you. Your aircar driver will be Beta Ten."

An almost audible sigh of relief rippled through Beta. Boudicca was not to command us—some good news at least! And Redhawk would be our air jock—couldn't complain on that!

"Badboy." Psycho leaned over to me and whispered. "Deadman! How do they come up with these names?"

The screen flashed. Mongera disappeared, replaced by a skeletal black city enveloped in flames, burning brightly under a glowing orange night sky.

"Century City," Lowdrop said quietly. "A few days ago it was a prosperous, modern settlement. Millions are now attempting to flee via the starport. The O are closing in. You will be dropped in here. Your mission is to kill an O—any O—survive, and return to tell us about it. If you get one it will be a first, and could change the outcome of the conflict."

We thought about that. Heavy duty.

"Do you all understand the mission?"

"Does ConFree know about this mission?" Boudicca asked suddenly.

Lowdrop looked at her sharply. "The highest levels of ConFree have been briefed on this mission."

"Well then, screw 'em!" Boudicca snapped. "Why should we die for ConFree? Let those Inners drop in to Mongera themselves and kill an O, if they think it's so important!"

Lowdrop paled with rage, then turned to Snow Leopard. "What the hell is this?" he demanded.

Snow Leopard gazed back at Lowdrop, a trifle uneasily. "I told you what that Systie dip said about ConFree. You didn't respond. Everyone in my squad knows about it. Perhaps an explanation might be in order."

Lowdrop stared at Snow Leopard, then turned away. One hand went to his comset, then hesitated. Finally he turned his gaze back to us.

"All right. I suppose you deserve to know, if anyone does. This information is not to go outside this room. It's true, ConFree did learn about Oplan Gold, about ten stellar years ago. What they learned was that the Systies had a sustained, continuing contact with the Omnis. That was about the most important news we'd ever had. Can you imagine the implications of a Systie alliance with the Omnis? It would have meant System supremacy, and the death of ConFree and the Legion. And you know what that would have meant for humanity."

The capmod was as still as a tomb as Lowdrop continued. "The trouble was, we did not know where the contact was taking place, and we also had no details about it. We did not, for example, know about the unitium. And we had no idea that the contact was taking place in ConFree vac. We naturally assumed that it was somewhere in Systie vac. ConFree has been searching for the zero for ten years.

"When we first learned about the contact, from a highly reliable source, we approached the System, and threatened to publicize it. That got instant cooperation. They promised information about the O's, in return for silence. ConFree couldn't turn that down—reliable information on the O's was hard to come by, and in great demand. Naturally, the Systies told ConFree as little as possible over the next ten years—but what they did tell was totally accurate. ConFree was disappointed in the product, but it was always just enough so we'd want a little bit more. It was certainly better than nothing."

"And the original mission to Andrion Two," Snow Leopard asked, "did anyone know the Systie star track was associated with Oplan Gold?"

"No. ConFree had no idea Andrion was the site they had been looking for. They regarded it as just another Systie intrusion."

"When did the Legion learn about all this?" Boudicca asked.

"We weren't briefed on Oplan Gold until we reported what Gravelight had seen in that Mocain's mind. It was only then that they told us."

"So ConFree approved the attack on Andrion Three?"

"Of course they did! Locating and destroying the site was the ConFree objective all along."

"I don't believe a word you're saying," Boudicca declared calmly. "Cubes told us that ConFree resisted the decision to attack Andrion Three. And ConFree was in bed with the Systies all along! That Systie dip said he briefed a ConFree rep, in STRATCOM Hqs! I'll bet ConFree even knew the location!"

"You shut your mouth!" Lowdrop leaped to his feet and leaned forward toward Boudicca menacingly. "Shut down and listen! ConFree urged caution, but did not call off our attack. I believe that Systie dip was lying to you, but the Legion is investigating your story..."

"It's not my story!"

"Shut down! We are investigating! It's ludicrous to think ConFree is cooperating with the System to protect their contact with the O's. But if there is any truth to it, we will discover it; and there will be serious consequences. And in the meantime, you keep your big yap shut! If this story leaks, I will personally throw your ass into the brig!"

We were quiet. Lowdrop's explanation did not ease my doubts about ConFree. ConFree was a civilian outfit, and they were Inners. Who knew what went on in their minds? I certainly didn't. It didn't seem right to me.

"All right," Lowdrop resumed. "If there are no further hysterical outbursts, let's get back to the mission. With luck, you might not even be downside longer than a few hours. You all now have access to the complete mission orders and ops plans. I'd suggest each of you start on them as soon as you hit your cubes, but I'll leave that up to your One." He paused and took a sip of dox. Calmly, as if he was discussing the weather.

"There are two more details—equally important. As you know, we are in a state of undeclared war with the Systies. However, both the System and ConFree are somewhat busy lately—the Systies are dealing with a full–scale Omni invasion, and ConFree is gathering its strength to defend our own vac from the O's. Neither ConFree nor the System has much energy to devote to another human civil war. Despite this, a Legion warship will not be welcome in the skies over Century City. They're shooting anything that doesn't have port clearance, no questions asked. So you're not going in on one of our ships." Lowdrop smiled, a cold grimace.

I had never seen that before—it was kind of scary.

"Secondly, you won't be going in alone. You're going to have some help, people who know the O's a lot better than we do. They will brief you during your journey to Mongera. I'd advise you to listen to them carefully. They will also be accompanying you downside on your mission. These are VIPs—Very Important People. I expect you to keep them alive during the mission, and return with their hides intact."

"Can't these people take care of themselves?" Boudicca asked, cold and expressionless.

"No, they can't. There are fourteen of you. I'm sure you can handle it. Beta One knows the problem, and he will give you a detailed briefing. So—to summarize: Your mission is to proceed to Mongera, drop in covertly, zero and kill an O, and return—with your VIPs—and report on the results of your mission. Beta One will tell you how this is to be done." Lowdrop glanced at his wristmod. "I've got to go. Badboy, it's quite a mission. I wish I was coming with you, but they've got other plans for me. Beta, it's yours. I know you can do it. It's tricky, but you can do it. Make them understand—tenners?"

"Tenners." Snow Leopard was pale and tense. He rose as Lowdrop left the room. Then he slowly resumed his seat.

Silence settled over the capmod.

"That was fun," Dragon declared.

"The dox is not bad," Psycho observed with a wry smile. The others were silent.

"Well, let's hear it, Snow Leopard," Dragon said calmly. "Don't keep us in suspense."

"We're not going to like this, are we, One?" Merlin had probably already figured it out.

"Make them understand..." Warhound repeated. "I liked that part. He was talking about us, wasn't he?"

"If it involves killing O's, you won't get any problems from Gamma," Boudicca observed quietly. "So let's hear it, Beta."

"Right, listen up." Snow Leopard let his gaze wander over us all. "You're right, Merlin. Nobody's going to like it. But that doesn't matter. This mission is of critical importance to the entire war. This is the most important mission which has ever been entrusted to us. And we are going to accomplish it or die—it's that simple. We're not going back without killing an O. You can all just make up your minds about that— there's only one way back. And I don't want any bitching and whining along the way. We're not going to argue with any aspect of the ops plan—even if it upsets us a great deal. We're just going to keep our mouths shut, and follow orders, and do our best to survive, and accomplish the mission." One was really working himself up. His hot pink eyes were almost spitting sparks, and his pale face was starting to glow red.

"You understand that, Gamma?" Snow Leopard glared at Boudicca.

"I speak Inter!" Boudicca snapped back, the color rushing to her face.

"Good—because these orders are in Inter, and they are perfectly clear."

"You don't have any right to question Gamma's loyalty!" Boudicca objected. The Legion cross on her forehead was throbbing.

"I just want to make it clear—to everyone in this room—that we are going to follow our orders, to the letter. These orders are NOT open to debate. With that clearly understood, I will now inform you of a few details which Two Four One did not mention."

I could hardly wait. Snow Leopard had our respect and he knew it. He was not in the habit of lecturing us on the necessity of following orders. Whatever he had to tell us had to be very shaky.

Snow Leopard slowly took a sip of dox. He carefully put his cup down, and spoke. "We're going in on a Systie–registered private freighter. It will have a crew of Systie civs, but they'll be under Legion control. There'll be a Legion half–squad on the ship for security—they'll be topside when we drop. The ship will have port clearance—it's a profiteer, dropping in to make a fast fortune evacing refugees. We'll drop in a Systie aircar. Some of you are familiar with the aircar. It's the same girl who took us off Andrion Three. Redhawk assures me it's now a very hot ship."

"That's a big ten, sir." Redhawk lit up like a lamp. "She's panting on the sheets."

It didn't sound so bad to me. A Systie ship, but under Legion control. We could do that.

"Who's the half–squad?" Boudicca asked.

"Two–Three Delta. They're a good bunch. They were on the Andrion Three drop with us."

"And the Systie crew—they're with us?" Coolhand wanted to know.

"That's a ten. They're under Legion control."

"What does that mean?" Boudicca interrupted.

"It means they'll be there when we ask for extract," Snow Leopard replied. "That's what it means."

"We can do it, One," Dragon concluded. "It's a bit unorthodox, but we can handle it. What's the problem?"

"The problem," Snow Leopard said, "is the VIPs who will be accompanying us, and who will be teaching us about the O's, prior to our arrival. The people we are going to be keeping alive. They're Systies, too."

"What?" Boudicca looked as if she was about to explode.

"You heard me."

"Systies?" Boudicca snarled, "Systies! Systies are going to be telling us what to do? Systies are going to accompany us on the drop?"

"That's a ten—three of them. They are official reps of the United System Alliance, and they are just as interested in the success of this mission as we are."

"Deto!" Boudicca exploded. "Who cares what the System wants? They caused this mess! Official reps? Are you crazy? Is the Legion crazy? We're going to teach the System how to kill O's? Who's the lunatic who thought that one up?"

"The Systies know all about the O's, trooper! Or at least they know a lot more than we do. They are going to share this knowledge with us—knowledge that could keep us alive! And we, in return, are going to share with them what we learn about killing O's. That's the deal! The orders are coming at you from the highest levels, but they're coming through me. You have a problem with your orders, you see me, trooper—but I wouldn't advise it!"

Laughter. Evil, guttural laughter, from Sassin the Assassin, Gamma Seven. His sharpened white teeth flashed as he spoke. "Dead meat. They're dead meat." Valkyrie raised a fist in agreement.

"Let's understand one thing," Snow Leopard said quietly. "I will personally execute—on the spot—anyone who harms these Systies. Badboy is charged with their safety. I've given my personal word to the Second that these three Systies will accompany our survivors back to report on our mission. I have never before had to threaten my men, and it upsets me that it appears to be necessary this time, but that's the sit. You got that, Seven?"

"Yes sir." Sassin was suddenly quite subdued.

"Gamma Two, you get that message?"

"Yes sir." Valkyrie was cold and distant.

"I am completely serious," Snow Leopard continued. "You have no idea how important this is. A successful mission could forge an alliance with the Systies against the O—and it could also lead to the collapse of the System itself—since their policy of appeasement directly led to the Omni invasion. Failures on that scale have consequences. Important consequences."

"Snow Leopard—I don't quite understand one thing." Merlin said.

"Yes, Four."

"If the System is with us on this, then why the elaborate cover story, the civilian freighter—why are we worried about port clearance, if the System is with us?"

"Four, this mission is top secret, both here and on the Systies' side. Nobody on Mongera will know what we're up to. The System has always been more afraid of its own people than of anyone else. If it got out that the System was cooperating with the Legion to solve a problem it had created in the first place, it could lead to political problems of the highest order."

"But if we're successful, won't it get out?"

"I'd say—offhand—that the Legion will publicize it heavily. No matter what we promise the Systies."

"The Systies must know that."

"I think they do. But I believe they have reached the point where they feel they have no choice. And if the mission fails, they've lost nothing. We're dealing with the highest levels of the Systie regime. They apparently believe the potential benefits of this mission outweigh the possible political backlash. I think they're wrong—but what I think doesn't matter."

"May I say something?" Boudicca was trying to control her temper.

"Go right ahead, Gamma." Snow Leopard was tense and touchy. They might have been lovers, in bed, but there was no love showing in the capmod that day, between those two.

"Just for the record, I want you to know what I think. I think this stinks. I think this is a rotten setup. I think if this works, and we get the O, those three Systies are the only ones who will return to the ship, and the Legion is never going to get the word. I don't like Systies. I don't trust Systies. And they feel the same about us. I'll make a prediction. If our O goes down, the Systies turn their guns on us. Immediately. And if that happens, Gamma is shooting back. Do you have any problems with that?"

"It won't be necessary, Gamma. This is a Legion op. The Systies will be unarmed."

Boudicca was quiet. Stunned is more the word. Unarmed! Going to face the O's, unarmed. They were certainly putting themselves at our mercy. I wouldn't do that, with Systies. No—I was not that trusting.

"Right, if there are no more bitches I'd suggest we get to work."

Snow Leopard stood up, aggressive and confident once again. "Hit your quarters and start working on the mission orders. See the ship for your bunks. When I want you, I'll let you know."

Chapter 8

Volunteers

"How'd you like a ship like that?" Dragon asked.

We were in a troop shuttle from the *Spawn*, gathered around the screens, approaching a prize of war. A private starship, a fabulous toy for galactic plutocrats; a wonderful, shimmering white ship, stunningly beautiful. It was a slaver and had been seized by a Legion interceptor. Now a Legion prize crew was aboard. This was to be our transportation to Mongera. I knew this ship. I had visited it in orbit around Coldmark. This was the Personal Ship *Maiden*, and it was Tara's ship. My heart beat faster as we approached. It was a ship of light, a beacon of hope and life floating in an infinite, black ocean of death. How could such a lovely ship be a slaver? Tara—how could she possibly be involved in such an unholy venture, even as a Legion asset? I could hardly comprehend it. I had attended midschool with Tara in our own impossible past. How long ago it seemed!

"Slavers!" Merlin remarked. "Nice company we're keeping."

"We need them," Coolhand commented, "to get port clearance. So let's be nice!"

"Slavers and Systies!" Boudicca spat. "Scut! Some mission!"

"Thinker," Dragon was right next to me, grinning happily. "You meet any hot slave honeys when you were on board her?"

But I didn't really remember much about the slaves at all. What I remembered was Tara, her face glowing out of the dark. She was certainly cooperating with the Legion—but at what cost? The Tara I knew was as bright as a sun—compromise was not in her vocabulary, and slavers only lived until they met the Legion. She would have gladly shot them dead, herself, and felt good about it.

"Prep for docking! Secure all personnel!"

Stone cold beauty, a ship like a burning star glittering in the dark. What horrors had it known? How many hopeless slaves had seen those portals? How many tortured souls had Tara delivered into the unknown? Tara, Tara, Tara, my hopeless, dark angel—what will be your fate?

Priestess squeezed my hand, smiling up at me, a child of the Legion, blinking warm dark eyes. A shot in the heart. Priestess was mine, totally mine, and she was all I ever wanted. Just to be alone, with Beta Nine—how could I want anything more? But life was not that easy, could never be that easy. Tara awaited me, in a ship of slaves, and back on Andrion 2, a Dark Cloud princess was going to have my baby. Moontouch, Moontouch, Moontouch, my secret obsession. What was I going to do? It was all dark to me—in the Legion you live one day at a time.

* * *

The Legion never told anyone a thing they didn't need to know. Snow Leopard certainly knew about Tara, and so did Delta One. I only knew a little.

Delta's half–squad came on board with us, and the Spawn's prize crew was ferried away. We went into stardrive immediately—there was no time to waste. While Delta took charge on the bridge, Badboy fanned out through the ship, looking for trouble. It was a palace in the stars, still and lifeless except for the padding of our boots in the carpeted halls and the sighing of the conditioners. The odor of perfume still hung in the air. A pleasure palace, full of memories. Now it belonged only to the Legion—what would we do with this ship of lights?

We found the brig—they had locked the humanoid inside. I had heard about this creature, but had never seen him. Gildron, they called him.

He snarled at us, his eyes dark lifeless pools. A giant, he was clothed in the ship uniform, elektra violet. Thick hair covered his huge body. The prize crew had said he was the Commander's personal bodyguard. I tried to reconcile this half–human beast with the girl I had known, and could not. Tara had taken a very strange road to the present. I sighed, and turned away.

The Cyrillians were all unarmed, but it was their ship—we didn't trust them for an instant. They snapped to when we approached, and tried to be helpful. We were all armed, at all times, and prepared to fire. They knew it. The Legion was not a trusting bunch. The Cyrillians watched us with suspicious eyes, and whispered to themselves in their own language. They had jet black skin, yellow slit eyes, and sharpened teeth. Cyrillians were mercs, refugees from a savage, violent world that had been effectively destroyed by the System in a series of nasty civil wars. They were survivors. Gamma had one Cyrillian in their squad—Sassin the Assassin. He was a survivor, too. And so was I.

* * *

I was on aircar watch when she came. Our Systie aircar was safely tucked away in the launch bay of the *Maiden,* and we were not about to let any of the slavers near it. So we watched it. I sat there under its great black belly, my E at my chest, nightmares rushing through my mind, and there was nothing at all I could do to stop them.

She came as silent as a ghost and at first I thought I was imagining her, a vision from my past, glowing softly out of the darkness. Then she moved, just a little, and her auburn hair slid over her shoulders like silk, and she blinked hot exotic eyes and wet her lips with her tongue. The shadows highlighted her high cheekbones and her skin was like brown satin. She was dressed in black. I rose to my feet.

"Hello, Wester." That soft, slightly husky voice.

Adrenalin, my heart exploding. She had always called me Wester.

"Tara! Hello." It was the best I could do, under the circumstances. I tend to freeze up in the grasp of angels.

"Are you worried about the aircar?" A faint, faraway smile.

"Yes. Yes, we are."

"There's no need to worry. My Cyrillians are very enthusiastic about this mission. They will do exactly what I tell them to do."

"And what will you tell them to do?"

She blinked, looking right at me. "We'll do the Legion's will. Isn't that what it's all about? We all do the Legion's will."

"Even you, Tara?"

She looked around, uneasily. "Especially me, Wester. Are you going downside in that thing?"

I looked up at the aircar. "Yes, I'll be downside."

She looked at me again, a soft, faraway gaze, full of longing and regret. I didn't need it; not then, not ever. "...all the more reason." Her lips found the words, but I could hardly hear her.

"Say again?"

"All the more reason..." She tossed her head back, and her hair hissed around her shoulders again, silk on silk. "...for the mission. I can hardly believe it, Wester. Surely it must mean something."

"What do you mean?"

"I mean we're tossed together again, two grains of sand in the wind. You're going downside, and I'll be watching over you, from above. Doesn't it give you a thrill?"

"Tara..." There was only one thing I wanted to know from her. "You'd make it easier on me if you'd explain something. You command a slave ship, your alias is in our Black Book, and you pass secret messages to the Legion. I suppose that makes you a Legion asset, but it doesn't explain a thing to me. I knew a girl called Antara once...a long time ago. She wouldn't do what you've done. Why, Tara? Why? You used to tell me everything. Remember?"

She looked up at the aircar again. "Remember...yes, I remember. How could I forget? Yes, that was a long time ago, wasn't it? A girl called Antara...life was simpler then. I was just a girl, and you were just a boy. Now you're a soldier of the Legion, and I'm...well...a lot of things, I suppose. I see the Legion has told you nothing. Yes, of course they wouldn't. I can't answer your questions, Wester. You want more than I can give."

"The Legion has taken your ship, Tara. Are they going to execute you? You can surely tell me that."

Her dark eyes smouldered briefly. "I can take care of myself, Wester. They were going to kill me and all my crew, when they captured us. But they didn't. Perhaps it would be best if you thought of me as being dead already. Yes—maybe she is dead, maybe Tara is only a memory, just like that boy Wester. But I can tell you this much, Beta Three. I've got plenty of names and I can assure you that Cintana Tamaling is very much alive, and she's going to be watching over you when you're downside. You can depend on that." She turned abruptly and faded into the dark. A hatch hissed open, and she was a shadow, outlined against the light. "Good luck, Beta Three," she called out softly. "Good luck." And then she was gone.

* * *

A Legion interceptor delivered our Systies, in great secrecy, in the pit of the vac, endless light years from nowhere. There was no hint where the interceptor had come from. We were definitely in Systie vac by then, and getting closer and closer to Mongera. Whatever the Systies were supposed to teach us about the O's, they would not have much time. Not that it mattered to me. I had already decided I was not going to be listening.

"Leave your weapons outside, Badboy. Delta will babysit." Snow Leopard made the announcement, his face pale and grim. Whatever was on the other side of that door was bad news. A couple of Delta troopers stood by with E's. We propped our weapons against the corridor wall. Delta was at the bridge and would watch over the Cyrillians. There was nobody in the conference room except the Systies.

"You sure they're unarmed, One?" Coolhand whispered.

"They're unarmed—but you're not going to like it. Nobody's going to like it. Right, Badboy! File in and take your seats! Go in there and sit down and shut down! You hear me? I want you to act like a Legion squad—keep your traps shut!" Snow Leopard's face was flushed, his hot pink eyes glaring at us.

I noticed One's mini was still holstered at his waist. We filed in.

There were three of them, dressed in STRATCOM red, Systie silver and SIS green, sitting together calmly at a large conference table. A huge Mocain soldier, tall, shaved bald, well–muscled, pale greenish skin, flashing dark eyes, no eyebrows. Another Mocain, a female, as pale as death, short military hair, speckled, mottled skin, her face in shadows, as still as a statue. The third was an Outworlder, slender and wiry, shaved skull, blinking nervously. It was all wrong, and warnings were going off in my mind. I paused before an airchair. Then I realized what it was. The girl, dressed in SIS green—there was a huge purple scar at her throat, and ugly shrapnel splotches all over her face. It was that Mocain bitch, what was her name—Millina! She had taken Valkyrie, and almost killed us all on Coldmark. Merlin had lost his legs in that raid. We had rescued Valkyrie, but had failed to recover Millina...we had thought she was dead, but here she was, cold green flesh, sitting right there.

And the Outworlder! It was that simpering, fast–talking diplomat we had captured on Andrion 3, right in the Omni's starport. He was scared of his own shadow, and terrified of the O's. These creeps were going to teach us about the O's?

No, this was not going to work.

Beta and Gamma filed around the table, but nobody sat down. We stared at the Systies. Valkyrie turned pale, locked on to the Mocain female like an E on laser. Her lovely mouth snapped open in a savage snarl. Boudicca seized her arm, but Boudicca was also glaring at Millina, the blood rushing to her face.

"It's that Systie dip!" A hoarse whisper from Psycho.

"It's the bitch!" Boudicca exclaimed. "That Mocain bitch! Scut, I thought we killed her!"

"It's not too late..." Valkyrie trembled, leaning forward, both hands on the table, and it looked as if she was going to climb right onto the table and throw herself at the Mocain. Boudicca grabbed her by the shoulder to hold her back. The tall Mocain soldier stood up, and Snow Leopard appeared by his side.

"Silence!" Snow Leopard shouted. "Badboy, be seated! I want silence!" He was furious, his face bright red.

"Can it not control its own units, squad leader?" The Mocain soldier was openly contemptuous, speaking Inter with a thick Mocain accent. He was dressed in STRATCOM red.

"Take your seats, gang," Coolhand quietly ordered. We obeyed. I think it was a combination of Coolhand's low–key tone and the contempt displayed by the Mocain. We were not at all pleased by this development. Valkyrie was just barely under control; Boudicca was still holding her back.

"Do you recognize me, Millina?" Valkyrie called out. There was no stopping her. Millina blinked her cold reptilian eyes and focused on Valkyrie. She gazed at her for a few fracs, her face cold and set.

"Legion," she at last concluded. "It's our Legion. Yes...yes, we see you now. You've changed a little. We like the cross. Yes, it suits you!"

"I'm sorry you didn't die, Millina."

"Yes, we know. You're a lot stronger now than when we first met, Legion. We think we were good for you—don't you?" A faint smile appeared.

I could hardly believe it.

"I'm not good for you, Millina," Valkyrie replied. "You'd better keep your distance." She twitched, pale and sweating.

I knew if Valkyrie had her E that would have been one dead

Mocain.

"All right, blackout," Snow Leopard ordered. "So now we all know. Some of you have met Systie Cit Millina, of STRATCOM Information, on Coldmark. Others have met Systie Cit V–Four Carollus, of the diplomatic service of the United System Alliance, on Andrion Three. Colonel Calgan of the Fifteenth DefCorps is new to us all. Millina and Carollus we met under very trying circumstances, for us all. But that was the past. The past is dead and gone—maybe some of you have heard those words." Snow Leopard paused, and looked up at the ceiling. His eyes glowed, and his voice was hypnotic.

"I'd like you to think about that. We are engaged in a great historical event—we are soldiers of the future, and we're walking point for our race. This is no ordinary mission—it requires great courage to set aside the past and step into the future. It requires courage and faith. Faith in the Legion, faith in your leaders, faith in your comrades, faith in yourselves. I know we can do it, Badboy. These people have lived with the O's; they know their capabilities. They know exactly what the O's can do. And they're going to tell us all about it. I want you to put aside the past, and open your ears and your minds, and listen to what they have to say. It might—it just might—save our lives. They're coming with us, downside. Unarmed. That says something, Badboy. We must cooperate—we must. Together, we can defeat the O's. The Gods of History are watching us—right now. We have a great responsibility, and we will prove equal to the challenge—we will!"

Beta One was a visionary. When he got onto the subject of history, it was all over. He was convinced he was a direct participant in momentous events, and we were his squad. We were all going down in history, whether we wanted to or not. I always enjoyed listening to him, and I often wondered whether he was right. But it was truly wonderful, knowing that our leader had such great faith in his cause. He had enough faith for us all.

"Is it trying to convince its own units to obey it, squad leader?" the Mocain Colonel asked. "Why doesn't it just order them to do what it wants?" He seemed vaguely amused by One's speech.

"My units—as you call them—will do exactly as I say," Snow Leopard replied. "If I ask them to shoot you through the forehead, they will do so. If I ask them to safeguard your life, they will do so. What you do not understand is that the Legion is composed of free volunteers. There's not one Legionnaire who hasn't chosen to be here. And we like to tell them what they're fighting for."

The Systie Colonel laughed. "Is it telling us its troopers are in the Legion of their own free will?"

"Is that so hard to comprehend?"

"It is hard to believe. But let us not argue. We have much to tell it about the Variants. Let us begin. Each of us has something to contribute. We all spent a very long time on Andrion Three, under the power of the V. We will brief it on what we know of their military capabilities. Cit Millina will brief it on the V's psychic powers. Cit Carollus will brief it on what we know about the V's decision–making processes. Together, we believe we can prepare Legion to face the V— or the Omnis, as it calls them. Then, it will be up to Legion. We do not know how to kill the V—but we can tell it everything we learned."

Dragon grimaced. He looked over at me and slowly shook his head. Dragon was not buying it either. We would listen, but we were not going to be easy to convince. As the Systie Colonel droned on, my mind drifted away. Priestess sat off to my left, an angel in a litesuit, blinking dark wet eyes. What was she doing here? A volunteer—yes, she was a volunteer, just as One had said. We were all volunteers, immortal fools, walking death's dark road. Mongera grew closer every frac, and all we could do was wait for it, and prepare.

Chapter 9

Mongera

"Mongera Port, this is P.S. *Maiden*, exiting stardrive and requesting port clearance. We are here to evacuate refugees in response to its regional nova. Please give us a sitrep on the starport and vicinity." Cintana Tamaling was cool and efficient, once more in charge, sitting in the command chair. Her first officer, Whitney, was beside her in the exec's chair, cruising on mags, quiet and calm. Snow Leopard and I huddled with Delta One just out of view of the d–screens. The idea was to keep an eye on the slavers.

The main screen flickered and filled with light. A Mocain officer appeared, his faintly green skin covered with a tracery of pale white scars. His suspicious eyes focused on the screen under naked brows. Identification data from the P.S. *Maiden* filled his databloc and hopefully matched up with the registration data in his files. The officer would be viewing two young females on his screen. The Commander was a stunningly beautiful creature with pale brown skin and lustrous auburn hair. The exec was a pale blonde, as cool as ice. The biotech should have been flashing confirmation of the genetic ID—this was the P.S. *Maiden*, and these were the principal officers.

"P.S. *Maiden*, this is Mongera Port. It has port clearance. The port is secure. Appreciate its assistance. Request it hard–land inport. Mongera Port is our evacuation center. We are sending it landing data."

"Negative, Mongera," Tara replied briskly. "We will not risk our ship downside. We will do the evacs with our shuttle, call sign *Highroad*, repeat *Highroad*. Please note we are a commercial firm and will be charging a fee for this service. We are sending it our price list, terms, and guarantees. We will be happy to evac everyone we can carry."

Delta One was just out of view of the main screen, a shadow with an E. He was a young trooper with long black hair; dark tanned skin; and alert, wary eyes. He'd be in charge on the ship when we were downside.

"P.S. *Maiden*, this is Zemband Station! We are surrounded and need evac fast! The skies are clear—request its shuttle land here, please send us its terms."

"P.S. *Maiden*, this is Century City main aircar terminal! We request extraction right now! We'll pay whatever it wants! Just get here quick! We've got over seven hundred people here and no more aircars!"

"P.S. *Maiden*, this is the Cairnsport Police. We have a group of two thousand refugees on the move in darkside—we're sending it our zero. These are women and children, *Maiden*! The V are closing in, and the military can't help us. It is our last hope, *Maiden*. We'll give it everything we have! Please don't abandon us!"

"P.S. *Maiden*, land at the National Trust Commercial Center in Torrens City. We're a group of bankers and lawyers, treacherously abandoned by the military. We'll pay twice what it's asking! Its highest profits are right here! We're sending it our zero."

"P.S. *Maiden*, our town is cut off and our aircars are all gone! This is Forest Hill—we're a squad–sized DefCorps unit and the V are cutting us to pieces. Maiden, the schools were never evaced! All of the children are still here, and the V are closing in! *Maiden*, there are hundreds of children here! We can't pay it. Just save the children, *Maiden*. Please! We're willing to die. Just save the children! We're sending it our zero."

"This is Mongera Port! Clear this channel! P.S. *Maiden*, its shuttle is cleared to land at Mongera Port—we have hundreds of thousands of refugees processed for evac, right here. We'll meet its terms."

"Sounds like the bankers and lawyers have got it," Whit said with a faint smile. "We guess we could call this a profit–rich environment."

Tara was silent but she was in a white–hot rage—I knew her well. She cut the commo and turned to us. "Are you people ready?"

Snow Leopard picked up his E. "Keep an eye on things here, Delta."

"You watch yourself, Beta."

"Death." Snow Leopard and I started to move out. Whit got up from her chair. Tara ignored me. She looked up at Whit.

"Take care of the *Highroad*, Whit. It's the only shuttle we've got." Tara avoided her eyes.

"Yeah, we love Cit too, Commander. We'll be careful."

"Sub will be fine, Whit," Tara said carefully. "Don't worry."

* * *

"Helmets on! Tac mode! Systems check!" A cool green glow bathed the interior of my helmet. All systems were ten high. Beta One lowered himself into the aircar from the overhead escape hatch. He was metalman, a great dull black soldier–ant, studded with antennae and weapons. We were all in A–suits. I checked my E. It glowed with life and death—this was a special E, as special as you could get. All the twisted dark science the Legion lab rats could cook up was in that E. It was a very nasty bag of tricks and if this didn't work, there was nothing left except to say our prayers.

"Seal the car."

"Shuttle prepped for launch."

"Badboy, Delta, all secure." Our aircar was poised in a launch tube in the belly of the shuttle, the *Highroad*. The other tube housed Cinta's personal aircar. Two of Delta's best were riding the shuttle, watching the pilot and the crew. The *Maiden*'s exec, Whitney, was piloting the shuttle, and she was bringing a few Cyrillians to help with the refugees. All of Badboy—Beta and Gamma—were packed into the aircar, along with the three Systies.

"Just another drop, gang." Coolhand was in a good mood—he was always a calming influence.

"Keep your safeties on, Psycho, or this is going to be a very short trip." Warhound sat behind a manport atlauncher, modified to counter the O's psypower. He sounded a bit nervous, with good reason. Psycho grinned back at him through his faceplate. He was burdened with a massive weapons system, a heavy chainlink skysweep attached to a backpak shoulder rig. Quadruple ammopaks were strapped to his back. The chainlink was normally mounted in Legion fighters. In addition, Psycho had a specially modified manlink secured to his chestplate. He was a walking arsenal, a city buster. We hoped it would bust the O as well, but there was only one way to find out.

"Separation!" A heavy metallic explosion rang through the aircar and we were falling, hearts in our throats, stomachs floating, falling down into the dark. The shuttle had separated from the *Maiden* and was carrying us down to our fate.

"Good luck, Whit."

"On course, Badboy."

"Omni ships continue combat tracks last reported. Looks like another Starfleet attack shaping up."

"Ignition—stand by!" A warning tone sounded, and the launch's drive exploded to life. The gravs pressed us into our chairs.

Into the dark. We could see the future on the screens as the *Highroad* fell towards the planet. Mongera glowed before us, a massive, luminous presence, icy blue, drawing us in, sucking us in to our doom, so beautiful it hurt, so great, so awesome it was like the face of God. We were microbes, struck blind and deaf and dumb by the light, falling, helpless, into the future.

"Good angle, Whit."

"Look at all that traffic!"

I shifted my gaze to the port datascreen. The planet was ringed with starships, thousands of ships, a great rescue force, freighters and liners and yachts and cargo tramps and even a great fat colony transport. And a whole fleet of warships, cruisers and fighters and interceptors and probes and scouts and drones. Thousands of tracks, glittering golden tracks, orbiting the planet like rings of dust. And, here and there, popping in and out of stardrive, darting into the planet on hot combat drops were evil little ruby fireflies like falling stars, exploding into whole fleets of ships, hundreds of deceptors hiding their tracks—these were the Omni ships. And Starfleet was after them, immediately. But there was no hope for Mongera—none at all. Great numbers of Omni transports had already landed, discharging hordes of aliens—and nobody could stop them, on the ground. Nobody.

"Good drop, good drop."

The skin started to glow cherry–red as we entered the at. I was sweating inside my A–suit. No mags required, I decided. I was ten high. The stars faded behind us. I hoped the pilot knew what she was doing. Mongera filled the screens.

"Look at that—Starfleet fighters attacking the Omni ships." Hopeless. A gallant last stand. They might get the ships, but no matter what happened, Mongera was doomed.

"Squad leader, it is responsible for our lives. We will help it as we can, but it must protect us," the Mocain soldier said. The three Systies were clad in dull bronze–colored Systie armor. They weren't really expected to do anything, I knew. They were just along for the ride, watchdogs for the System.

"Yes, squad leader," Millina hissed in agreement, "protect us from its squad." Snow Leopard ignored her. We were all going to be watching over them, but Beta One had recruited me as a special watchdog. I was not happy about it. I had been told that the Legion had looked into the Systies' minds, and that there were no plans to betray us. It did not reassure me.

"Is that thing going to work, Merlin?" Ironman asked.

Merlin smiled, and held his weapon up to examine it closer. It was a heavy biobloc fieldfaxer, another special toy, just for us, fresh from the lab.

"It'll work," Merlin replied confidently. "It'll cook an O like an egg. Those samples you guys brought back from Andrion Three were conclusive. We've finally zeroed the O's genetics. But I can't get through the mags. That's up to the rest of you. Get me through those mags and I'll cook your O."

"Make it well done, Merlin," Dragon said. "Raw meat can be dangerous."

"You get me through those mags and he'll be chargrilled."

The ship began to vibrate wildly, blitzing its way through the atmosphere. Outside we could only see the interior of the launch tube, but Mongera was right there on the screens, coming right at us, irresistible and final. We could see the shuttle's skin, white–hot, and I was strapped in. It was every childhood fear–of–falling nightmare I'd ever had turned up to max, like a killer dog tearing out my throat. Cold sweat trickled down my temples.

Yes, get us through the mags—that would be the trick. The O's walked around in personal force fields, and we did not know how to counter them. Yet we had done it—somehow—last time, and Warhound had drawn blood, when the field went down, briefly. Now all we had to do was do it again.

The ship shook, banging around wildly. Somebody laughed. You have to be in the Legion awhile before you can appreciate that type of humor. I wasn't quite there.

"Thinker, Warhound. You know what I think about that O we met?"

"No. What do you think?"

"I think it was unarmed."

"Yeah—it was."

"It was probably somebody's aged grandmother."

"Yeah, or a pregnant lady," Psycho cut in. "Or a little kid, pissing in its pants."

"Thanks, guys," I said. "I needed that."

"It's a ten, Thinker," Psycho assured me. "When we meet a real O, fully armed, we'll be able to give all this hardware a good field test. Otherwise we're wasting our time."

"Wouldn't want to do that."

The ship was shaking itself apart, a falling star, a meteor, hurling itself at Mongera's tortured surface.

"We die today," Valkyrie said dreamily.

"We die together," Boudicca replied quietly.

Outstanding leadership, I thought glumly.

"That O is going to die too, guys," Sassin announced. He was armed with a massive plasma manlink, another horrendous new toy for our O to ponder.

"I'm staying right next to you, Sassin," Scrapper said. "I've got no plans to die."

"Nobody's going to die," Snow Leopard cut in, "except the O. Listen to me and follow orders, gang. We came back from Coldmark, we came back from Andrion Three, and we're coming back from Mongera. Nobody dies!"

That was the difference between Beta One and Gamma One. I'd walk into Hell for Beta One, but I wouldn't cross the street for Gamma One.

"Drop successful. Levelling out."

"Got the port."

"Watch out for those O's."

"Get down on the deck."

"*Highroad*, it is cleared for softdock in Mongera Port. Please note the zero."

"Acknowledging landing instructions."

"Priestess," I said, "You stay close. Don't stray." My mind was a whirl of wild emotions; my heart was thumping.

"I'll be right there, Thinker," she replied immediately. "It's going to take more than an O to split us up."

"Thinker." Warhound was on private.

"Yes, Warhound."

"I know for a fact that Scrapper hates me."

Oh no, I thought. Not now. Poor old Warhound.

"Well, I know for a fact that she doesn't hate you, Warhound," I said. "Don't be silly. Look, we can talk about this later. Sometimes things just don't work out. It doesn't mean she hates you."

"She hates me. I know it."

"Come on, Warhound. We need you, right now. You've got to concentrate on the mission; we need that psybloc!"

"Don't you worry about that, Thinker. I'll be right there!"

"Good!" The awful thing was, Warhound was right. Scrapper had told me herself that she hated Warhound and was sick of his bumbling efforts to romance her. I felt so sorry for him. I'd talk to him after the mission.

"Get right down on the deck," somebody said.

"Badboy, prepare for aircar launch."

Adrenalin kicked in. The *Highroad* was almost at zero altitude now, flashing at blinding speed over a cold grey forest, bouncing lightly over forested hills, flattening out again, hugging the contours.

"Hang on to your stomachs, gals!" Redhawk shouted.

"Launch aircar!" The warning bell bleated.

A sudden chill to my flesh. Then a sharp explosion shattered my ears and the gravs smashed at my chest and my vision blurred and I was paralyzed and helpless and praying for survival.

Redhawk shrieked for joy as my vision slowly returned. Weak sunlight dazzled my eyes. The grav eased off. The aircar was free, flashing over a forest of bleak wintry trees under cold grey skies. I craned my neck and I saw the *Highroad*, a blunt white wedge, fading into the distance. We were on our own now—down to business! The aircar was crammed full of troopers and everyone was suddenly having second thoughts about the readiness of their weapons and equipment, checking it all once again.

"Weapons check—mark!"

"Weapons all—hold it. What's the story, Gamma Seven?"

"Yeah, just a frac..."

"Tenners, all weapons ready."

"Look at the horizon."

It was past dawn, but the sky was dark. Up ahead, the horizon was aglow under smoky black clouds.

"That's Century City. We'll find our O there."

"Badboy, Big Kid. We've got you on scope." Big Kid was Two Three Delta, back on the P.S. *Maiden.* Delta's mission was to watch us die, or maybe even live, and report it all back to the Legion. We didn't answer.

"Look at all those O's—Deadman!"

The *Maiden* had flashed us a view of Century City, and each individual O glowed red. The suburbs were spotted with hundreds of little red dots, like an infectious disease. A scattering of dots were in the city. There did not seem to be any order behind it—the O were wandering around by themselves, all over the place.

"What do you think?" Snow Leopard, to Coolhand.

"The East—there's hardly anybody there. Look at that one."

"Yeah. Yeah. Target selection. You see him, Merlin?"

"Right. That's the one!"

Mountains flashed past, taking my breath away. We were between two great mountain ridges, hurtling to our deaths. The sky was dark with smoke. I caught a glimpse of the city up ahead, burning brightly. We had our O zeroed. Introductions would be made, shortly. And one of the two parties was going to die. Either the O, or Badboy. We burst free of the mountains and Redhawk took us down as low as he could get. The aircar was a fat black bullet splitting the air apart, a supersonic knife, now over darkened meadowlands, now flashing through black smoke, the land below all on fire, a dirt road snapping past, a glimpse of a moving groundcar.

All the power of the Legion was with us. I could feel it glowing inside me. And I knew that O was in trouble. I didn't know if we were going to kill it, or it was going to kill us, but I knew, for certain, this was not going to be one of its better days.

"See it?"

"Right, Badboy. Let's get our O. By the numbers! Prep for decar!" Snow Leopard was out of his seat and ready to go, death in an A suit. He would be the first one out the door and the closest to the O.

The ZA came flashing at us on the screens, and the gravs were again pulling at us, and then we softly glided, weightless, floating like a dream, an armored bat, hovering over the ground.

"Badboy—decar! Death." Snow Leopard added the last part almost as an afterthought.

"Death!" We echoed him, in unison.

The assault door snapped open and we threw ourselves out at once, into swirling smoke, an entire reinforced squad dancing in air for just an instant, dull black armor and winking red faceplates and exotic weaponry, all on display, all together, charged and hyper, coiled to strike. Then we hit the ground and I ran, following the track etched onto my faceplate. We were going starburst, immediately. The O was going to have to kill thirteen of us, and then he'd still have to deal with Redhawk in the aircar.

Thick black smoke, all around me. Flames, up ahead. I jogged through a muddy field. It must have just rained.

My darksight gave me the edge. The Systies were slightly behind me, off to the left. Snow Leopard was a little further to my left, ahead of us. He had told me to keep the Systies between us, if possible. I signaled the Systies to move up. Burning buildings loomed ahead of us. I intercepted a hard surfaced road, and started down it—it led right to our O. I could see it up ahead, on the tacmap.

"Keep awake, Sweety," I cautioned my Persist.

"Sit is fine, Thinker. Humans approaching on the road—unarmed."

Thick black smoke swirling past me. I saw them on the tacmap. I set my E to xmax.

"Refugees, Badboy. Let them pass."

"Everyone in position, sir."

"Tenners. Keep moving."

"Badboy, Big Kid. We've got you on scope."

"Badboy, Badass. You let me know when you need me." Badass was Redhawk, Beta Ten, in the aircar.

"Keep on the move, Badass, and keep low."

"Tenners."

The refugees appeared out of the smoke, all on foot, hurrying along the road toward us. They saw Snow Leopard first, and scattered off the road into the fields, screaming. Children ran into tall grass. An old lady fell, somebody stopped to help her up. A toddler, lost and crying.

"They're humans!" A shout on the wind.

"Soldiers! It's the DefCorps!" The refugees thought we were Systies. We continued marching along the road. I could see the O on-screen. Flashes lit the sky ahead. It was like lightning, but I knew it was the O.

As the word was passed, the refugees straggled back to the road, and we could see the horror in their eyes as we passed them by.

"Aircars! Does it have aircars?"

"Groundcars! We need transportation!"

"Are there more soldiers coming?"

"The V's are right up ahead, they've got Fernveldt City—the Police stayed to fight them. Right up the road!" A madman, spraying spittle.

"Kill them! Kill them all!" A young man, in tears.

"Our daughter! Can we find our daughter? We've lost our little girl!" A young mother wandering in a dream, hand outstretched.

"Is the port still open?"

"Is it true that Century City is being held?"

"It should have let us have weapons! Cowards! Cowards! We die, for its cowardice! We spit on the System!" Another young male, convulsed, spitting his hatred at us.

Stalking down the road, we ignored them: holy pilgrims bound for death, clad in the armor of our God, carrying his terrible swift sword, fire from the core of a star. And death to all our foes! That's what I was thinking, hot and cold and terrified, as we got closer and closer to the O.

And I knew the refugees were wrong—there was only one O in Fernveldt City.

Burning buildings, roaring with flames. Corpses, blown to bits, body parts scattered all over the road. An explosion up ahead. A dull boom, a sharp shock wave, debris in the air.

"See him? See him? That's him!"

"Destructive little critter, isn't he?"

"All right, Badboy. We've got him zeroed," Snow Leopard said. "Two, move your element left. Gamma, move right. I've got the center. Nobody fire until I give the word."

The city of Fernveldt was right up ahead, and the road led straight to it. I was with Beta One's element. When we were through, the O was going to be in the center of a u–shaped cordon of Legionnaires, and we planned to keep him very busy.

Lightning flashed ahead. The crack of doom snapped all around us. We could see the city—Fernveldt, a suburb of Century City. Burning, wreathed in clouds of fiery ash.

"Right, first volley. Five, hit him." Snow Leopard was going to say hello.

I went to one knee, my E up and ready. It was all green, all around me, in the darksight. Hopeless refugees, a man with a baby, two girls, running frantically into the dark dawn of the System's end, veering away from me.

Flashes to the left. Tacstars crackled sharp and eerie, whistling downrange to the O. White–hot micronukes burst ahead of us, three, five, seven—a tremendous shock wave and a horrendous ripping noise hit us. Psycho put seven tacstars right on the creature's head. A huge, luminous, rolling mushroom cloud writhed up into the dark skies. Bolts of lightning snapped wildly all around the clouds. Introductions had now been made. We knew the damned tacstars couldn't hurt the O, but we hoped it would give him something to think about—and maybe just a little concern.

"Six, psybloc." Snow Leopard was calm and his voice was clear.

Warhound was off to my right, out of sight. I craned my neck to see it. There was a faint flicker, a sudden flash and then a sparkling comet shot high into the sky, lost in the clouds.

"Bloc away."

"Badboy—forward."

Forward, right. I got up and continued the advance. Then the skies lit up. Fireworks, a bright, white–hot starburst, high above. Then another, phospho green. Then another, glittery red. And another, sparkly gold, until the sky was a glittering tracery of hissing streaks. And then each streak exploded at the tip, hundreds more flashing explosions high overhead, lighting up the world, and the fireworks fell like hot, slow rain. A great rattling, moaning roar filled the skies. This was our psybloc, falling slowly from the sky. Atom had assured us it would interfere with the O's psych projections, and protect us from its psypower. Otherwise, we were dead. All our fancy weapons were useless without the will to use them.

"Good—good! Now we attack, squad leader! Now we attack!" The Mocain soldier was a fighter, that was certain.

The three of them were just to my left, advancing cautiously. They had been told to keep me in sight. I wondered if the Systie dip recognized me as the one who had nearly executed him back on Andrion 3. He had been silent so far.

"Tacstar!" Sweety's warning and the explosion came almost simultaneously—a pulsating white sun burst to life just to my right and the shock wave bounced me off the ground. The sun rose into the sky, crackling and hissing, shooting off glowing white streamers.

"Tacstar! Tacstar!"

Two more evil, white–hot flowers just behind me. Two more shock waves, banging off my armor.

"That was the O."

"Looks like Warhound upset him."

"Six, One, are you tenners?"

Three nuclear blossoms, radiating heat and light, glittering in the sky. Psycho's micronukes still hovered up ahead, and Warhound's fireworks still fell, lovely multi–colored sparklers. It was truly beautiful.

"Enemy probes!" A fine tracery on my tacmap, lower left plate. Six, seven, eight, damn! Coming right at us, from the O.

"Auto xmax! Tacstars! Shoot 'em down fast! These are the guys we did before. Five, let 'er rip!" One was eager and excited.

They came in fast and low, just like before, splitting up, seeking out individual targets. Psycho's chainlink spat tacstars, autofire. The vibes crawled on my skin. My heart was in a vice. It felt good. It was like having a Legion fighter on call, bringing in the death from the skies.

I raised my E to my shoulder and found a probe and fired, auto xmax, and Psycho's tacstars filled the skies, nuclear airbursts, poison toadstools of power. Shock waves pounded at my armor. My E shrieked, everyone suddenly firing, an auto xmax morning, death whistling all around us.

The probes ran into a solid wall of fire. They exploded all around me, sharp flashes and glittering tracers as they blew apart. I kept my E on auto, following the nearest probes on my faceplate.

"Four down—more! Three, fire to the right!"

"Got him! Got him!"

"He's firing more!"

"Coming around—Valkyrie, get that one!" It was Boudicca's strident voice. "Watch it! Lasers!"

"Scrapper, to your rear!"

"Tenners, got him!" There were two more behind us, coming around in Gamma's sector, firing lasers, snapping past us, hissing into the dirt.

"Easy...easy...fire!" Scrapper was talking to herself. The two probes winked off my faceplate. "They're done for!" Scrapper sounded elated.

A sparkling flare shot up into the sky and exploded, shocking blue, stunningly beautiful. Then crimson and golden and phospho white and silver, filling the skies. Warhound was still with us, and our psybloc was going strong.

Flickering green lightning up ahead—tremendous explosions shook the earth, very close, two rolling white–green phospho fireballs.

"What's that?"

"That's the O."

"Undefined power source, laser guidance, biotic field, human range, extremely dangerous!"

"Damn! That's new!"

"Psycho, blow those green bastards apart as soon as they appear—tacstars!"

"Tenners." Psycho's chainlink shrieked, and the tacstars flashed and ripped over to the front, and a new field of white–hot nukes appeared, glowing, to mark our progress.

Psycho poured it on and the horizon erupted, flaming nuclear skies, and the green fireballs vanished immediately, swallowed up in the apocalypse.

"Advance." Snow Leopard, as cold as ice.

The O was still on scope. Then the world exploded, drilling me right into the ground, a horrible grinding roar in my ears, a white–hot sun dazzling my eyes, a massive shock wave—I struggled to raise my head. My faceplate was white–hot. The sky burnt phospho green.

"Five!" Tacstars burst to life, a nuclear sky, right over my head. The O had hit us, direct hit, airburst, and Psycho was exploding tacstars right above us to disperse the biotic field. My body burned, the skin crawling, contracting, blood bursting from my nose, eyes going dim, my guts twisting inside me. Biotics—deto! We were dead!

"Advance! Get up, Badboy! Fire all weapons! Let's get that O!"

"We won't go on! It's crazy!" the Systie dip shouted. "We can't help it! This is wrong! It's wrong! They're intelligent! It should..." Someone screamed. Lasers snapped all around me. A blinding green fireball erupted in the sky to my right. The O was playing with us. Psycho's chainlink came to life again, and white–hot tacstars exploded within the fireball, blowing it apart. I don't think anyone was listening to the dip.

The skeletal frames of burning buildings drifted in and out of the smoke. We were getting closer to the O. I could see. I could move. Blood was dripping down my chin. I advanced. The Systie soldier and the Mocain female were still with me, just to my left. The dip had disappeared.

"Gamma, are you still there?"

"Tenners, we're moving up."

"Beta Two, report."

"We're tenners—all here!"

"Rising energy levels from target—high mag levels! High rad levels!"

Lasers, brilliant red laser light, flashing, flickering over our heads, touching down, ten, twenty, thirty, countless glittering streams, snapping and crackling, darting all around us, and any one could end a life with a gentle touch.

A blood–curdling scream.

"Who's hit?"

"Heads down!"

"Fire! Fire! Let 'er rip!" I raised my E and fired auto xmax, and off to my right there was more firing, sheets of lovely xmax. To my left I saw Snow Leopard, alternating laser and auto xmax, and further left Psycho's chainlink snarled, and the earth cringed and shook, and all our fire was centered right on that one O. The O was still firing lasers, ruby red lasers, snapping all around me. I was in the ruins of a great factory building full of burning groundcars. Splintered glass ground under my boots and smoking cables and shot–up robot arms dangled loosely from the ceiling. I found a good spot by a fiercely burning groundcar and switched my E to canister. We were getting close, and it was time to try out our new toys.

"Rising mag levels!"

"Six, do it again!"

"Enemy launching aerial device!" There was a soundless flash up ahead, and something rocketed up into the glittering sky. Off to my right Warhound launched another psybloc, a sparkling trail shooting skywards. Warhound's fireworks and the O's device exploded at about the same time. Then a solid sheet of light from Psycho's skysweep lanced up to erupt, six, seven, eight, ten tacstars, golden flowers of the Legion, as scary and beautiful as angels of the Lord, and the sky was a great bowl of glowing light, flickering and flashing and throbbing with every color of the spectrum.

"Launch deceptors." Snow Leopard was as calm as if it was all a training exercise.

I was terrified, huddled in my armor, icy sweat trickling over my skin. I switched to deceptors and fired on auto. The sky was a shrieking, frantic beast, full of raging metal, and the tacmap was all trash.

"Tenners, what's the O done?"

"Unidentified aerial devices approaching! Attention! Enemy launching energy spheres! Unidentified devices approaching from high altitude, energy spheres approaching from low altitude!"

Damn! I could see it on the scope now, spidery lines on the tacmap, lazily approaching us. This was the weapon that had decimated Gamma on Andrion Three. But there was something else as well, coming at us from above!

"Gamma Seven, Beta Four, Five, you all in position?"

"Seven ready!"

"Four ready!"

"Five all set!"

One wanted to go after the O, but something was whirling overhead, a strange buzzing noise that turned my flesh cold.

"Genetic energy weapon, low–mass, twenty–one separate strands approaching," Sweety announced. "Recommend auto stunstars and v–max to disperse these energy masses."

My blood ran cold. This was something new, too. I stepped out from behind the flaming wreckage and brought my E up to my shoulder, switching to v–max.

"V–max, gang! Five, Gamma Seven, stunstars!" I could see them now, sparkling aerial strands of biotic death, falling gently down from the sky, slowly snapping and whirling in the breeze, floating towards us, living death, coiling and uncoiling like snakes, tails snapping, programmed to wrap around the appropriate genetic material and merge with it. We were the appropriate genetic material. I knew it could penetrate our A–suits and the result was an awful, hideous death. I fired at the nearest strand, auto v–max. It was taking hits from Merlin and Warhound to my right. It writhed blindly in the air, whirling wildly. The v–max appeared to be working—the strand was being blown apart, a shower of sparkling fragments.

Four stunstars burst over our heads almost simultaneously, a tremendous ragged quadruple boom, scattering the strands all over the sky. I fell to my knees.

It felt as if I had been hit by a speeding aircar.

"The spheres! Get the spheres, then do the O!"

"Who's the casualty?" Priestess asked.

"Look out! The snakes!" A glittering sheet of raw flame swept over my head.

"Use flame on the snakes! They burn like gas!" Dragon shouted. Streams of fire shot up from his position, and the genetic snakes burst into flames.

Thank God for Dragon!

"Energy spheres approaching! Six spheres! Recommend immediate counterfire!"

Lasers snapped past me, missing by mils. The spheres approached. Closer and closer. I struggled to my feet.

"Counter those spheres—now!" Snow Leopard was still on top of it. We'd have to put off our hit on the O until we dealt with the spheres. A shriek of raw terror, right in my ears.

"Use flame! Burn it!" One of the strands had touched down, and had somebody in its grasp. Things were happening so fast I could not even look at the sit.

"Sphere approaching, Thinker!" Scut!

"Spheres!" Snow Leopard commanded. "Biodee, canisters, chainlink, plasma, now!" It was coming right at me, glowing like a comet. I switched over to biodee and fired, shaking with terror.

Chapter 10

Advice for the Dead

The sphere came right at me, glowing like a sun, drawn by my own genetics, and I knew nothing at all could stop it from merging with the nearest mass of human flesh and consuming it utterly, burning fiercely from outside until all life was gone. This was what had happened to Gamma on Andrion 3. This was a high–tech, self–guided energy weapon, unlike the snakes, and neither v–max nor stunstars nor flame were going to turn aside this relentless, mindless sphere from its murderous mission.

I was almost frozen with terror, but I fired biodee right into the glowing mass just before it hit me and it exploded right in my face, a brilliant white–hot glare and a crackling bang, lighting up the battlefield for one stark instant.

"Biodee works!" I croaked, staggering in relief. I blessed the warped genius who had come up with the device, and all the nameless toilers in the Legion death factory who had integrated it into our E's. It eats people, fine, we feed it people. Genetic bullets, biotic life and death, human genes to set off the spheres, and superflash moeboid reproduction of the genetic material, driving the sphere to consume to its own destruction.

"Biodee!" Snow Leopard commanded, "Biodee!" Another white flash behind me. A nightmare landscape of twisted, skeletal black buildings was wreathed in dark smoke, fires burning all around us, nuclear clouds glowing overhead, our psybloc flickering in the sky, a lovely, multicolored rain slowly floating down through the dark.

"Snake approaching, Thinker!" Above me, twitching in the air, seeking me out.

"I want canisters on the O—now!" Snow Leopard commanded. It was time to tackle the O. I fired flame up to the snake and it writhed, the fire running all along its airy body, burning brightly.

"Help us!" It was the Systie soldier. A sphere, darting at him. A blood–curdling scream.

"Fire biodee!" The sphere exploded, another white–hot crack.

"Canisters!" We were closing in on the O—he was dancing on my tacmap—right up ahead! The building just to my right exploded, showering me with debris. Laser snapped and popped past me from the O's position. Boudicca and Valkyrie passed me like shadows, heading for the O. What were they doing up here?

"Seven! Plasma! Now!" Snow Leopard ordered in a cold dead voice. Terrific ripping explosions and a blinding tracery of glowing streaks—several troopers opened up on canister. I raised my E and trotted forward to meet the O. I switched to canister and fired on auto. The recoil almost knocked me down and the flash dazzled my eyes. A glimpse of an A–suit to my right; I recognized the weapon, a biobloc fieldfaxer. It was Merlin, moving up, all set to cook his O. But we had to get through the mags first. The canisters were designed to do that. They fired cenite slivers, hundreds of miniature darts of cold death, crafted to slide between the madly whirling molecules of the O's mag shields, and tear open a hole for us to explode.

Another scream, a flash of lasers, a sharp explosion behind us as a tacstar cloud rose to the sky, a sparkling trail rocketing up. Warhound gave us one last psybloc, and the earth shook again to Psycho's chainlink, spitting autofire, then rattling to a stop.

"Get it off! Get it off!"

"More canisters! Autofire!" Sassin ran past me and his massive Manlink spit plasma, glowing pulses of pure energy, straight to the O. Canister! I fired canister, finger holding the trigger down, the E dancing in my grasp.

We walked forward to the O. Snow Leopard and Psycho and Coolhand appeared to my left, firing nonstop.

A black wall loomed between us and the O. It exploded, disintegrating into fragments, and the O spit death at us, a sudden firestorm of laser and tacstars.

Explosions erupted all around me, and suddenly I was on the ground, my head spinning wildly, my helmet glowing red, tacstar skies burning into my eyes, and Sweety calmly relaying data into my ears.

"...left arm no longer functional. Get up, Thinker! Fire canister! The O approaches!" I struggled to my feet. The left side of my A–suit was smoking. I felt nothing but I could not move my left arm. I did not want to look—I aimed my E with my right arm and fired canister.

"Death, Gamma!" Boudicca hurled herself at the O. Sassin fired again, plasma flashing, again and again and again, right into the O. Full auto canister fire deafened me as a deadly hail of cenite darts filled the air. Psycho opened up again with the chainlink and for the first time, I heard the shrill grating whine of Merlin's biobloc fieldfaxer. An airburst flashed just over my head and hot metal hissed down all around me.

The O appeared, looming before us out of the smoke, tall dark body parts shimmering in a pulsating violet haze; is that armor? It fired, a flash, exploding just to my left, my faceplate going dark.

"I'm hit, Two. Take command." Snow Leopard, detached, a message from Dreamland.

"One is down," Two reported calmly. "Fire all weapons—canister, chainlink, plasma, biobloc."

The O erupted, winking like a star, firing everything it had—laser, tacstars, spheres, xmax. Highways of light came right at me, and then I was down again and the world was aflame, a hot white sky.

"Three's hit."

"Seven is hit."

"Nine?"

"Get the O."

I struggled to my feet. Focus, a cloud of black smoke. Fire rippled above me. The O stood before me, enveloped in a hazy violet field, cold air shimmering all around it, ice forming on my A–suit. The head, moving; armor, it's in armor; the eyes, glowing red, right into mine. Something came down, a weapon, writhing like a snake in hazy air. My life flashed before me. Tara, and the Legion gate. Hell and Valkyrie and our landing on the New World. Priestess appeared before me, glowing like an icon. I saw Moontouch, the Princess of the Dead, holding up my baby—what a beautiful baby! I fired canister, right into the O's ugly face. The world exploded, a tremendous flash, and hot sparkles danced in my vision. I was on my back now—the world was spinning around, and I was blind. The battle raged around me.

"Canister! Biobloc! Pour it on!" Multiple explosions deafened me. The transmissions were fading.

"Biobloc! Get him, Merlin!"

"No...no! He's gone."

"Get the O! Get the O!"

"Use flame!"

"No—not the tacstar!"

"Canister! More!"

"Don't stop! Don't stop!"

I struggled to my feet. My vision was coming back; I was still alive.
I spat blood and aimed with my good arm. I saw A–suits in the smoke,
walking in flames, firing into the dark. Something writhed in the
shadows. Four leaned into his fieldfaxer; and it was shrieking, whining,
howling biotic death at the thing in the shadows. Plasma dazzled my
eyes; Sassin firing full auto from his Manlink, full auto plasma, spitting
and burning, lighting up a wild thrashing form like a great metal snake
in its death throes. Pulsing violet flashes, on and off, a dying star.
Coolhand fired canister, the air full of humming death, riddling the
target, full auto canister. Psycho, the snout of his chainlink almost
touching the creature, firing auto xmax; we're much too close for
tacstars. The shield is down! I switched to auto xmax and fired one–
handed and kept my finger down on the trigger, a death grip. Someone
fired flame, and the O ignited.

"Burn the bastard!"

"Blast him!"

"Don't stop!"

Junk, the O was flaming junk, whirling in a firestorm of cenite,
dancing in the lightning of xmax and melting in the plasma's hot breath,
cooking in the biobloc. The buildings came down around us, falling
down on our armored backs, but we didn't care. We kept firing until we
knew, beyond a doubt, that the O was dead.

"Don't die, Boudicca! Oh my God, please don't die! Priestess!
Priestess! Help me!" It was Valkyrie, frantic.

The world whirled around me. I found Valkyrie on the tacmap and
staggered dizzily to the site. She was on her knees, cradling Boudicca
in her arms. Hell burned all around them. Boudicca was horribly
wounded, her frontal armor burnt away and smoking, white–hot, her
abdomen a bloody mass of melting cenite and bubbling gore, her legs
two black, shredded metal stumps. I wrenched at her visor with my one
good hand and got it up. She was pale and still, in shock.

"Thinker! Thinker, you're hit!" Valkyrie exclaimed. She was also in
shock, breathing shallowly.

"I'm all right. Gamma, speak! Priestess, where are you?"

Boudicca's eyelids fluttered and she tried to focus on me. "Beta?

Three? Did we get the O?"

"We got it, Gamma—it's stone dead!"

Blood spurted out of Gamma One's mouth, and she began coughing.

"Valkyrie, get my medkit!" I couldn't seem to get it open with my one good hand.

"Don't die, Boudicca! I love you!" Valkyrie was clinging to Boudicca and crying, hysterical.

"The medkit, Valkyrie!" Priestess suddenly appeared, slamming a bloody biotic charger on to Boudicca's charred and smoking chest. Priestess hit her with a max charge, and did it again, and again.

"Valkyrie...Val..." Boudicca was trying to speak.

"Boudicca! You're going to be all right!" Valkyrie replied. "Priestess is here, you're all right!"

"No, Val...I'm dying...I'm done." Her face twisted into a painful grimace. "But we got the O! Gamma got the O...you put that on my grave, Valkyrie."

"Don't die, Boudicca! Don't leave me!"

Gamma One's eyes turned up to the sky. The color was fading from her twitching, frightened face. Her lips moved. "Forming a new squad, Val..." she whispered throatily. "I'll save you...number two." And then she shuddered and the life ran right out of her, and Priestess kept banging away on the biotic charger, but it made no difference—another immortal was dead.

"Priestess! Medic! Medic! It's One!" Coolhand was calling for help—it was for Beta One. Priestess leaped to her feet and disappeared into the dark. Snow Leopard! I gritted my teeth. This was not going to be easy.

"Are you all right, Valkyrie?" I asked.

Valkyrie did not move. She silently held Boudicca in her arms, and said not a word. I made the sign of the Legion over Boudicca, and then over Valkyrie, and then I left them, to see about Snow Leopard.

I found him in Coolhand's arms, with Priestess working frantically on him. They had unlinked his upper armor. It was red with blood. Horrible sucking chest wounds, blood spurting everywhere. It looked as if he had lost an arm as well. His visor open, pale face, his eyes blinking—he was as pale as death, gasping for air.

"Is he going to make it, Priestess?"

"Shut down—hand me a fleshpad. The breather!"

I could see, behind his visor, Coolhand shaking and crying silently. I prayed to the God of War for Snow Leopard's life. And all I could think was that he was a great warrior, and he was our One; and if the Gods let him die, I would curse the Gods, and believe in nothing, and face a future as dark as a black hole.

"Ten, Two...damn! Badass, Badboy, we're through here. Get us out. Big Kid, we've done it. Acknowledge, please." Coolhand had taken charge. Snow Leopard screamed, in sudden agony. Blood spurted all over my faceplate.

"There..." Priestess's armored fingers were digging in Snow Leopard's chest for something. The medpads were soaked in blood.

"Is he stable?"

"Badass, Badboy. Respond!"

An armored hand on my shoulder. It was Dragon. "Thinker, you'd better come here." I turned to follow him. Flames licked at our feet and the sky was dark with smoke. I did not want to see whatever it was Dragon had for me.

"Badass, Badboy. Scut! No response."

"Badass...kid....to pick up Badboy. Acknow..." Shot full of static. That had to be Big Kid, trying to relay our message to Badass. At least somebody was getting the word. A dark sky. Shadowy figures in A–suits, moving in slow motion around me like a dream. Something flaming, a charred pile of junk—the O. Dragon's heavy hand was still on my shoulder. He was guiding me somewhere.

"Badboy, Beta Two. Count off! One, wounded. Two, present—count off!"

"Three," I said mechanically.

"Four." A whisper. Merlin was alive!

"Five." Psycho! Bulletproof, the magnificent little maniac was bulletproof!

Silence. Silence, from Beta Six. The remnants of his psybloc were still falling, ghostly lights in the sky. And out of the smoke a vision appeared. It was Psycho, on his knees, cradling another trooper in his arms. I saw in an instant that it was Ironman. Smoke drifted slowly around the scene, and a faint halo of light illuminated them from behind. I sank to my knees and touched Ironman's helmet with the armored fingers of my good hand. His face was still and pale behind the visor, and his eyes were open. A ragged laser track ran through his armor from the neck down through his chest and left arm. The cenite armor was still smoking.

I couldn't speak. It was like a dream.

"Priestess..." I finally said. "Priestess."

"She's already been here," Psycho informed me. "He's gone. Ironman is gone."

Dragon leaned over and made the sign of the Legion before Ironman's faceplate. "He was a warrior," Dragon said. It was the highest praise Dragon could give.

"He was advancing and firing when he was hit," Psycho said. "I saw the whole thing. He was walking right into the O. Nobody could have died better than that."

Ironman, Ironman, Ironman! I could not see, my eyes were full of tears. He was our child, our innocent, our only link with a lost world. With Ironman at our side, we knew we were fighting for something worthwhile. Now he was gone.

"Count off! Count off, damn you all! I said count off!" Coolhand was losing patience.

"Six," somebody said. But it was not Warhound's voice. "Six is...he's here—with me."

"Beta Seven," Dragon said, "mission accomplished. Eight—present."

"Nine." A haunted whisper. My heart leaped.

"Gamma One—she's gone! Gamma Two—present!" It was Valkyrie's cold, lost voice, a cry in the wilderness.

"Gamma Five is wounded. Gamma Seven here."

"Systies! Let's hear it!"

"May God have mercy on your soul. My friend, my friend...how can you leave us?" It was Merlin, talking to himself. I got to my feet, in a trance, and followed the tacmap to locate him. He was squatting in the dirt, his fieldfaxer on the ground beside him. Warhound lay before him, his A–suit glowing cherry–red. I stopped, stunned. Warhound's atlauncher was at his side. His faceplate was burnt black.

"Don't look in," Merlin warned. "Don't. It was a sphere. It came in behind him. He had just flamed a snake that had started to wrap itself around one of the Systies. I fired biodee, but it was too late. Too late."

Not Warhound, I thought. Not Warhound. Warhound never asked

anything of anyone. He just wanted a home, that's all, and we were his home. He was faithful and dependable. A good soldier, I thought—a good soldier. There was a roaring in my ears and the world was spinning around. A burning pain enveloped my chest. It felt as if I was on fire. I reached out my good hand for Warhound, my friend, and fell into the dark.

* * *

"He's conscious," Priestess whispered in my ears, and the pain was gone. "Can you get up, Thinker?" I tried. I got up. Flames rolled in the sky. Agonizing pain. I could not move my left arm.

"We're set, Thinker. The aircar's here. I've got to help the others." A dark aircar hovered before us in a whirling cyclone of smoke and dirt. Priestess was gone. I checked my E—still there.

"Board! Bring our dead—we all come back! Board, board! And bring that O!" Coolhand was not going to leave anyone behind. We were all going back together, and we were even bringing the O. It would be an incredible prize for the Legion. The lab rats would be ecstatic, and the ultimate result would be more dead O's.

Coolhand and Merlin hauled Snow Leopard toward the aircar on a camfax cloak and Priestess was with them, leaning over to check on him. It was an unreal picture on my faceplate, glowing green A–suits moving through the smoking dark. It started to rain. And three Legion A–suits were lying side by side nearby, light rain dancing off the twisted metal. A strange holy glow hovered all around them. A shadowy group of figures dragged what was left of the O out of the burning ruins in which it had died. The O was charred, just as Merlin had promised, and as Psycho and Dragon pulled, its limbs broke apart in a shower of ash and sparks.

"Its squad leader has done it, number Two—one of its units saved our life!" The Systie soldier was just as shaken as we were.

"He lost his life doing it, Systie," Coolhand replied. "His number was Beta Six. Remember it!"

The aircar hovered, haloed by rain. The assault door popped open. A Systie in an A–suit stood in the door with an SG. He fired, and I watched in horror as the xmax exploded white–hot right on Coolhand's chestplate, glittering streaks of phospho shrapnel ricocheting off his armor, more xmax, full auto, multiple explosions. Priestess was blown aside like a rag doll, flames spitting off her A–suit, and Coolhand fell, his arms outstretched, and the Systie was out the door jumping to the ground, still firing. Another Systie stood in the door, his SG at his shoulder, the barrel coming down. It was happening in microfracs but I could see every speck of dirt on the Systie's A–suit and it was unrolling in extreme slow motion like a horrible nightmare. My E was up and my finger tightened on the trigger. A Systie A–suit to my left—it was Millina, the Mocain. She reached down, it seemed to take forever, to seize Coolhand's E, her armored fingers wrapping around the stock. I pulled my E around to blast her, traitorous bitch! She had the E now and in the far corner of my eye I caught a glimpse of a Legion A–suit, Valkyrie, bringing her E up to her shoulder, aiming right at the Systie bitch. My E was on xmax and just as the laser confirmed the target, Millina fired and the first Systie staggered, his faceplate exploding as Millina walked the xmax down his chest. I didn't even try to understand it, but I snapped my E back to the aircar's assault door and fired.

* * *

Someone screamed right into my ears, shrieking in agony. Then the deceptors drowned it all out and a spattering buzz filled my helmet. Lightning, close overhead.

I crawled in the mud, burrowing like a worm, and lasers snapped mils above my head. The earth shook again and the air crackled— Psycho's chainlink, a magnificent symphony of death, full auto, a flickering in the sky and then a rolling flash, lightning, and the world split open as the tacstars hit. Debris spattered all around me. A dark aircar slowly passed overhead, right over me, and it was burning, spitting sparks, and as I watched, horrified, a barrage of tacstars erupted on the car, one two three four five six, flash flash flash flash flash flash, perfect shooting. The aircar erupted, six micronukes, a multiple crack, the end of the world, white–hot streaks lighting up the sky, and an A–suited figure fell in fantastic slow motion down from the car, flaming like a meteor. The aircar tumbled wildly, falling apart, flaming chunks of metal raining down to the ground. Then a stunning explosion and the sky lit up and the earth shook.

"...least twelve." It was all I could hear—the sky was full of deceptors. I could not move my left arm but my right was still good and I had my E.

Sweety was relaying data to me, and her I could hear. "Target ahead, one Systie, on the ground. Fading in and out, keep crawling, Thinker!"

I was shaking with horror and hatred. My world was ending, the only world I had ever loved, and the Systies had done it, and a Systie squad was all around me, and they were all going to die. If Beta was finished, I did not want to live. There was one Systie right up ahead, and I was going to kill him.

Auto x rattled all around me. I had glimpses of the Systie in the tacsit, a faint green glow, drowned in static. Laser, flickering in the dark—he was firing laser. I paused behind a chunk of masonry, my head roaring, pain overwhelming me. "Sweety...xmax. Give me the target."

I balanced the E against the rubble and pressed my faceplate against the sights. Smoke drifted past. Someone screamed. Priestess was out there somewhere, lying in the mud, fate unknown. Deceptors crackled close overhead and a defeaning explosion split the sky to my left, showering me with shrapnel, hits pinging off my A–suit. The scope was full of glittering junk. More lasers, up ahead—there! I fired, and xmax erupted up ahead, white–hot flashes, phospho streamers.

"Hit," Sweety informed me. "Good hit, Thinker." I rolled away from the site and began crawling into flame and smoke. A building collapsed just to my right, a rising cloud of smoke and ash.

"I'm hit! Oh God, God, I'm hit! Medic! Medic!" A horrible, bloodcurdling scream followed. I thought it was Sassin, but I was not sure. I only knew that there was no medic, any more.

"Soldiers of the Legion!" The message crackled in my ears. "You are doomed! Surrender immediately and we will assist your wounded and grant you official PW status. We repeat, surrender immediately and save yourselves and your comrades! You are completely surrounded and further resistance is pointless!"

"Give me a zero, Sweety..." Soaked in sweat and blood, I kicked myself over onto my back to free my E. My left arm was completely useless. A burst of auto x, laser slicing overhead.

"That target just went off–scope, Thinker," my Persist informed me.

"Someone made a good hit."

"Sweety..." the pain was so bad I was ready to pass out. "Give me a mag, then find Priestess. Now!"

Worming through black mud on my back, gasping, burning, raindrops burst on my faceplate like shrapnel as a wild smoky sky flamed overhead. The deceptors whirled all around me, but Sweety still had Priestess on scope.

"You can't get to her, Thinker," Sweety informed me calmly. "The Systies have that site well zeroed. You will die if you try."

"Shut down, Sweety!"

"Beta, Beta...any Beta, answer!" Roaring with static, but I knew the voice. Dragon!

"Eight, Three!" I shouted. "I'm going to help Nine and Two and One. Cover me!"

A tremendous roar of static. Someone was saying something. It did not matter. No, not at all. I rolled over onto my chest. Green hell, swirling all around me. There, up ahead, Sweety had them zeroed. Lumps of clay—black clay, flickering in the laser. Lumps of clay, my God, it's all we are! They pulsed on my faceplate, B2, B9, B1.

"...don't do it!" Advice for the dead.

I waved my E into the dark and fired full auto xmax. I crawled, a worm in hell, brainless, blind and deaf and dumb. The earth shook, the air crackled and burned, the sky lit up—chainlink tacstars! Micronukes exploded white–hot right in my face, rising into the sky, glittering, golden, magnificent. I scrambled to my feet and ran right into it and the shock wave knocked me flat. I gasped and reached out my good arm. B2, B2, B2 flashed on my faceplate. I had reached Coolhand. A smoking A–suit, a pile of metal junk in the mud.

The chainlink spoke again, and I cringed. Someone gurgled in my ears. Was Coolhand alive? I caught a glimpse of his face behind red plex—still and cold, eyes open, covered with blood. His mouth opened—a silent scream.

Excruciating pain, glittering white–hot stars— a massive crack hurled me bodily into the gates of Hell. I was dead, on my back, burning. My ears rang—I was hit, again. My hearing was gone. It was strangely calm. I saw Priestess, in the mud. Smoke, curling from glowing cenite. I crawled to her. My E was gone. I reached out and touched her hand. I had it now—hand in hand, we would go out together. I was so tired I could not speak. A wave of exhaustion swept over me. The lights were gently going out.

* * *

The next thing I knew I was floating overhead, looking directly down at my body. It was such an astounding sight that I was stunned and awestruck. I could see everything in excruciating detail and in total silence. I was lying on my chestplate down below in a sticky sea of mud, and my A–suit was riddled with hits—the armor on my left arm was smoking and glowing. My right hand was linked with Priestess's and she was on her back—her chestplate was twisted and punctured, white–hot, splattered with bubbling blood. Coolhand sprawled nearby, his A–suit riddled with hits. I could see every tiny speck of dirt, every splash of mud, every evil smoking scar on our armor. It was raining, and every raindrop that hit our cenite burst into steam. I couldn't quite understand how I could be down there while observing myself from overhead, but then it slowly dawned on me. I was hovering at the doorway to death's cold road, and I was only a soul, floating on the wind, balanced precariously between one dimension and the next. That clay down there—that had been me!

It was probably only a split instant of time that I was out of my body but in that brief frac I saw everything. It was truly astounding—it was almost like being a God. One glance and I saw it all, the entire battlefield winking and flashing with xmax and laser, an insane tacstar sky rolling overhead with nuclear clouds burning and throbbing like Armageddon, spitting phospho debris hissing down to explode in geysers of black mud. And then I heard it, a horrific rumble, the Thunder of the Gods.

I saw Psycho running like a rat, splashing through mud on hands and knees and feet, the chainlink dangling, streaking through smoking flaming buildings, scrambling and crawling through the rubble. Lasers and xmax followed him, and the buildings shuddered and came down around him as he ran. The sky was getting darker. It was raining, fat hot drops splattering in the mud. Psycho found an opening in a collapsed wall and snaked forward on his belly, the chainlink nosing slowly out ahead of him. Rain, hissing on hot metal. He was a tiny figure on my field of dreams, but I could even see the blood on his lips.

"Give me a target, you bitch. Give me just one target!" He whispered it. I heard every word. The sky was rotten with deceptors, and the tacmap was trash. But they were close—he'd spot them soon. Green trash, flickering on his faceplate. Three Legion A–suits, down and out—that was me! Xmax, exploding off to his left. They had left him behind—perfect!

"Give me that..."

"Target, Psycho! Fire!" The tacmod illuminated what it had seen in a flash, the source of the firing—a faint green blob, hidden in a collapsed building.

"This is for Warhound." Psycho fired full auto tacstar, a rasping screech. He scrambled away immediately, cursing, back the way he had come, a rat on the run.

Less than a heartbeat—that's probably how long my soul was hovering there, but I could see everybody, I could hear them and feel them—all of Beta, and all at once. We were one, you see. It isn't surprising. I saw Valkyrie watch Five's building detonate a block away, a series of white phospho flashes and suddenly the nukes rose into the sky and the earth shook. She scrambled to her feet and ran through the shattered building where she had been hiding, up the fiery staircase to the second floor. She lay there for a moment quaking. No response. The entire building was burning. Most of the outside walls were gone, but the basic structure was intact. Valkyrie crawled through burning desks and chairs and d–screens spitting sparks. She slithered to the edge of the building and found a good position by a riddled masonry column. She slid her E ahead of her and guided the stock into her shoulder.

"Deadman, give me a kill," she prayed. "Show me a Systie." The tacstars burnt on her faceplate, and she had a great view—almost as good as mine. All of the buildings around her had been hit. Groundcars burnt in the streets. It was raining, a black sky lit up by flashes of xmax and laser and deceptors and the lovely flaming flowers of nuclear hits, rising to the sky, the flowers of the Legion. Deadman, they were beautiful!

"Deadman, you bastard, give me a target, for Gamma!" She was crying and her flesh was ice cold.

"Beta, Beta..." the rest was lost in static.

"Eight, Five..." a long roar of static. "...move, but I can't..." hopeless static. No, there's no sense in trying for commo, Valkyrie, I thought.

It's hopeless. Just kill Systies, and die. That's the mission, now. Kill, and die.

"Target!" her tacmod cried out, "Marked!" There! A Systie, sprinting through an alley from one building to another, now hidden behind a massive pile of rubble. No matter.

"Auto xmax airburst," she instructed the tacmod, "right over his head." She touched the trigger gently, lovingly. A long burst of auto x exploded right over the rubble. Then she was off, running frantically back through the gutted office, hurling herself face–first down the stairs, crashing down to the ground floor as the building exploded above her with a tremendous boom. She hit the ground hard, running, gasping, sweating, moaning—running for her life. And the xmax followed her as she ran.

I could see Dragon as well—he had also sought high ground, a burning apartment mod flaming like a torch, wreathed in black smoke. Dragon was on the fifth floor now, kicking in a smoking door, moving through a fierce fire. Bodies lay on the floor all around him, a whole family sprawled in sudden death, a man, a woman, three children, their flesh smouldering.

Dragon took a position by a shattered window and watched his tacmod. He was slowly zeroing the Systies—he had ID'd three positions already from the third floor. If only he could reactivate the squad!

"Beta, Gamma—Beta Eight. Respond! Respond!" He squatted in the flames. His armor was beginning to glow. The building might collapse at any time. I wanted to respond to him, but I couldn't.

"...got two Systies spotted..." the voice was interrupted by a massive burst of static. "...to try to take..." More static. "...goodbye, Eight. Good..." Static. It was Merlin, I realized. Beta Four, the tech, the lab rat, taking on the Systies alone. At that precise moment, Dragon's tacmod spotted another Systie in the whirling chaff from the deceptors.

"Target! Mark!"

"Confirm!" Dragon pulled away from the window. He had four Systies zeroed now. He moved quickly through the flames and out the apartment and along the glowing halls and down the smoking stairway. If he fired from the fifth floor, they would have him. I knew exactly what he was thinking. He could see it was hopeless to try and organize the squad. No, it was all up to him. He was going to go from one target to another until they were all dead, or he was. As he walked carefully down the smoking stairs he set his E to canister. I was suddenly overwhelmed with sorrow for Dragon. Death was here, to claim us all...Dragon's old companion, Death, stalking him still, tracking him all the way to Mongera. Death ultimately embraced all his comrades. He had told me about his curse—some evil crone had branded him for life. "Death will be your shadow!" she had said. "You will bring Death with you like a plague, and everyone you love will die!" He had shot her in the face, but it had all come true—and now he could add Beta and Gamma to the list. It didn't matter, I thought. I was confident Dragon would kill our Systies. All that was important at that moment was to kill Systies. And Dragon was a first–class killer.

I saw Merlin as well. Thinking back on it, I guess all this was instantaneous. But I still remember every last detail. Merlin was almost frozen with terror—I could tell that much—but he was forcing himself on, crawling through the mud like a worm. It was raining heavily and his faceplate was splattered with mud. He was shaking and crying. He must have known he was going to die, he could surely taste it, but he was not whimpering in a hole. He was crawling forward, seeking death like a moth hurling itself into a naked flame. The Systie was right up ahead—Merlin had zeroed him, and Merlin knew the Systie could not spot him through the crumbled wall of rubble that lay between them. All he needed now was a clear shot. Beta Four, the Wiz, Merlin, our own lab rat. He was stalking the Systie like a jungle animal. Boudicca had been right all along, I thought—never trust a Systie! They had waited until the O was dead, and then they had struck. It was treason against humanity. That O was drenched in the blood of the Legion, and the System wanted to steal it away. Beta was gone, sacrificed so that others might live. Merlin was terrified, but he was not going to let the System get away with this.

There—the Systie was in sight. A Systie A–suit, half buried in a pile of rubble behind an SG, wreathed in smoke and ashes as the rain poured down on the fires. Merlin pushed his E out ahead of him and slid the stock into his shoulder. The biobloc fieldfaxer was no good against Systies; he had lasered the weapon and left it smoking in the mud.

The Systie moved—Merlin switched to xmax auto and the laser sight lit up the target. Raindrops danced on his faceplate. Life was so sweet. Merlin must have been insane to join the Legion. He surely did not want to die, but Beta was dying, and he was Beta Four. I watched him gently squeeze the trigger.

It was pouring now, black clouds scudding close overhead, lashing the burning city, a smoking moonscape. I sensed that my soul was fading—something was happening. But there was Millina! She lay in a widening puddle of muddy water behind her E, trembling with hate and terror. A wave of sympathy swept over me. She had switched sides! It was almost miraculous—after all that Valkyrie had said about her. Why? What could have motivated her? Of course they would never have told her about the plans for the aircar—such knowledge is dangerous. They would have simply listened to the progress of the op, and then suddenly neutralized the aircar, and shown up themselves in an identical car, to collect the results. No mess, no fuss.

A brilliant op. Millina knew the System well. And she had switched sides!

The sky flickered and laser snapped over Millina's helmet. Death, we had said, launching the op. Yes, death it was, death for us all, Legion and Systies and O's, death for everyone, without favor or prejudice. And I suddenly understood about Millina. Death was Millina's goddess—Death, a remote pale blind goddess with a black cloth wrapped around her eyes, and a huge sharp sword. And whenever she heard a noise, she swung the sword.

The Hand of the Mocain, suddenly awakening to the truth, after a lifetime of service. I knew Valkyrie was part of the answer. Millina had hit at least two of the DefCorps soldiers as they leaped from the aircar, but they must have had two squads in that car, and most of them made it out before the car had been shot down. One of them was right up ahead, hiding in the energy field of a fiercely burning groundcar. It was time for Millina to play her dangerous game.

"It's Millina! Millina! DefCorps, hold its fire!" Millina shouted it out, her skin crawling as she crept forward. If even one DefCorps soldier had seen her firing at them during the landing, she would die as soon as she exposed herself.

She scrambled to her feet and charged forward into the rain, her E held low. The DefCorps soldier was on his belly in the flames from the burning groundcar. His SG was up and scanning. He motioned Millina down with one hand. She hit the ground, breathing hard. Rain hissed off her A–suit. She switched to laser. All those years, in the service of a false god. All that misdirected hate. It wasn't enough, to betray humanity. Now she had to betray the System as well. I felt an indescribable sadness, for Millina. Then she stood up and fired laser, right into the DefCorps soldier's A–suit.

* * *

It came out of nowhere in a heavy sheet of rain, spitting tacstars, booming past in a heartbeat, gone, back into the dark sky. Micronukes erupted in its wake, sudden flashes, the earth shaking, and a winking forest of phospho fireballs, rising to the sky. Lightning flickered wildly, and there was a stunned pause as a great crackling roar rolled over the battlefield.

My head was throbbing. My faceplate was covered with mud. I strained to move—a black cloud of pain. I squirmed over on to my back. Tacstars rose all around me. I smeared the mud around on my visor and stared out stupidly. Alive—I was alive! And back in my body!

"Cover me, gang..." Who was that? It was Merlin, suddenly up and running towards our tragic pile of shattered A–suits, Coolhand and Snow Leopard and Priestess and me. Merlin, for God's sake, throwing himself away, for Beta. Behind him, Psycho suddenly appeared, running forward firing his chainlink, full auto x, hosing down everything in sight to cover Merlin. Tacstars erupted in great, glowing flashes. Psycho hit every building in the vicinity. The buildings disintegrated, spitting phospho streaks, the sky full of junk, the buildings falling slowly in massive clouds of dust and Psycho crouched there, a perfect target, panting and screaming, finger fixed on the trigger, firing right over Merlin's helmet.

It was a nuclear morning for Fernveldt.

* * *

The escape pod hovered a few mikes over the smoking earth of what had once been Fernveldt City, and the access door snapped open and a girl appeared, an E in one hand, the other hand covering her mouth. The girl was unarmored, her hair blowing in the backblast. She paused briefly in the doorway, then leaped to the ground. I was still in the mud beside Priestess, too weak to move. I had ripped open my medkit and spread medpads all over her wounds, but the blood was bubbling up around the bandages and I didn't know what to do. I couldn't understand why nobody was helping me. What had happened to Merlin? Perhaps we were still fighting. It slowly dawned on me that the escape pod had strafed the Systies and probably turned the tide of the battle. And then I recognized the girl. It was Tara.

Dragon faced her with his E. Behind her, in the escape pod's doorway, a second person appeared. A savage face, heavy brows, violet uniform, also unarmored but wielding an E—it was the humanoid, Tara's pet! What was his name? Gildron! How had he gotten loose? He leaped to the ground, snarling and holding his E up warily.

"You!" Dragon exclaimed to Tara in total surprise. "Good shooting! We need evac, now! We've got dead and wounded!"

Tara stood there gaping at the scene of devastation around her. The entire city had been nuked. Not a building remained standing, and the sky was a poisonous brew of writhing fireballs. Fierce fires roared up to the sky. Nuclear light glowed on her face. A hot breeze carried a misty rain, stinging her flesh, and the fires flickered all around her. It was a miracle anyone had survived. The A–suited delegation before her was covered with mud and blood.

"Bring me your casualties," she responded.

"I've got life!" Merlin and Valkyrie were hauling shattered A–suits through the mud to the escape pod.

"Where are the others?" An eerie silence settled over the battlefield. There was only a deep rumbling from the sky. Psycho stopped firing. Smoke curled all around him—his chainlink was glowing.

"Everyone to the escape pod! Where's Gamma Five and Seven? Check the casualties! Quick!"

I was vaguely conscious of A–suited figures struggling above me. Then I was moving, under luminous skies. Priestess, don't forget Priestess, I struggled to say, but I could not. Someone's faceplate came close to mine. Horribly scarred plex, but I could make out the face— Valkyrie! Just for an instant she was there, and it was like a kiss, the kiss of life.

"Thinker...Thinker! Stay with us, Thinker!" Then she was gone. A quick glimpse of Merlin, and I was on my back again, and a hot wind was blowing debris all around us.

The escape pod exploded with a tremendous crack, dazzling and deafening me, the shock wave knocking everyone flat. When I struggled to my elbows in the mud, I saw the escape pod had been blown into the sky and was disintegrating, separate sections flaming through the air trailing white phospho smoke. The wreckage impacted several K away, testifying to the force of the hit, multiple flashes, multiple booms. My tacmod shrieked. A tacstar had exploded right on the escape pod. Dragon brought his E around in a slow motion blur towards a Systie soldier staggering from a smoking pile of rubble, Manlink at his shoulder. Dragon fired, Psycho fired, Merlin fired, Valkyrie fired, even the humanoid fired—another nuke shimmered and rose and the Systie was gone, snuffed out like a candle.

Tara was face–down in the mud, stunned. The humanoid was on his knees beside her, his eyes glazed over. I couldn't even get off the ground, but Dragon was there. He gently turned Tara over and held her in his arms.

"They got your ship—I'm sorry," Dragon said. The tacnet was working now and I could hear every word. It was like the crack of doom. It was hopeless now, I knew—Redhawk had to be dead. There would be no evac for us.

Tara's lips moved. Her hands came up. She activated her wristcom. "Whit—Whit, come. Come." It was a whisper. How could anyone possibly hear her, under this nuclear holocaust? Impossible.

"Coming!" The reply came immediately. "On the way, Commander!" My heart leaped. The Gods were there after all!

A huge, hairy hand placed itself on Dragon's armored chest and gently pushed him away from Tara. Gildron reached down and took her in his arms and stood up, Tara's arms and legs dangling, Gildron's E hanging loosely from one arm, a light hot rain hissing down all around them. Gildron looked around the sky in despair, rolling his eyes and snarling quietly. It was as if his whole world was ending.

Chapter 11

Ghost Riders

The aircar appeared in a halo of rain and mist, a pale, fragile vision, hissing magically up to Badboy's position, hovering in the air, spraying a storm of mud and water. My head whirled. Lying on my back, I thought I had never seen anything more beautiful in my life. It was a pure white aircar, Tara's personal car, which had ridden in the *Highroad* down to Mongera. It did not belong out here, I thought, in the firestorm.

I tried to move my limbs. A bloody, glistening cenite arm appeared before me, then fell away. Bad idea. Voices echoed in my helmet.

"Get in! Get in!"

"Faster!"

"Oh my God."

"Cinta, three DefCorps aircars, coming quick!"

"Aircars!"

"Systie aircars!" Dragon exclaimed. "Psycho—cover us! Load 'em up, gang!"

Psycho charged off into the rain, his chainlink going up. Merlin and Dragon, splattered with mud, seized me under the arms and tossed me effortlessly into the aircar with a crash. I did not even feel it. Valkyrie pulled me to one side, then stepped over me.

Full auto tacstars whistled and ripped through the air, tingling my skin, the stars hissing and roaring. The sky exploded, airburst nukes, a sky of fire for the Systie aircars.

Someone screamed. Someone else was crying. Armored bodies slid along a bloody metal floor. Frantic activity. I tried to raise my head—I could not.

"That's One, Three, Two—Gamma One—Nine!" Dragon and Merlin were hauling Priestess towards the aircar. I knew her wounds were bad.

"Gamma, I think she's alive." Valkyrie helped drag Priestess into the aircar. There was blood everywhere.

"Coolhand is critical!"

"Snow Leopard is still bleeding!"

"Hurry! DefCorps aircars are here!" Tara's exec Whit was in the pilot's seat all by herself, calling out to Valkyrie. "They're here!"

Psycho was still firing outside and the sky was full of nuclear clouds, spitting an unholy white light. The humanoid leaped into the aircar, carrying Tara in his arms.

"Gamma! Help us!" Dragon and Merlin struggled with a body. Valkyrie helped them drag it in. It was Warhound, who died for us all, his A–suit horribly burned. Then there was another—Ironman, a helpless, dead A–suit. Valkyrie slipped in the blood and went to one knee.

Another scream. Who was alive, who was dead? Whit was out of her seat, hurrying to her Commander. "Oh my God! Cinta! Oh! Hurry, hurry! They're circling!"

"Get back in your seat, pilot!"

"Coolhand is hit bad!"

"I've zeroed Gamma Five and Seven!"

"Where are they?"

"Wait for us! Be right back!" Dragon and Merlin whirled around and disappeared into the smoke, splashing wildly through the mud.

"No! No! Come back! Oh my God!" Whit was ready for a complete breakdown.

Out the open assault door Dragon and Merlin paused at a glowing tacstar crater full of rubble from a collapsed building. They found two Legion A–suits trapped in the wreckage, one covering the other.

"Get them out." Dragon frantically tore at the rubble with his hands. Merlin pulled at the first A–suit.

"It's Sassin."

"Is he alive?"

"Don't know."

"Help...help." A whisper.

"Five!" Scrapper, stunned but alive.

"Aircar attacking!" Psycho fired his chainlink again, white–hot tacstars ripping overhead. Dragon and Merlin raised their E's and fired into the raging sky. Nuclear airbursts, hot hail splattering all around them. Merlin dropped his E and pulled Sassin from the rubble. Dragon got ahold of Scrapper. A flaming inferno above, splitting into fragments, trailing black smoke.

Psycho stood alone in the mud, watching the Systie aircar break apart above him. Direct hit! The sky was his! He let loose another burst, giggling to himself. His sky—his! The other aircars circled, warily.

"Systies! Systies! I'm here! Right here! Can't you see me? Closer! Come closer! I want to kiss you!" Psycho burst into demonic laughter. "Just a little kiss! Here—taste it!" He let loose another burst, up into the burning sky. He was staggering in the mud, looking up and laughing.

Two more shattered A–suits, Dragon and Merlin dragging them, splattering through the mud. Gamma Two reached out to haul them into the aircar.

"Bring the O."

"We don't have time!"

"Bring the O!"

Another corpse, this one charred and smoking, obscene black unreal armored body parts, all wrong, still sizzling, falling apart as they slid it into the car. Alien limbs, twitching. Alien blood, hissing onto the deck. A revolting stench.

"Scut! Is that it?"

"Another attack! He's launched!" A warning from Whit.

Psycho fired immediately, a long tacstar burst. The ground shook. The aircar shrieked.

"Board, Psycho—now!" Dragon and Merlin leaped in. Then Psycho hurtled in head–first, his chainlink slamming against the ceiling. The aircar moved, picking up speed, rain and spray hissing over us from the open door.

"Wait! Don't leave us! Take us! We helped it!" A Systie A–suit was running alongside—it was Millina.

"Shoot her," Dragon said, reaching for his E. I came to life, my one good hand locking onto Dragon's arm.

"No!" I shouted, "Help her! She shot the Systies! I saw her!"

"What do we do? God!" Whit hesitated, the aircar gliding forward slowly, barely moving, the Systie aircars already on their firing runs.

Valkyrie leaned out the door, extending her E in one hand, barrel out. Millina ran alongside, her arms outstretched. Only an instant, for Millina to decide. Gamma Two, Legion, her slave, leaning out with her E, the barrel pointed right at Millina. Pale green eyes, a whole new world, life or death, reach out and taste your fate. Millina seized the barrel of the E with both hands. Her feet left the ground. Valkyrie and Dragon hauled her in. She collapsed on the deck, gasping, hysterical. Whit hit the throttle and the aircar spat flame and the assault door slammed shut and Fernveldt blurred and vanished in a flash of tacstars.

"Thinker's stable."

Stable, stable, stable, echoing in my helmet. Someone opened my visor. It was Valkyrie, a flash of her pale face, icy green eyes. She turned away. Pandemonium erupted. I desperately tried to get off my back and crawl over to Priestess—the pain was overwhelming. Somebody screamed, and I think it was me.

"One's bleeding. I can't stop the bleeding!"

"Give me the cyro!"

"Hold still there—don't move it!"

"Open the visor."

"Coolhand—Deadman! Help Coolhand!"

"Priestess! Can you hear me?"

"Gamma, gimme a charge!"

"Priestess is hit bad!"

"He's not breathing!"

"Sassin! He's alive!"

"The charger! Quick!"

"Deadman! Hold still!"

I forced myself over to Priestess's prone A–suit, the car whirling around me, cold sweat on my brow, acid burning in my mouth.

"Priestess—Priestess!" Her visor was open. Her eyes were open. She gasped for air. Valkyrie was unlinking Nine's armor—she had been hit in the chest. Blood oozed out of the armor. My crude medpads fell away, soaked in blood.

Another scream. This time it was not me. Dragon tossed Valkyrie a bloody biotic charger. She pressed it onto Priestess's scarlet chest. Priestess's eyes flickered and closed. She breathed deeply and shuddered.

"Don't let her die!"

"Get out of the way, Thinker—you can't help. I need a cyro!"

"Deadman! Sassin is in bad shape!"

"What about Coolhand?"

"He's dying, Gamma! Gimme the charger!"

"Unlink, unlink!"

"Ohhh no—no!"

"Stop the bleeding!"

"Coolhand, Coolhand, can you hear me?"

"He's not breathing!"

"No! No! God no!"

"Biotic charge! Quick!"

Valkyrie bent over Coolhand, frantically working to unlink his bloody armor. Blood was splattered everywhere. It was a charnel house, a butcher shop. I struggled to retain consciousness. It whirled around me. I found Priestess's hand and took it in mine and closed my eyes and prayed. Just let her live, I thought. Just let her live! I'll do your will, I'll kill Systies the rest of my life, whatever you want! Just let her live.

"Sassin! Critical! Now!" Another mad scramble.

Shattered, scarred armor, black blood on the deck, a massive, alien limb, burnt to a crisp—the O! Its head was at my feet, encased in melted armor deformed by plasma.

The humanoid sat beside me, cradling Tara in his arms. She was pale and still, her eyes closed. Lord, she was just like an angel, a wounded angel. The humanoid was crying, running his blunt, hairy fingers through her silken hair.

"DefCorps aircars closing!" Whit shouted. "What do we do?"

Millina scrambled up to the cockpit, sliding on the blood, tearing at her visor. "Is it on Mongeran freaks?" Millina asked.

"Affirmative—two of them!"

"ATTENTION! WE ARE BEING TARGETED FOR ATTACK! HOSTILE LOCK–ON!" The aircar boomed out the warning. Millina hit the transmit tab.

"DefCorps aircars, attention! This is Millina, repeat, Millina! Hold its fire! We have seized control of the aircar! Repeat, the System has control of this aircar! Enemy units all terminated! Acknowledge!"

"Acknowledge it has control of the aircar. Slow down and land, Millina. Does it need assistance?"

"Negative. Negative, we have seriously wounded here, please escort us back to Mongera Port, acknowledge."

"They're still locked on!" Whit reported.

"Lock on lifted," the ship corrected her.

"Slow down, Millina! We're coming alongside. Who is on board?

Report!"

"DefCorps, our comrades are dying! Escort us in! Alert the port!" Millina took her hand off the transmit tab. "Don't slow down! Fast as it can! The bastard is coming alongside us."

"Psycho," Dragon said cautiously, "take position by the door. Pilot, you do exactly as I say. Be prepared to take evasive action."

"Affirmative! Do it quick, whatever it is!"

An enemy aircar slid close in behind us, easing in to our left.

"Nobody move! Heads down! Millina, wave at him or something."

Right alongside us now, an ugly wedge of burnt black armor ramming its way through the air, hot cenite death, all the power and pain of the System, functional and deadly and excruciatingly lovely, so lovely I could hardly believe it. Millina waved from the cockpit. The Systie pilot could see her and Whit sitting together up front.

"Millina, report its status and casualties immediately!"

"He's not buying it!"

"Whit, open the door! Psycho, chainlink! Hold on, gang!" The door snapped open suddenly, a great roar as a typhoon of air rushed in, loose gear exploding all around us. The Systie pilot's eyes widened as Five fired full auto tacstar, and the enemy aircar exploded, a blinding nuclear flash; and our own aircar was blown aside like a leaf in a storm, falling, rolling, chaos, everyone screaming, upside down, then back again, crashing down towards the deck in a wild pile of bodies. Whit regained control of the car. Dragon landed on top of me. He scrambled off, stunned.

"Deadman! Is everyone still here?"

"The door! The door!"

The door slid shut. Chaos reigned.

"Help me! It's Sassin!"

"Oh no! Where's the medkit?"

"Where's the other aircar?"

"Badboy, Big Kid! We've got a distress beacon—it's your aircar jock, Beta Ten. Badboy, Big Kid, repeat, distress beacon from your aircar jock—do you read it, acknowledge?"

"Oh, Deadman!"

"Aircar closing—this is..."

"Evade, evade!"

"That's Ten! Beta Ten! Are you getting that signal?"

"Badboy, Big Kid—we've got you on scope, one Systie aircar behind you, closing fast. What's your status, over?"

"Oh, we're fine—SCUT!"

"No life signs from Coolhand!"

"Mag charge! Keep him alive, Valkyrie!"

"Sassin—critical!"

"Oh damn! Damn damn damn damn!"

"Deadman, don't let him die!"

"Deceptors!" Whit slammed a tiny fist down on the controls and the sky exploded all around us and we were in a hot drop to the deck and suddenly in a forest, crashing through the underbrush, a leafy green cathedral all around us, black tree trunks flashing past like ancient stone columns. Whit took us to a faint stream and we followed it into the woods, mikes above the water, trailing a shock wave of water vapor and shredded leaves.

"We've got to pick up Redhawk."

"Keep going, pilot! You're leaving him behind!"

"Coolhand, Coolhand! Please! Live, damn you, live! Coolhand!"

"We go to pick up Redhawk, now! Do you have the beacon on scope?"

"No response! There's no response! Hit it again!"

"Affirmative. Just let us shake this aircar." Whit's face was beaded with cold sweat. The deceptors had done the trick. The DefCorps aircar was wasting time dealing with phantoms.

I could taste the mags on my tongue—it was all that was keeping me conscious. Priestess was curled in a foetal ball under a tangle of equipment. I tore it away, frantic. Bloody fleshpads, all over her chest. Her eyes were open—she was breathing!

"Priestess, Priestess—answer me!" Her eyes focused on me. Her mouth opened.

"Thinker..."

"Don't talk! I'm right here! You're all right—stay awake!"

"...hurts..."

"Gimme that medpack!"

A hand on my arm. It was Merlin. "She's had a charge, Thinker. No more!"

"You stay awake, Priestess!"

"Faster! Have you got the zero?"

"Got it, got it!"

"No response!" A muffled scream from Valkyrie. She hit the charge again, again, again. "Please...please...please...." It was Coolhand they were working on, I slowly realized. I watched, stunned. It was like a fever dream, and Dragon and Valkyrie were armored demons hovering over one of their own, the A–suit still glowing, scarlet blood bubbling.

"No response."

"No! No! No! No!" Valkyrie continued triggering the biotic charger. Coolhand's blood splattered all over his A–suit, but he was not there any more. He had joined the phantom army, the Legion of the Dead. I turned my head away.

He had been my first friend in the Legion. I could not believe it. I simply could not grasp it. It was a mistake. Surely it was a mistake.

The humanoid still had Tara in his arms. She was gasping. I moved over to her in a trance, and opened my medkit. I pressed a biomag onto one arm and triggered it.

The creature did not object. Tara stirred, and her eyes fluttered open. She looked so fragile, like a lost child.

"Wester..." she whispered, "...it's you."

"Yes, Tara—it's me. Don't try to talk—you'll be all right."

"You're wounded."

"It's nothing." It's only my heart, I thought, and my soul.

"I came for you, Wester."

"I know you did."

"I'm sorry, Wester—I'm sorry!" There were tears in Tara's eyes. The humanoid put his ugly face right next to Tara's—he was giving her a big, wet kiss. He was beaming.

"Gildron!" Tara flashed a beautiful smile. She was coming around. "Gildron, you're all right!" The creature was whimpering and drooling.

"We're closing on that beacon," Whit said. We were out of the forest. The sky was dark and cloudy—raindrops spattered against the plex.

"Faster!" Millina urged. "That aircar will be on us soon."

"Again! Again! Biotic charge!" Valkyrie and Dragon and Merlin and Psycho were struggling over Sassin's bloody form. He was slipping away, fading away, and all the magtech wonders of the Legion could not bring him back.

"He's gone!"

"Keep trying! Keep trying!" Valkyrie was in tears, hysterical, banging away with the charger. They had a breather in his mouth and the charger had ahold of his heart, and his lungs were still going, but it was hopeless. The life signs were all flat.

"Negative life."

"No! No! No! Keep trying!" Smoke was rising from Sassin's scorched flesh.

"Valkyrie—he's gone. He's gone. Valkyrie, please." Merlin gently pulled Valkyrie away from the body. Her armored hands were scarlet with blood.

And Sassin the Assassin, Gamma Seven, was at last, truly, immortal. I was so stunned I could only lie there, sprawled on the deck between Priestess and Tara, ice cold flashes rippling over my flesh inside the A–suit, waiting, under siege, for whatever was to come next.

"Badass, Badboy. Respond!" Dragon was in the cockpit now between Whit and Millina, calling Redhawk. We were out of the forest. A road flashed past below, then grasslands, then a series of forested ridges.

"Badboy, Badass! Am I glad to hear your voice! Get me outta here!" He was right up ahead. The forest was burning, strewn with wreckage. A greasy cloud of black smoke shot past us. Then we spotted Beta Ten, hobbling out of the woods in a scorched A–suit.

"Enemy aircar heading this way!"

"Oh no—hurry!" The door popped open as we hovered in a whirling cloud of smoke and leaves. Dragon and Merlin hauled Redhawk in. He collapsed on the deck.

"Get out of here!" The door slammed shut.

"Enemy aircar closing!" Redhawk scrambled to his feet and forced his way into the cockpit.

"Give me the controls!" he demanded. Millina relinquished the seat next to Whit. Redhawk punched the power and we were off in a dizzying arc, up, then down, the forest rushing at us, then whipping past as we proceeded at treetops back the way we had come.

"It's going the wrong way," Whit objected, "It's headed right for the DefCorps aircar!"

"I know," Redhawk responded quietly. "Where's the freakin' armament? Is that..."

"Yes, it's a DefCorps chainlink, but it's not going to shoot it out, is it? We've got to get out of here!"

"Somebody shut her down," Redhawk requested, dropping the car below treetop level. A green blur flashed past all around us—my heart was in my mouth.

"Don't interfere," Dragon cautioned Whit. "Redhawk knows what he's doing."

"If it knows what it's doing, how did it get shot down?" Whit asked shakily.

"There were four of them," Redhawk retorted angrily. "Now shut down."

"DefCorps aircar closing!" the car warned.

"Come, you bitch." Redhawk muttered. He snapped the controls up. We burst through the forest roof up into the clear; rainclouds close above.

"We are on a collision course!" The aircar called out.

I had seen Redhawk do this before, and I never liked it. The enemy aircar glowed on the screen.

"Come to Daddy, come, you bitch."

"Chainlink functional—lockon! Enemy has locked on!"

"Missiles! Ignition!" Redhawk squeezed the trigger. A sharp burst, then we made a ninety degree turn and I almost blacked out and suddenly we were back in the forest, back in the shadows, trees flashing past, a luminous green roof flickering overhead. Redhawk released deceptors behind us.

I closed my eyes and gritted my teeth—how in the world did he do it? A series of explosions reached our ears, shockwaves shaking the car. The scope was littered with junk.

"Direct hit, gang." Redhawk pulled the aircar brutally out of the forest, exploding through the treetops, rain hitting the plex.

"That was not bad," Whit said quietly.

"I'm good in bed, too," Redhawk replied.

"Head for the shuttle," Dragon ordered. "We've got to lift."

"*Highroad*, Whit. How goes the loading?"

"We just finished."

"Good! Prep for liftoff—we're on the way back. As soon as we dock, we want liftoff!"

"Got it, we're sealed already."

"Any signs of trouble?"

"Negative."

"Psycho, get back in position by the door," Dragon ordered. We may have to shoot our way in."

"We didn't know about this," Millina said suddenly. "There would be a very limited number of people who would be aware of it. Maybe only the bunch in those aircars. It could be that nobody in Mongera Port knows what it's all about. We might have no trouble at all."

I picked up an E with my one good hand. Tara was conscious. Priestess breathed heavily, her eyes blinking. I struggled to a sitting position, facing the door. Psycho and Merlin were all set. Dragon was in the cockpit, watching Whit and Redhawk. Valkyrie was checking the wounded, leaning over Scrapper.

"Scrapper's stable. You'll be all right, Scrapper."

"Sassin...how's Sassin?" Scrapper sounded as if she was already in Dreamland.

"Don't talk. Rest. I've given you a mag." Valkyrie turned to Priestess. "How are you doing, Priestess?"

"How are the others?" Priestess asked weakly. "Is Snow Leopard all right?"

"Try to rest. We'll be home soon."

I was ready for whatever happened, my E fixed on the door. I did not want to know about Snow Leopard. My mouth tasted like acid. No, I did not want to know.

* * *

The transmission came in as we were nearing the Port. "Millina, it's the First. Millina, respond. Is it wounded? Repeat, First to Millina, please respond."

Millina reached over between Whit and Redhawk and triggered the transmit tab of the comset. The laser spot of my E roamed over her back. "Excellency, Millina. What a surprise. We were not told of its presence here."

"Millina! It's wonderful to hear its voice! We were very worried. Has the mission succeeded? Those fools that attacked it thought it was a Legion raiding party. We only just found out about it—an unforgivable mess! Is it all right?"

"We're fine, thanks, Excellency."

"We're sorry about the foul–up. It was a stupid move and somebody will pay for it. Was the mission successful?"

"Yes, Excellency, fully successful."

"Good! Good! That's wonderful news! Well, carry on as planned. I'll notify everyone that it was successful. Sub cannot imagine how anxious we have been to hear this news. Congratulations, Millina! It's a brilliant coup, and we will insure that its designation is mentioned prominently in the official reports."

"Our thanks, Excellency."

"We hope the cooperating units were not upset about the attack. It realizes we could not inform anyone of its presence. We suppose it was a natural reaction by the DefCorps. We thought we could stop anything like that before it got started. But the situation here is extremely chaotic—we did not hear what was happening until it was too late!"

"We understand, Excellency."

"Please explain to them what happened. We are compiling a full report."

"We will do our best, Excellency."

"We know Sub will, Millina. And, again, congratulations! First out."

Millina cut the commo on the aircar's instrument panel.

She hunched over between Whit and Redhawk. Mongera Port came into view ahead, swarming with activity. A liner thundered up into the dark sky. "Burn in Hell, Excellency," she said quietly. "Burn in Hell. They must be out of assets. Otherwise, they wouldn't be talking." She had bought us a few more marks.

"Whit," Tara gasped. "Did it pick up those children? Forest Hill?"

"Affirmative, Commander. Squalling brats! They're all safe aboard the *Highroad*. Cit is getting soft in its old age! The bankers and lawyers would have paid us." Whit was twitching with exhaustion, but she obviously worshipped Tara.

And I thought she was right, about Tara—picking up doomed children, in the midst of this chaos. That was the Tara I had known.

"*Highroad* aircar, Mongera Port Customs. Please proceed to Inspection Bay Orange Five, as marked. We wish to examine its cargo."

"I knew it!" Dragon snarled. "Ignore them."

"Stinking bureaucrats!" Psycho exclaimed, "The world is ending and they want to fill out forms!"

"Whit..." Tara was conscious, still in Gildron's hairy arms. "Refuse, cite our agreement with the Government. Our terms, accepted by them...ah, para ten, our right to pick up any special case refugees, any location, to be determined by us, no inspection, free access to and from the shuttle and the ship."

"Commander, it is a genius!"

"We know." Tara closed her eyes. She looked truly weary. Whit repeated it, firmly, to Mongeran Customs.

"Hold one, *Highroad* aircar."

"Keep going," Dragon ordered. Someone was moaning. I was just barely conscious—it was a red haze. An aircar flashed past outside. Tara was pale and her eyes were closed. The humanoid was stunned, staring into space, holding on to Tara protectively. Priestess grimaced in pain, icy sweat all over her brow. Millina looked sick, still huddled between Whit and Redhawk in the cockpit. Whit was grim and tense. Redhawk was silent. Valkyrie and Merlin were watching over Snow Leopard, keeping him alive. Dragon and Psycho had their weapons pointed at both doors. Scrapper was feverish, talking to herself. And the others were all around us, I thought, a whole squad of A–suits. All my comrades are here—living and dead, we are all here, riding back from the mission. Ghost riders, I thought, still with us, the living. Everyone has come back except the two Systies, the soldier and the dip. And in view of what had happened, we would not miss them. I was still by the assault door behind my E, fighting to stay conscious in a gritty, throbbing wave of raw hot agony. I knew my left arm was gone, but I didn't even care. Priestess was on the deck beside me, her chest bubbling black blood. Her eyes were shut tight and she was trembling and I could read the despair in her face. I put the E down, and the armored fingers of my one good hand closed over hers.

"I'm here, Priestess." I whispered it. She answered with a faint moan, clutching my fingers tightly. And I vowed to love her forever, and never leave her. I didn't want to see the future anymore, I suddenly realized. I wanted to extinguish it. But even as I held Nine's hand, I prayed to Deadman for revenge, against all our enemies. I wanted blood. I wanted to see the corpses of our enemies floating in rivers of blood. My mind whirled with images—our holy dead were with us, riding home. We would burn them, under alien stars—I could see the death ceremony, hot green nuclear flames licking around my A–suit, I was on the pyre as someone chanted the death song..."Missing in action, we join you soon!" Perhaps we, the living, the immortals, were the real dead. The others were free, at last, but we would never be free.

Moontouch appeared before me in my agony, a hazy image, holding up our child, calling out to me over the light years. I was certain I would never see her again, and I would never hold my own son in my arms. I was shaking with rage. Someone was going to pay for this—I didn't know who, and I didn't know when, but someone was going to pay for Mongera—I would see to it if it was the last thing I ever did.

"*Highroad* aircar, Mongera Customs. You may proceed to the *Highroad*."

Whit did not even bother to answer.

Priestess squeezed my hand. We were both alive—who could possibly ask for more?

PART III

FEVER DREAMS

We stood the night watch together, you and I, against the rest of the universe. Call out for me, in two hundred years. Do you think I'll have forgotten?

Night Watch, Born in the Outvac

Chapter 12

Cold New Worlds

Rain. Warm heavy rain from dark skies, to wash away our sins. A muted roar, a faint tingling on my skin—a tropical downpour. It was wet season on Veda 6. The jungle was awash, shuddering behind heavy sheets of rain. I was thinking of her even then. Strange, that the rain should bring her back. I stood silently on the walkway gazing into the forest, protected by the overhanging bulk of the base. I was walking perimeter for Minos Station, an E at my chest, dressed in litesuit camfax, alone with my mind. There used to be entire squads walking perimeter here. But now there was only me.

I was just a regular guy, I thought. Perfectly normal. Except for being immortal. And being a professional killer. And being insane! But, aside from that, I was perfectly normal. Just like the rest of the guys! So why did I feel that Deadman had me in his sights?

No, the rain was not enough to wash away our sins, I concluded. Not nearly enough. Maybe a tacstar would do it, or a laser track through the brain—but nothing less. Until then, we remained immortals, survivors, sinners in the eyes of the Gods of Fate.

"Three, One." That's how it started, a call from Snow Leopard. Just another call. We are microbes—we are clay. Immortal, for an instant. The Gods breathe, and we die.

"One, Three," I answered.

"Report to Opcen."

"Tenners." I turned back to the main entrance. There was no rush. Perimeter duty was just make–work for us. Nothing was going to come at us on Veda 6. And if it did, Snow Leopard would know about it without my help. Perimeter duty was just therapy, I thought, for Beta. Whether it would help or not was debatable.

Inside I walked empty halls, boots echoing down gleaming, half–lit corridors. Dark doorways lined my path like crypts. I felt like an intruder in the tomb of a long–dead emperor. Minos Station was a top–line Legion base—they didn't make them any better than this. The Legion was not into opulence, but the cold stark beauty of a major

Legion station always gave me a charge. There was a sense of limitless power in a Legion station. And to see it as it was then, completely deserted, was downright eerie.

I took an elevator to topsides. It was silent except for a faint whistle as I shot upwards. The floor numbers flashed past on the panel. My camfax leaked water all over the deck. I made sure the E was set to safe.

Beta One sat alone in the Station opcen, a pale statue in a little pool of blue light surrounded by a vast darkened room of sensors and comsets and megadeath weapons systems. We were atop the base. Armored plex gave us the view, a dark morning, low grey clouds shedding rain over our own jungle. Once this opcen had teemed with life, once this had been the heart of a vast Legion hive. But now it belonged only to us, only to Beta.

Snow Leopard looked up as I approached. He was pale as death, hot pink eyes blinking at me under long straight blond hair, hair so blond it was almost white. Faint blue veins throbbed at his temples. He was dressed in a camfax litesuit. Beta One, our own Snow Leopard. Our heartbeat, our brain—our soul. Speak, One, and it will be done. Without thought, without regrets. We had all been together too long, and seen too much. We were in it now to the end, and Snow Leopard was on point. We had almost lost him on Mongera. We had all left little pieces of ourselves on Mongera, but Snow Leopard had left more than the rest of us, I knew.

"You've got a message," Snow Leopard said. He sat before the Station Commander's conmod. He slid a datacard to me along the console without further comment.

"A message?" I picked up the card and stared at it stupidly. "What kind of message?" I was truly mystified.

"A personal message. Star tracer." Snow Leopard looked up at me briefly, then turned back to the screens, vaguely troubled. "What's the latest on the port?"

"Merlin is still working on it," I responded. "Says he'll be done soon." It was not easy to keep a full Legion station functioning smoothly at low power with only one squad. The problem at the port was one of many. The war was stretching the Legion's resources, and Veda 6 had been stripped of almost all personnel. We were on hold, far from anywhere even remotely important—a ghost squad guarding a dead station, standing night watch for a deserted world.

I left Snow Leopard behind me alone with his own phantoms and took the elevator down to ground. I walked through a cavernous cold hall wreathed in shadows and found my way to the library. It was dark. I found a cube and hit the lights and sank into the airchair.

I was tired. We were only wasting time here, I knew. I wasn't sure if we deserved it or not. I placed the datacard on the desk before me. A personal message, from the unknown. A personal message, hurtling through the light years, sparkling through alternate worlds, blasting past all the magical barriers of reality and extinction, into the out and out to the in, matter and antimatter, all the way to Veda 6, all the way to Beta Three. Who did I know who would send me a personal message across the galaxy? Who did I know who could afford it? A star tracer could eat up your life's savings. My past was dead—I could think of no one from the past who would want to contact me, for any reason. Joining the Legion was like dying—you left the world of mortals, for some other place. People did not normally send messages to the dead.

The card had my Legion serial number glowing on the address line. It was for me, all right. I placed it on the tray and pressed it on. It was a genetic ID—for me alone. More expense. The message came up immediately in cold white light on the cube screen: "Come quickly. I need you now. Mica 3, 252–042211. Cite private A/C Black Rose 172472, valid CR 66,000. Tara."

Tara. Tara! I should have known. Who else? Tara, coming at me like a nightmare. My very own past, coming right at me again. A wave of cold prickled over my skin. I had thought I would never see her again. She last appeared to me through a fever dream, when I was down and out in the body shop of the P.S. *Maiden.* She was pale and weak, standing only by sheer willpower, her brow beaded with cold sweat. Her humanoid pet was hovering by her side, anxious to hold her up but forbidden to touch. That was vintage Tara.

"Goodbye, Wester," she said softly. "It's a big galaxy. I doubt we'll meet again. I hope you will remember Cintana Tamaling, who came to you when you needed her, on Mongera. I'll be out there somewhere— and thinking of you." She blinked hot smoky eyes and reached out her hand and touched my sweaty forehead and made the sign of the Legion. It was a blessing.

"Tara," I said groggily, "call me. If you need me...call me. I'll be there!" I was not sure if she was really there, or I was hallucinating, but that's what I said, and that's what I meant. She smiled a sad little smile and turned away with the beast. And when I awoke I was in the C. S. *Spawn*, and she was gone.

I need you, the message said, now. This was Tara at her very best. No please, no explanation. You've said it, boy, now let's see it. Lord, what did it mean?

I knew immediately I had to go, no matter what. It was surely impossible, but I had to do it anyway. Somehow. Mica 3—where the hell was that? It was a Legion world, I knew. And a number to call, upon arrival. Now what was the rest—an account number, an access code—66,000 credits! What the hell! That had to be for the passage. It was personal business, not official. Oh Tara, what are you doing to me? I'm a soldier of the Legion; I can't go shooting off across the galaxy on personal business whenever the mood strikes me.

My mind flashed with frenzied images of Tara, exotic Assidic eyes blinking at me in the dark, long luxuriant auburn hair, pale brown satin skin, and teeth like white pearls. Stone cold beauty. It was an image I did not need, haunting me forever. What could she want? What could she possibly want? Only my soul. I was sweating, cold sweat on my brow. I accessed Center.

"Give me route and costs, here to Mica Three, personal travel." The screen flickered and glowed with the data. Twenty-two thousand credits. Pricey. So what was the rest of the money for? That was Tara, too—it was a test. Figure it out, Wester—then do it! I could still hear her voice. She was always playing with me. I wasn't as bright as Tara. I knew it and she knew it. It had never mattered, in the beginning. But that was long ago—we had taken different roads to the present.

The screen was a hot white glow, my eyes were no longer focusing. I picked up the datacard. I did not need to look at it again. "Come quickly. I need you now." Deadman! The Gods were here, again. Tara—blessed, holy Tara. I knew I had no choice—no choice at all!

* * *

The squad drifted into the room slowly. Snow Leopard sat behind the desk in the Station Commander's personal office. It was a huge, semi–circular conference desk, inlaid with comsets and d–screens. Snow Leopard was like a sinister white spider at the center of a vast web of power and pain. His gaze flicked constantly over the screens as the remaining squad members filed in. The lights were down, and he was partially hidden in the shadows. A panoramic window port gave us a view of the approaches to the base. The starport was visible in the distance, partially obscured by the forest. It was a grey cold day, still lightly raining.

I was seated, still a little tense after my talk with Snow Leopard. I had decided to throw myself on his mercy. There had really been no other way. But Snow Leopard always did things his way. I still didn't know what he had decided, but he was calling in the squad.

Dragon showed up first, dark and silent, dressed in wet camfax, sliding an airchair out from the desk and settling in without comment. He rested his E against the desk. Dragon moved slowly but menacingly, like a great snake, a constrictor, poised to strike. His ears and hands were covered with dark tattoos from a dark past. Lost faces looked up at me from his knuckles. I knew some of the faces—four of them decorated my own knuckles. Dragon was a first–class killer. I always felt better when he was around.

"The beacons are operational," Merlin announced, slipping into a chair next to Dragon. He was soaking wet, pale and tense, dripping water from a floppy camfax hat, sliding a wet techscan onto the desk top. Merlin was a science freak. He understood everything. Central had recently approached him, asking him to return to Starcom to participate in some new research effort on the O's. It was a big opportunity for Merlin, a chance to do something close to his heart. Something he was born to do. He had turned them down. What a tragedy. He would die in the mud with the rest of us. Died in service, it would say—died in service. I thought it a terrible waste. It made him just as crazy as the rest of us—but after Mongera, nobody was going to walk away.

"Good," Snow Leopard replied. "Redhawk, did we get that shipment off to Narra Base?"

"Tenners. Should keep them happy for awhile. I threw in some sex holos." Redhawk pulled his chair out, smiling, looking around. He had an unruly head of extra–long, tangled red hair, a scruffy beard, and a pale splotchy face. He was certifiably insane—a good soul.

"So what's the word?" Psycho dropped his Manlink noisily onto the desk top. He was always doing things like that. Psycho was another mental case, but I suppose he had his good points. The Manlink was certainly all right—we all owed our lives to the weapon.

"Put it on the floor," Snow Leopard said quietly. He was used to dealing with Psycho. Psycho complied, grinning happily.

Priestess took the last seat at the desk, silently. She was a pale slim child, soft dark hair, blinking liquid eyes, wearing wet camfax raingear. She always took my breath away. Beta Nine, Priestess, my own child, my own future. We had vowed to die together—I could not imagine living without her.

"We all here?" Snow Leopard looked around the room. Valkyrie and Scrapper had taken up positions together, sitting on the floor against the wall. Valkyrie had an arm resting on Scrapper's shoulder. Valkyrie had been Gamma Two, and Scrapper had been Gamma Five, but that was all done now—Gamma was history, annihilated on Andrion 3 and Mongera. Now the two survivors were part of Beta, but Snow Leopard could not bring himself to use the proper designations—Beta Two and Six and Seven were still with us, in our minds. It would seem strange, maybe sacrilegious, to call out their numbers and have someone else respond. So Gamma Two became Beta Eleven, and Gamma Five became Beta Twelve.

Valkyrie was stunningly beautiful, a pale blonde girl with icy green eyes and a black Legion cross burnt right onto her forehead. Scrapper was another heartbreaker, a thick mop of tawny hair, grey eyes, a freckled face, and heavy breasts. Valkyrie had been mine once, briefly, in another time and place. But now she belonged only to the Legion—and Scrapper belonged only to Valkyrie. Since Mongera, Valkyrie's eyes had glowed with hatred and her cold, perfect face was radiant with a strange, powerful energy. It was frightening—it was almost as if her dead fem lover Boudicca had secretly returned and inhabited her body. I knew how hard to resist Valkyrie had always been for me. And now Valkyrie seemed to have appropriated Scrapper for herself, with no effort at all. Scrapper was stunned and shattered by what had happened. There were now only the two of them left from Gamma, and Scrapper did not appear to have the will to resist Valkyrie. In the mornings they would appear together at breakfast, Scrapper with bruises all over her neck. Valkyrie was lovelier than ever and burning with a savage sexuality. I prayed she would not turn her smouldering eyes to me again. Priestess watched Valkyrie the same way you'd watch a highly-poisonous snake. I guess she knew I could never summon the courage to resist Valkyrie. All I could do was stay close to Priestess and pray for protection.

I suppose it was a very strange squad, when you really thought about it. We were walkers, the walking wounded. Maybe that's why we had been dumped on Veda 6. The Legion probably wanted to insure we were still under control.

"All right, gang," Snow Leopard said quietly. "Thinker has got a problem. I've listened to him, and I've made my decision. I'd like the rest of you to hear this, as it concerns us all. Thinker, tell them what you told me." Snow Leopard turned back to the screens, tracking the sit. He had a lot to worry about, even in a backwater world like Veda 6.

I activated the control, and the message filled the wall screen. The squad took it in silently. Finally Dragon spoke. "So who's Tara?"

"Tara," I responded, "is Cintana Tamaling. I believe you all remember her—the slaver, Commander of the P.S. *Maiden*."

"The girl with the pet ape," Psycho remarked with a wry grin.

"That's right," I said. "The girl who saved us all. The girl who dropped out of the sky firing tacstars. The girl who got us off Mongera. Right—the girl with the ape."

The message glowed on the screen. "Come quickly. I need you now." It wasn't complicated. The most important issues rarely are. Tara herself had taught me that.

"The way I see it," I said, "she came when we needed her. Now she says she needs my help. I think I should go."

"Why you?" Merlin asked.

Why me. How could I possibly explain that? Tara and Wester— people from the past. She was Tara, and I was Wester, in a warmer, simpler world. And now we were out here at Chaos Gate, and Tara was calling in the past. I wasn't Wester any more, but I would always be hers—that was certain.

"We're old friends," I replied.

"She helped us," Valkyrie said, from her post by the wall. "We should help her." Then she turned her eyes away, bored.

Yes, Tara helped us. We would all be dead, without her divine intervention. She fell from the sky like an avenging angel and struck down our enemies with thunderbolts from Hell. We owed her our lives. How could I not go?

"You should go," Dragon said. There was a general murmur of

agreement.

"What kind of trouble can she be in on Mica Three?"

"That's a Legion world."

"She's a slaver—it could be bad."

"Probably something illegal."

"It doesn't matter—we should help."

"I thought she had some kind of in with the Legion."

"What does she want, Thinker?"

"All I know is what's in the message," I replied. "Just that. So what's the word, One? Do I go?" I had already decided I was going—it was not really an issue. The only issue was whether or not I got Snow Leopard's permission. It would be a lot easier with it. Without it, I was going to call in all my cards—Dragon, Merlin, Priestess, Redhawk, Valkyrie—they were all going to help me. I already knew what each one was going to do to help me get off Veda 6. I couldn't see anyone turning me down. We had been through a lot together.

"Tell them the rest," Snow Leopard said.

I turned back to the screen. "As you can see, she's given me funding. I presume it's for the trip. If you're not on official business you can still travel, even on Legion ships, if that's all that's available. But it costs plenty. The current fare to Mica Three from here is twenty-two thousand credits—one way. You can't pay return fare in advance, because the route might not be the same. As you can see, she's forwarded exactly three times what I need."

"Sounds like she's trying to tell you something," Merlin commented.

"That's what I think," I said. "I think she wants me to bring a couple of buddies."

"Why didn't she just say it?" Dragon asked. "If she can afford to send you close to a million credits, she can afford a few more words in the star tracer."

I shook my head. "That's just the way she is. She never says anything straight out."

"It sounds pretty straight to me," Psycho laughed. "I need you—ha! We may never see Thinker again!" Psycho could be counted on to say something like that. Everyone ignored him. Snow Leopard stirred, partially hidden in the shadows.

"All right, this is it," he said. "We certainly owe her. Thinker, you get three weeks sick leave—Priestess will prep it. That much is within my power. If you choose to travel during that period, it's your business. It's highly unusual, but there's nothing illegal about it. What happens after you get there, we don't know. It's true that Cintana Tamaling has close ties to the Legion. But she's on a Legion world. Whatever problem she has evidently cannot be solved officially. It may be illegal. All I can say is use your best judgement, don't get caught, and be back in three weeks at the latest. Earlier, if you can. We're not staying here forever. We'll be moving soon—I'm expecting a big offensive against the O's. And I don't want to have to explain any missing troopers."

I was light–headed with relief. I should have known Beta One would come through! It was so much better this way. Finally I found my voice. "I owe you, One. Can I take two guys with me?" I figured I might as well press it—Snow Leopard owed his life to Tara, after all.

"Who do you want?" Snow Leopard was expressionless. I knew it would hurt, asking for Dragon.

"I want Eight—and Nine." I wouldn't be afraid of anything, with Dragon at my side. And Priestess—yes, she was for protection as well.

"Nine!" Psycho exclaimed. "Thinker, you scut! You're just afraid to leave her here with me!"

"You wish!" Priestess shot back at him.

"Dragon?" One asked.

Dragon was staring into space. He told me later that at that instant he had flashed back to Tara, leaping from the escape pod on Mongcra holding an E, covering her mouth, a hot nuclear wind blowing her hair around. Dragon blinked, and turned to me, then back to Snow Leopard. "Sure, I'll go," he said.

"Priestess?"

Priestess wet her lips. "Tenners." Her gaze flashed over to me. "I'll come."

"Priestess," Snow Leopard said. "Sick leave for the three of you. I'll approve it. Now get moving. First leg is that freighter to Aran. If we're not here when you get back, I'll expect you to find us."

* * *

I brooded alone in my cube, trying to decide what to take. I didn't like it one bit. This summons from Tara was exactly the last thing I needed. We had enough problems, trying to regenerate the squad after the disastrous mission against the O's on Mongera. And now this. Yes, we owed her, we all owed her, but it wasn't fair. My mind whirled with terrifying images, echoes from the past.

After Mongera they had sent us here, to a medmod on Veda 6, a backwater garrison world reserved for the truly lost, where the air tasted of sweet rain and forest and the nights were still and cold with a billion stars glittering in a deep black sky. We had time to think.

Priestess and I didn't need any words. I kept my new arm around her, although I guess it was really the Legion's arm. The damned thing felt fine. We'd lie out there on the terrace of the medmod on deckchairs under the stars, and the rest of Beta would be all around us, silent. I wondered why we were there, but Priestess knew exactly why she was there. She had always been stronger than I. The Systies had almost killed her, but she had survived. She had taken x–max right in the chest and was still badly scarred. She worried that it meant she was not beautiful any more. I told her it was the mark of the Legion, and that it made her more beautiful than ever.

She was closer to me than before, but more distant at the same time. It was not easy to talk—we preferred not to talk. It was enough just to be together.

They saved our dead for us. When we were all out of the bodyshop, we burnt them in a still dark night lit up by nuclear flames. Five bodies, all in their A–suits, just as they had been when hit—Coolhand and Warhound and Ironman and Boudicca and Sassin, laid out side by side on the platform under dark stars, and all the brutal horror of their deaths came flooding back. Snow Leopard and Valkyrie held the torch and touched it gently to the pyre and the platform flashed and burst into white–hot flames and the Gods of War consumed them, five nuclear pyres glaring in the night like miniature stars. I cried like a baby.

Snow Leopard survived—so they said. Better than new, the body shop claimed. I was not at all certain about that. Snow Leopard was always a bit distant. In the old days, he talked with me. Later he talked with Coolhand and Merlin. Now he didn't talk at all. It didn't matter. We'd still follow him to Hell.

Shortly after our arrival at Minos Station, One called each of us into his cube, where he sat at his desk with printout tacmaps of the battlefield at Fernveldt. He asked each of us to go over, in exhaustive detail, what we had done and where we had been and what we had seen. We answered him, he thanked us, and that was that. Since then he had stayed by himself. I figured he was going over the action to see if he had done anything wrong. To see if he should blame himself, for all our dead. I knew he was bleeding inside for his lover Boudicca—and for the others too. Foolish—nobody could have done better than our One. Nobody! I'd follow him tomorrow—today! Just give me the word.

We may have been walkers, but we were all there. We had all changed. Dragon was harder than ever. He had added some new images to those strange pale miniature faces which adorned his hands and knuckles—the dead, faces from his past. I knew their images and numbers were on the monument as well, the Legion Monument to the Dead, with that final line: Died in Service.

Died in Service—that fate was reserved for us all. They died facing the enemy. They died for us, I thought, for all of us, for the Legion, and the Legion is us.

I touched a holcard that was lying on my desk and both squads flashed to life in miniature, mils from my face. We grinned at the holscan, splattered with the mud of Planet Hell, celebrating some mindless triumph. Beta and Gamma, living and dead—we were all still there. My heart burned with grief. Psycho was smirking, seemingly ready to plunge a hot knife into Dragon's back. Psycho would be all right—wielding a Manlink was his destiny. He'd be a little tougher, a little nastier, after Mongera, but he'd be all right. I knew he had been especially depressed by Warhound's death. It had been the same with me. Both Warhound and Ironman were special. They were innocents, I thought, in the service of a savage God. I'd never told either one how I felt. And now they were gone. And Coolhand—Deadman, Beta Two was my blood brother. The Gods had snatched him away, and it didn't seem right. They were all in the picture—Coolhand and Warhound and Ironman. Children, grinning in the face of death.

If it doesn't kill you, it makes you stronger. Old Legion saying. Yes, that was Mongera all right. I could still see Millina, the Bitch, raising Coolhand's E and blasting that Systie soldier right in the face. Lunacy—she was just as crazy as we were. She was a Mocain, our enemy, but she had turned on her masters and now she wanted to join the Legion—to walk through the Gate, just as we all had done. She had said she just wanted to carry an E, only that. Then she leaned over and kissed Valkyrie tenderly on the forehead, right on the Legion cross, and said goodbye. A new life, for Millina. I knew she didn't have to worry about the psych. She was exactly what the Legion was looking for.

Our dead were still with us—they would always be with us. Nobody here dies in vain! The Second had said that right after the Coldmark raid. But what had we died for? The lab rats had wet their pants with delight when they saw the dead Omni we brought back. Millions of O's would die, I was convinced. But the System would not pay for its betrayal of humanity, or even for its betrayal of us. ConFree had decided to pass everything we had learned about the O, and everything we were to learn, to the Systies—despite the Systies' attempt to steal all that knowledge away, knowledge we had paid for in blood. It was too important, they had decided, to keep. Our struggle with the Systies could wait—this was a war for the survival of humanity, and every world the O's seized from the System was a direct threat to us. That's what they said. I didn't follow their logic—the United System Alliance was a totalitarian obscenity, founded on slavery and coercion. The Confederation of Free Worlds and the Legion had always opposed everything the System stood for. Pass vital military information to the System? It was treason, I thought—a betrayal of everything we fought for. I knew I would never trust ConFree again—not ever. I wondered what Boudicca would have said—or done—had she known. It seemed there was nothing that could be done. It was out of our hands. But it was not going to end there as far as I was concerned. The Legion stood for justice—that's what they had told us since the very beginning. And this wasn't justice.

Ironman was in the front row of the holo. I had done a star tracer to Alpha Station, asking them to tell Moontouch that I was alive, and Ironman was dead. She would relay the news to Ironman's Taka girlfriend, Morning Light. Someone had to speak for the dead. In my world, even some of the living might as well be dead. I knew Moontouch awaited me on Andrion, praying in the dark to strange Gods, and there was not a chance in a million that I would ever return to her. Moontouch was my lover, my wife, my lost future. I did not know what to do about Moontouch. She must have had my baby by now—I was starting a new race, all by myself. Half Legion and half Taka—he would be a tough little kid, a survivor. I could hear the Legion chant, echoing in my head.

"I carry my seed to cold new worlds
To raise me up strong children
Who will dwell in the stars..."

Moontouch—she was an enchanted dream, a fever dream. Yes, I had to make plans about Moontouch and the baby. It was not going to be easy. I would surely never see Moontouch again, and I would never have the pleasure of touching my own child. That was life in the Legion. All you could do was live for today, and stay out of the way of the lasers. I accepted it—I was a soldier of the Legion.

I had no idea what Tara wanted. What could I possibly do that nobody else could? There was only one way to find out.

Chapter 13

The Trouble with Katag

A wet cool breeze washed over us, tingling our flesh. It was a clear crisp morning. Mica was a white orb, glittering in a brilliant white sky streaked with wispy silver clouds. We wore Legion coldcoats, stepping carefully in light gravity. It was a magnificent morning, so beautiful it was downright eerie. I had called Tara upon arrival at the port, and she had told us to rent an aircar. Now we were at her villa, past a formidable sliding cenite gate set in a tall stone wall covered with razor vines.

It was quite a villa, two stories with lots of shaped stone and darkened plex, set in a garden of bright green grass and pale purple flowers and strange willowy trees.

Priestess hesitated on the walkway before the door, looking up to the sky. A faint shiver ran over her flesh. A few birds flew over, calling out. A sudden anger flashed over me.

"Forget it!" I hissed. "This is nonsense! It's all crap! None of this is real—so just forget it!"

"It's so peaceful!" Priestess exclaimed, almost in despair.

"It's a graveyard!" I said. "Of course it's peaceful. We don't belong here—so just get it out of your mind!"

Dragon touched the doorbell and chimes sounded, soft notes hanging in the air. The door hissed open. The ape stood there, Tara's man–ape, a huge retarded humanoid dressed in elektra violet, massive arms with big hairy hands. His lips went back to show his teeth. "Wer–kong," he said. He stood aside and motioned for us to enter. Dragon was measuring the beast up as if he was planning to challenge him to a little arm–wrestling.

The ape led us through the villa to a sun–drenched room overlooking an extra–large swimming pool that glittered like molten gold. Tara sat in a sofa by a low marble table littered with com gear and minicards and d–screens. An E lay on the carpeted floor. Tara looked up and smiled, a vision of languid beauty. She was so lithe and slender; she appeared to be not quite real, a girl from another world, a little bit closer to perfection than our own species.

"Hello, Wester! Glad you could drop by. Please have a seat. Would anyone like some dox?" She was so casual I started to burn. Did she have any idea how difficult it had been for us to get there?

We found seats around the table. The room was decorated with strange objects collected from many worlds. The ape disappeared to get the dox. Tara looked us over with a faint smile.

"This is Priestess," I said. "And Dragon. You may not remember them. But they remember you—well."

"I remember them both," Tara said quietly. She seemed suddenly very subdued.

I placed three expended farecards on the table. I tried not to look at her. There were too many memories. I suppose I was still angry. "We've used all your funds," I said. "How can we help you?"

Tara did not answer immediately. She picked up a datacard, then put it down. Her gaze fluttered around the room. She avoided looking at us. Finally she spoke. "It wasn't easy for me," she said, her eyes focused on the swimming pool, "sending that star tracer. No, it wasn't easy. I'm the sort of person who fights her own battles. I've never needed anyone's help before."

The ape reappeared with a tray of steaming dox. The aroma hit me as he set the tray down. "Thank you, Gildron," Tara said. She seemed happy with the interruption.

"Nartsing," Gildron responded. Then he padded away again.

"Please—help yourselves," Tara urged us. "I hope the trip was all right. This is Mica home brew—hot and sweet. They export it—it's pretty good."

I tried it. It was indeed very good. It was strange, seeing Tara this nervous. Tara did not shake easily—she was tough as cenite armor.

"It's funny," she continued. "I've made a lot of sacrifices in my life for the Legion. I've never asked anything, and I've given all I had. Now, for the first time, I need something—for myself. Do you know what they told me? They said no. No, for all my work. They gave me a lot of good reasons—but it was no." Her eyes flickered over us all, and she took a sip of dox. "And then I looked around to see who would help me—anyway. And you know what I found? I had Gildron, and a crew of loyal Cyrillians. They'd help me, if they could—but they couldn't, not in this case. There wasn't anyone else." She put down her cup.

"That's when I thought of you, Wester. I wouldn't have called you if I didn't need you."

I carefully put down my dox. "We're here, Tara. You asked for my help, and you've got it. So what's the problem?"

"You say the Legion wouldn't help you?" Dragon cut in. It was a troubling concept.

"No, they wouldn't," Tara confirmed. "Tell me...are you here officially or unofficially?"

"I'm here as your friend," I said. "Unofficially. And Dragon and Priestess as well. We're on sick leave—officially."

"And you won't be prepping any reports on this when you return?"

"No—we won't."

Tara looked out to the swimming pool again. Her eyes were misting over. She licked her lips once, pale pink tongue. My heart gave me a jolt. I sure didn't need that.

"You realize..." she said, "that I wouldn't have called you half way across the galaxy if this was an easy matter to resolve."

"We realize that," I replied.

Her eyes came back to me. Magical, swirling dark eyes, worlds of mystery, a hot typhoon of rain. A whirlpool, sucking me right in. "What are you prepared to do," she asked, "to help me?"

I glanced over to Dragon, then to Priestess. "We'll do anything you want," I replied. It was only the truth—we owed her our lives. I picked up my dox and took a sip. Good dox. The preliminaries were over. Now we would find out what this was all about. And how many laws we'd have to break.

Tara raised her chin, and long silky hair swirled around her shoulders. The fire was back in her eyes. The transformation was visible. Tara was back in command. She reached down and touched a datacard. A vision appeared to one side of our table, a holo of a slim pale girl, life–sized, dressed in elektra violet, shimmering in a field of light. Wispy short blonde hair, watery blue eyes—I recognized her. It was Tara's assistant, the P.S. *Maiden*'s exec.

"Maralee Whitney," Tara confirmed, "my exec, has been with me several years." Her voice was clear and steady. "It seems more like twenty years, but it's only been about three. Whit has always been something of an idealist—she truly believes that money can buy happiness, and she's devoted her young life to achieving that goal by acquiring as much wealth as she can, as quickly as possible. It's her major weakness. I should probably explain, first, that Whit does not know about the Legion connection—and we have to keep it that way. To her I'm Cintana Tamaling, phenomenally successful slaver and galactic criminal, wanted by every law enforcement agency around for crimes against humanity, but protected by the System itself as a useful source of slaves and funds. Secondly, I should explain that, although our relationship is strictly super–sub, the two of us have been through a lot in those three years." Tara paused, and reached down to touch the datacard again. The holo disappeared in a flash of light. I could see the old Tara coming back, rushing over her like an aura of the past, the mouth setting, the color draining from her face, the eyes burning with cold rage—this was the Tara I remembered. When she spoke she was in complete control. "My reasons are not important. I'm going to help her. I'm going to do everything in my power to help her." Her gaze flashed over to mine. "I'm glad you came, Wester! And your friends—yes, we'll need them. I want my exec back. And you're going to get her back for me!"

"Where is she?" I asked.

"She's on Katag," Tara responded. "Katag Two—a System world. Not a very pleasant place, I'm afraid. Very much a Systie outpost. And very much a garrison world. I'll tell you all you need to know about Katag Two. Whit went there, and disappeared. The deal evidently went bad. She was on her own, trying to open up a black infolink in cooperation with some local crims. I had advised her not to go, because we have some real problems with the authorities on Katag. But one successful infolink can set you up for life. She was determined to do it.

"I never should have let her go—I should have seen it. It was stupid. The authorities have a tremendous financial interest in controlling all infolinks, so it was a dangerous business. We already knew the locals were difficult to deal with on Katag, and it was certain they had us on a watchlist. We had run into trouble there before, you see. That's why I can't go anywhere near the Katag system. That's why I can't handle this myself." Tara's voice was hushed, almost a whisper, her eyes unfocused. It was almost as if she was talking to herself. I leaned forward to catch every word.

"She knew it was risky, going there. She went by commercial freighter. I set up good docs for her, even though I didn't approve of the trip. She went in alias as a regional inspector for a Systie microtech firm that had an office there. Mitomass—they owed me. It was not hard to arrange. And, although Mitomass was not into infolinks, it would explain any contacts Whit might have with the seedier elements of Katag's business community."

"How about the genetic ID?" Priestess asked.

"That was the weak link. She had excellent docs, but if they wanted to do a full genetic ID scan, the genetics on the docs would not match, and her real ID would be revealed. We were hoping it would never come to that. If the story held, there was no reason it should."

"Sounds like you went to a lot of trouble," Dragon remarked, "for a mission you had not approved."

Tara paused for a moment, then looked up out the window to the golden haze of the morning. "Yes...I suppose I did. I told her it was stupid, but I did all I could to make it work. It didn't."

"So what happened?" I asked.

"She never came back. Entry was all right at the port, and she checked into the hotel. She spent a few days at Mitomass, and did the inspection. Everything seems to have gone all right there. Then she disappeared."

"Just disappeared?"

"My Mitomass contact freaked when I told him his inspector had run into trouble. However, I did prevail upon him to make an official inquiry about his missing employee. It would have looked bad had he not done so. It resulted in the recovery of the personal effects she'd left in the hotel—nothing else. The authorities claimed to know nothing."

"Have you got the effects?"

"Sure, you can look them over, but there's nothing there to help us. Now, my problem is I've got nobody on the ground there to investigate this matter. It's a real mine–field. Highly illegal activity, big money, dangerous and desperate criminal gangs, a hostile government, and a girl who is wanted by both the Legion and the System for a host of illegal activities."

"And the Legion won't help you."

"No. She was engaged in illegal activity, there's a war on—they had plenty of reasons. They won't help."

"What was the original trouble the two of you had with Katag?"

Tara smiled. Lord, she had a dazzling smile—sparkling eyes, pale

brown face and phospho white teeth. A clock chimed softly on the wall.
It was still and peaceful. "The trouble with Katag," Tara said. "Yes, we
were young and foolish in those days. We were running slaves—Katag
was a source of supply. They had just had a war and the losers were
locked up and available. It enabled them to pretty much empty their
prisons and make big money as well. Well, the Minister of Law—a
nasty little bureaucrat called Fornos Cabra–Marist—decided, at the last
moment, that he wanted twice as much as had been earlier agreed. Of
course, we should have simply paid. But he was a despicable little
bugger who dealt with us as if we were dirty. So I simply informed the
Governor of the attempt. Got the little rat in a bad sit, I'm sure, because
the Governor was making plenty on the deal and didn't want trouble.
The only problem is that things change from time to time. Cit Fornos
Cabra–Marist is the new Governor. You have to expect things like that,
which is why you should simply shut down and pay. But we were
rolling in those days. We were impatient, invincible, and greedy."

"What do you think happened to Whit?" Priestess asked.

"On a world like Katag, there's no sense in speculating. Could be
the System's got her. If so, they wouldn't make it public. Cabra–Marist
will be waiting like a spider for me to show up. Or it could be she's had
a disagreement with the crims. That can be fatal. And they tend to get
crazy when large amounts of cash are involved. Or—it could be—
something as simple as street crime. As in every System world, crime is
out of control on Katag."

"What were the financial arrangements?" I asked.

"Never concluded," Tara replied. "Whatever happened, the infolink
deal never went through. Whit's bank account is still empty. And Whit's
infolink contacts—they're on another System world—are still waiting
for the down–payment from Katag before going ahead with the link.
The trouble is, all contact with the Katag infolink crims has to be on–
planet, for obvious security reasons. Gildron!"

The beast appeared in the doorway, snarling.

"Gildron, show our guests to their rooms. You will each find
extensive information on Katag Two, on Whit, and on the infolink deal,
in datacall. You may access these files with the code 'Lost Lamb.' I've
got a suggested ops plan in there as well. Please look it over. Now I
imagine you'll want to freshen up. Lunch is at noon. Do you have any
luggage? Gildron will take it to your rooms."

* * *

Gildron didn't strain himself carrying our luggage. Soldiers of the Legion travel light. The rooms were incredible—I had never before seen so much space for one person. It wasn't a room; it was a suite, spotless in soft phospho white carpeting, a warm golden haze from the morning glowing through the plex. There was a mini office in an alcove, screens on the walls, a desk studded with comgear linked up to a dozen worlds. The air was cool and clean.

"Quite a place. Mine's the same. Do you think the Legion pays for this?" Priestess came in silently, looking around the room. She was so slim and lovely I wanted to pull her to me and fall to my knees and cover her body with kisses. But I restrained myself. I got dizzy every time I looked at Priestess. She was a child, with gleaming black hair and warm dark eyes and small, ripe lips. Her beauty glowed right on her skin, and she didn't need any make–up to enhance it.

"I doubt it," I said. "Tara makes her own way in the world."

"Slavery—it must be good for her bank account, but bad for her soul."

"Yes—I'm sure it is. I've never understood that."

"You never told me you knew her."

"It was a long time ago," I said, "another time and place."

"They've got a fully–stocked cooler and a snackmod under the main screen."

"It doesn't surprise me."

"And my closet's got a clothing mod—I can order civvies in my own size!"

"That's Tara."

"I want you to sleep with me tonight."

"Well, I'll check my sked."

"It's not funny. You keep your distance from her! I know we owe her a lot—but there are limits. And you belong to me—remember that!"

I reached out and touched her hand and gently pulled her to me. She came, reluctantly. Morning rain, the scent of wildflowers, her heart beating against mine. She was all I ever needed from life. Only Beta Nine, and nothing more, forever.

"Priestess...if I had wanted to play house with her, would I have asked you to accompany me?"

"Well...no. I guess not."

"That's right. So let's just get the job done and get back to Beta, where we belong."

* * *

We had a light lunch on the patio by the pool. It was warming up a little, but the air was still crisp and clear. Dragon had found some swimjox in his closet and was trying out the pool after lunch.

"Thank you, Gildron," Tara said.

"Nartsing." Gildron was clearing away the trays. Dragon sat on the edge of the pool, spraying water off his hair just like a dog. Dragon had a hell of a build, and the swimjox didn't hide much. His brown body rippled with hard, wiry muscles, and strange dark-blue tattoos covered his shoulders. Fantastic dragons crawled down his arms, green armored beetles marched over his chest; and indecipherable symbols and runes covered his ears and hands, hieroglyphs from doomed worlds. Ghostly faces looked up from his knuckles.

"Where'd you get him?" Tara asked me, gazing hungrily at Dragon. She liked what she saw, I could tell.

"Where'd *you* get *him*?" I responded, motioned to the ape, now disappearing into the villa.

A shadow passed over Tara's lovely features. "It's a sad story. Too long to tell. He's lost his world. And he's a faithful companion."

"I guess I could say the same about Dragon."

"You'll have to get rid of those warnames. Have you had a chance to get into the ops plan?"

"Yes, it should allow us to move around. You've gone to a lot of trouble, Tara...Cinta."

"You be careful with ProScan. That crim Biergart is a real snake. He's the contact. You go to him first."

"I'm more worried about the Systies."

"Money talks. Just stick to the plan. It should work." Some birds were chirping from a tall tree in the yard. We could see them in the branches, pale blue birds.

"It's so beautiful here," Priestess said.

"Yes, it's very quiet," Tara responded. "It's a Legion world, there are no problems here."

"Idyllic, wouldn't you say?" I asked.

"You could say that." Tara looked up into the sky. Her pale brown skin was flawless, toasting in the sunlight.

"Paid for in blood," I said.

"That's affirmative," Tara said. "A lot of people died here. Yes, we paid the price."

"We?"

"The Legion. I mean the Legion."

"Is this your home?"

"No, it's just a hide–out. I'll be back in Systie vac as soon as you get my exec back."

"Back in business?"

"No, I'm through with all that. I've done enough. They can't make me go back. I'm going to make a new life."

"In Systie vac?"

"Yes...in Systie vac."

"Why don't you stay here?" Priestess asked. "It's so beautiful! Why leave?"

"You'd like to stay, wouldn't you? No, you wouldn't be happy here."

"Why not?"

"You don't belong here."

"Why not? It's a Legion world, after all."

"Yes—so it is." Tara looked off into space, again.

"Isn't that what we're fighting for?"

"Yes—but the people who live here are not part of your world."

"What do you mean?" Nine was insistent.

"What I mean...is that if people like you and me decided to settle down in places like Mica Three, it would not be peaceful for long. We might have some peace and quiet for awhile, but our children would pay the price. The O's are out there, cruising, ready to pounce on the slightest sign of weakness. Without the Legion, Mica Three would be extinguished like a candle, and the dark would rush in, and ConFree would die."

"You mean we just fight forever? Is that it? There's never any rest? It just goes on forever?"

"You already know the answer to that," Tara said calmly. "You don't need to ask me. You know the answer better than I. You came from a Legion world, too. Why did you leave? You could have stayed.

And now you're a part of it. Do you think you can just walk away? There's nothing to stop you—try it. You're welcome to stay here. I'll extend the lease on the villa, if you want. Try it for a few months. But I warn you—you'll have to look up at the stars, every night. The stars are beautiful here—dazzling."

Priestess was quiet for awhile. I took her hand. Finally she spoke. "I never told you I was from a Legion world. How did you know that?"

"I know everything," Tara said carelessly, "except what happened to my exec."

Chapter 14

Biergart

"Take you bag." He was a short, nasty looking creature with dark leathery skin, filthy greased hair, yellow eyes and dirty hands with long jagged fingernails.

"No, you don't." Dragon maneuvered the bag away from him. It was Nine's bag, an elegant plum–colored armorite creation that shrieked privilege and expense. We were out of Customs and heading for the aircar bay. I was on my comset to the hotel.

"The Lady Arbell does not appreciate waiting!" I shouted into the set. "Why is your aircar not here yet?" I was having a little trouble breathing. There didn't seem to be enough oxygen in the air, and the grav was too damned heavy.

"Take you bag!"

"You touch that bag and I'll remove your arm!" Dragon growled to the persistent porter. We were attracting a crowd. Several dusky, silent men drifted over to our vicinity, glowering. They appeared to be the same race, dark skin, yellow eyes, and thick matted hair.

"They say the aircar is on the way," I reported.

"You give the bag!" one of them demanded, pointing at Dragon. He was tall, with a wild, greasy head of hair. "We are porters—federal porters! You must give the bag!" The others growled in agreement. The short one reached out for the bag with a dirty hand.

Dragon hit him with a hard right to the face that came at him from above like a falling tree. I heard the cartilege in his nose crack. The porter bounced off the floor once and lay there stunned, blood smearing his face.

The tall greasy one snarled and came at Dragon with a metal pipe. I hauled out my vac gun and shot him in the face. It knocked him off his feet, and his head hit the dirty floor with a dull thud. The rest of them screamed in outrage, circling us like a pack of swarmers but now at a respectful distance. A policeman came running up to investigate the disturbance.

"Nice start," Priestess said. She was clothed in elegant civie casuals,

and she was a vision of heart–stopping beauty. I could tell she was
upset. It was, indeed, a poor way to begin our clandestine mission on
Katag.

"Why they have guns?" one of the porters shouted at the policeman.
"Guns are illegal! Why they have guns!"

"What's the trouble, Cits?" The policeman was an Outworlder,
eying us warily. He did not know whom to address. I stepped forward.

"This gang of savages attacked the Lady Arbell, and attempted to
steal its luggage." I said, gasping in the thin air. "There's no trouble.
They did not succeed." The porters howled in indignation, but still kept
their distance.

"They are porters, Cit," the policeman replied. "We are required by
law to allow them to carry the luggage. Please do not use derogatory
terms—we are all equal here on Katag, under the laws of the System.
Derogatory terms are highly illegal if applied to the historically
oppressed."

"We can understand why they've been oppressed," I said. "Still, we
meant no harm. We were merely defending ourselves. Is that illegal,
too?"

"Yes, it is. Where did we get the vac gun?"

"We brought it with us. We are employed by the Lady Arbell to
defend its interests and its person. We have System Interworld permits
for private weapons, fully cleared by Katag customs." Three of them,
actually, with hundred–C Systie credmarks slipped into each of the
permits for luck.

"That may be, but it's a legal matter when weapons are used and
people are injured."

"We think that's our aircar," Dragon said. He was glaring at the
porters and they were glaring back.

"The Lady Arbell must not be inconvenienced," I said. "It is here to
investigate business prospects, and plans to invest heavily in this world
if the circumstances are favorable. We'll be happy to pay for any
medical expenses suffered by the injured." I handed him my bogus
Systie ID. He examined it carefully, and when he handed it back
another hundred credits was gone.

"Very well, Cit. Our compliments to the Lady. Please go gently
with the Originals—they were here before we were, and deserve our
respect under law."

"Respect—under law, right. Thanks!" We entered the hotel aircar to the howls of the porters.

* * *

"We want that bitch alive!" Priestess was insistent.

"Yes, Lady—we'll get it!" I assured her. We were in the Nebula Towers, the Princess suite. It was a stunningly luxurious series of rooms done in green marble and soft pink carpeting. My skin crawled to see such waste.

"And if it's already dead, we want its skin!"

"Yes, Lady," I said.

"We want proof it's dead! We want its head! If it's buried, we want the corpse!"

"We'll get it, Lady—dead or alive!"

"If it's alive, we will personally torture it until it begs us to kill it. Then we're going to roast it alive—slowly!"

"Yes, Lady."

"And we record it all!"

"Of course."

"And exhibit its skull in the entry hall of Regulus Octo!"

"That might not be wise, Lady."

"No! It would be a warning—don't cheat Regulus Octo! We'll bill it as an archaeological find—but send the truth through the criminal community. That rotten bitch is going to pay! Nobody steals from us!"

"Yes, Lady."

"Secretary, we want to start on this immediately."

"Immediately, Lady."

"We will authorize all reasonable expenses. If someone is holding it, pay them. Enough so there's no trouble. But reasonable expenses, we repeat. If someone demands too much, we go over its head."

"Understood, Lady."

"What's that?" Priestess asked. Dragon had just unpacked something.

"The suppressor, Lady," Dragon replied.

"Do you mean you haven't activated it yet?" Her voice was edged in ice.

"Ah...not yet, Lady. We have just unpacked it."

"You stupid fools! Why do we employ you? What good are you? Turn it on, idiot! Turn it on!"

Dragon turned it on. It was a powerful commercial unit—nobody could hear or see us with it on. The hotel tapes would record only static.

"How did I do?" Priestess asked.

"Not bad, Lady," I replied.

"That was great," Dragon said. "A nasty, spoiled bitch! It was really kind of scary."

"I think that should do it," I said. "The System will conclude from our conversation that Lady Arbell is not here looking for investment opportunities, as stated, but is searching for someone who burned her badly on a business deal. And is willing to pay well for access to her target. If the Systies have her, the information should flow naturally to whoever has the power to release her. The story should make sense—it certainly fits in with Whit's background."

"And if it's the Governor?" Dragon asked.

"Hopefully the lower echelons won't let the info get that high. But if he's the one, we can only pray he buys our story. We know he takes money, and that's half the battle."

"He might be just waiting for us, grinning."

"The Systies may not have her at all," Priestess said. "It may be the crims—but even if the Systies don't have her, they will have a financial interest in locating her and presenting her to us."

"But they don't know who it is yet," Dragon objected.

"We'll let them know that after we pay a visit to Cit Biergart of ProScan—assuming it's then necessary." I said.

"Let's get back in character," Priestess said. "I find it difficult...that is, we find it difficult, using Systie terminology, if we're constantly switching back."

"Yes, Lady."

"Turn on the local networks, Security."

"Yes, Magnifico." The wall screen lit up. A gang of Originals were screaming and gesturing at the vidmon, clutching primitive weapons. They were almost naked, smeared with yellow powder.

"We kill you Outworld pigs!" one of them shouted.

"Burn you house!" Wild eyes, drugged.

"Crush you skull!" Sharp teeth, shaking a stone axe.

"Rape you daughter! Rape you wife!" Spittle flying.

"We cut off you bird!" Jumping up and down, in a trance.

"We eat you! We eat you!" Fade–out. A Systie announcer appeared, a young Outworlder female with a shaven head, calm and cool, dressed in USICOM blue.

"Citizens, please remember the Originals' righteous wrath is amply justified by their experience. Remember, the historically oppressed are fully protected under our laws. Race crimes against the oppressed will be vigorously prosecuted by the full force of the System. All allegations of elitist thought crime will be reported to the Federal authorities, and appropriate measures taken against the perpetrators. We cannot and will not permit crime against our egalitarian ideals. Remember—we are all equal under law, and the oppressed receive special protection.

"Next, local news; the death toll rises as major protests against police violence cause mass evacuations from Point Barrow."

"This really is a strange place," Dragon commented.

"The System is doomed." I said. "The O's are on their way here—now. There's no defense—and they continue bickering about their social problems. Wait until the first Omni ship touches down. Then they'll see some real social problems."

* * *

"ProScan." A female voice, bright and alert.

"We're sorry—wrong number." I clicked off. Our comset bypassed all the local controls—we could safely call anyone from our own hotel room with no danger of the call being traced back to us.

"ProScan is still there," I said. The suppressor was on. Dragon and Priestess were looking over some detailed maps of the area on their d–screens. One screen was flashing short–term rental properties. The market was down, and there was a lot available. We were going after Biergart first, then Mitomass, and finally the Government. However, we knew we had to approach Biergart with great caution. If the Systies had Whit, they would probably know about the infolink deal and could have Biergart and ProScan under surveillance. But it was just possible they didn't have her. So we would start with Biergart.

"How about this place here?" Priestess asked. A villa in the clouds, surrounded by forested hills. A huge terrace, spectacular view, stunning interior, warm and spacious. Razorwire fences to keep out the scum, a modern security system to guard the air.

"Looks good," I said.

"Looks very good," Dragon said.

"A bit pricey," Priestess commented.

"Regulus Octo can afford it," I reminded her.

"All right," she said. "Secretary, rent it. For a wealthy client who wants privacy. Rent it for a month." Priestess was getting a bit carried away with her role.

"Yes, Lady! As it commands."

"Now let's check out that Multimall," she ordered.

"Immediately, Majesty," Dragon replied.

"Oh, Shut down, will you! And turn off the suppressor."

* * *

We took to spending several hours at the Multimall every day. Lady Arbell would shop in the snob outlets, buying scandalously expensive and totally ghastly outfits presented by simpering sexboys, and later dine with her secretary—me—in outrageously pricey dox houses, with charmingly attentive fems serving exotic dishes from faroff worlds. It was a nice place, especially if you had the security to deal with the beggars and thieves that haunted the area. All the shops had armed guards.

Anyone following us would have noted that Lady Arbell's security goon hung around the underground aircar bay a lot, watching over her rented aircar. Sometimes he and the Lady's male secretary had drinks together or wandered through the malls while the Lady was shopping. The Lady did have a few appointments with high–powered investment bankers and Federal Chamber of Commerce officials who put on quite a show for her. But mostly, she shopped.

We didn't notice any surveillance, but that didn't mean much. ProScan's offices were located in the Multimall, on the 19th floor of one of the office towers. We didn't approach it directly, but on the third day we spotted Biergart in the aircar bay, arriving by car in mid–morning. He had an Original driver. After four more days, we were familiar with his routine and knew his aircar, his driver, his residence, and his route home. On the next day we were ready.

Biergart was later than usual leaving the office. Dragon and I were in the aircar bay sitting in the car, ostensibly waiting for our employer. Biergart hustled out of the elevator, looking around him, a doc case in one hand. He was heavy and balding, with shifty eyes and fat jowls. He wore a business suit. His driver was waiting, a somewhat large Original, oily hair and a scraggly mustache, wearing an uncomfortable– looking driver's outfit. There was a bulge in the front right pocket of his jacket that was probably a vac gun. He triggered the door of the aircar open for Biergart, then slipped behind the controls. It was obvious the car was armored.

We waited a few marks after they left the bay, then slid out into the weak sunlight and onto his route. In moments, we were out of town. He lived in a residential center about eighty K from the city.

"I've got him—he's up ahead." Dragon was driving.

"Keep this distance and altitude. This is about right."

We were so far behind him there was no way he would suspect he was being followed. A light mist hit the plex. The sky was darkening.

"Nobody else ahead..."

"Great!"

"Doesn't look like anybody behind us heading this way."

"I guess we go with it."

"He's over the forest." I hit the side window and it slid open. An icy wet breeze shot through the car. I leaned out with the vac gun. I had loaded a mini heatseeker probe with a contac tip. We had lots of contac. I fired when I acquired the target. Then we sat back to watch the fun. We were still a long way behind and it took several fracs for the probe to hit.

"He's going down."

"Right in the forest."

"Good shooting!" The contac would have exploded inside an exhaust vent, causing the engine to cut off immediately. The aircar's occupants may have heard a sharp pop but would have no way of knowing they were under attack.

Dragon dropped our altitude quickly. The forest came at us, stark and grey. With luck, they would be out of the car when we arrived. Otherwise, we were going to have to use the can–openers, and that would be noisy and messy.

We approached just over the tree–tops. We were hoping their instruments were all out—that normally happened with full engine failure on commercial aircars. It was quite a forest. We had reconned the area thoroughly in the last few days, ostensibly on our way to and from rental properties, and had found not a sign of life. Now the nearest aircar traffic was several K away. Nobody appeared to be paying any attention to us.

"They're down."

"Let's do it." Dragon dropped the aircar down below tree–top level. Trees flashed past wreathed in mist, leaves and branches exploding against our metal skin. Reducing speed now, just a faint whistle, the occasional branch snapping off to splinters. Closer, closer, right up ahead now. I leaned out the window with the vac gun. Cold rain stung my face.

They appeared suddenly out of the mist, a mud–splattered aircar parked incongruously in a field of shattered branches, surrounded by tall grim trees. The engine compartment was open. The driver turned suddenly to face us, his face going pale. Biergart was frozen for an instant by his side, then lunged for the open aircar door. I fired at Biergart first to prevent him from getting inside the car. He bounced off the aircar, spraying water, and fell to the mud. Back to the driver—I fired just as he was raising his weapon in a perfect two–handed stance, both feet planted solidly. Vac bolts flashed against his chest, knocking him over backwards.

I was out and running even before Dragon slid alongside the other car. Mud splattering, cold rain and icy air, adrenalin pumping. Biergart was getting up, thrusting one arm into the aircar. I fired again and he twitched to the ground. The driver moved. I approached him warily, aiming right at his face. He sighed and collapsed again before I had to fire. Dragon was suddenly by my side, his vac gun out, as cool as ice. I was out of breath and gasping helplessly.

"Good. Check the aircar dash," he said, "just in case they signalled for help."

"Tenners."

* * *

"It could at least have covered its faces," Biergart said. "That's the

least it could have done." His pale, quivering face was streaked with
sweat. He knew, better than I did, that he was doomed. He was tied to a
slave chair in a damp dark room lit by a single panel near the door. We
were in the basement of our newly–rented villa in the clouds.

Dragon and I were about to start the questioning—the driver was
secured in another room. It was cold. I knew it must have seemed a lot
colder to Biergart.

"Look, fellows—we've been around a long time." Biergart's gaze
was flicking around the room, avoiding our eyes. "We know the way
the world works. It's got us—all right. It wants something, it's got it.
Whatever it wants—it'll get no trouble from us. Just tell us what it
wants, it's done. It's working for Ginsa, isn't it? What does it want? Just
tell us!" The sweat dribbled off his nose and trickled down his neck.

I had one foot up on a chair. I just looked at him, silently. Dragon
drew up another chair slowly, scraping the crude wooden legs noisily
across the raw slab floor until the chair almost touched Biergart's knees.
Then Dragon slowly settled into the seat, his gaze riveted on Biergart.

A hot knife suddenly appeared in Eight's hand. Eight hit the control
and it flickered blue–hot, a glowing lance.

Biergart stared at it like a mouse before a snake. "There's no need
for that, boys!" he finally squeaked, "No need at all! Please—put it
away! We'll give it whatever it wants—we told it! What is it? Does
Ginsa want us dead? It can't be that foolish—we'll pay it! We'll pay!
There's no need for unpleasantness, boys—we can deal! We'll give it all
we have, just don't kill us!"

Dragon reached slowly up with his free hand and his fingers closed
over one of Biergart's ears like a vice. He pulled Biergart's trembling
head toward him, and the ear turned a bright red. The hot knife came up
glowing, the reflections shimmering off Biergart's sweaty face.

"Ear?" Dragon asked me. I nodded, without comment.

"Boys! Boys!" Biergart was frantic, his eyes popping almost out of
his head, "It's not necessary! We'll cooperate! Why? Why? Why do it?
Please! Whatever it wants! It's got it!"

I turned slowly to Dragon, and nodded slightly. He cut the hot
knife. The blade faded in the dark, still white–hot. Eight maintained the
death–grip on the man's ear. I turned back to Biergart. He was
trembling. I did not like this, not at all, but we had a job to do and we
had to start with Biergart.

"Why?" I spoke at last. "Why is because we wish to show you we are serious. Why is because we are pressed for time—we have no time for nonsense."

"Serious?" Biergart shot back. "Serious! Yes, serious, we know it's serious, boys; no need for ears to prove it. We accept it! It's serious! No need to show us! We have a wife and two children! We'll cooperate!"

I nodded to Dragon again. He released the ear, and Biergart jerked back in his chair with a shudder, covered with sweat. I did not think we would have any trouble with him.

"We wish to ask you something," I said quietly. I was using the Systie 'you', an impolite term which was reserved for inferiors or subordinates.

"Yes, yes—whatever it wants, just ask!" Biergart seemed very anxious to assist us.

"We want quick and accurate answers. Truthful answers."

"Of course! It's got it!"

"You were involved in an infolink venture not too long ago."

"The infolink?" His eyes flashed from me to Dragon and back again. "The infolink! Yes, so we were! We want to know about the infolink?"

"What happened?"

Biergart licked his lips. He was obviously puzzled. "We thought everyone knew what happened. It was a shame. The deal fell through at the last mark. But it wasn't our fault! It was the financing—the Northcom Consortium went bust. They were under investigation by the System, and the cash had to go elsewhere. They were to have financed the Eli Group. Eli asked us to come up with two million. Two million! Can it imagine it? An infolink, billions of credits at stake! And they're quibbling over a few million! So the whole deal falls in—we didn't have two million. We tried to raise it, but it didn't work. Can it imagine that? We tell it, Cits, this world is full of people of limited vision. Billions, we could have had. Billions! Is it with Eli? What does it want? We did our best! We didn't know Eli had a problem with us!"

"There was a contact from offworld—a Cit Ranwan Lima. It was your contact."

"Ranwan Lima..." Biergart hesitated, his eyes darting around the room again. Eight triggered the hot knife.

"It wasn't a question!" Biergart exclaimed quickly. "It was a statement! Ranwan! Yes, of course, we knew it! What does it want to know?"

The hot knife faded again, a dull white glow. Biergart was in agony, straining at his bonds, weaving slightly in the chair.

"Our employer," I said, "desires to locate Cit Ranwan Lima. Our employer is convinced that you know where it is. We hope for your sake this is so."

"Is that what it wants?" Biergart stopped struggling. His body went slack and he breathed out heavily. Something close to a smile flickered on his lips. "It's no problem, boys. Yes, we know where it is. Cit Ranwan Lima is in the tombs."

"The tombs? It's dead?"

Now he smiled—it was strange, that giddy smile on his sweat–streaked face. "No, no, not the tomb—the Tombs! It's what we call the federal prison here—Tombara Reformary. And, yes, as far as we know, it's alive."

"How did it get there?"

"We put it there, boys. Nothing personal in it, of course—just business. We even tried to get Ranwan to come through with the two million. Of course, it refused—that was not part of our agreement. We understood. But the collapse of the infolink deal did us in as well, financially. We were in up to our neck. And we knew the standing reward for turning in an infolink bandit. It was twenty thousand more than zero, which was what we had out of the deal at that point. And after all, it was an offworlder—no one cared about the deal once it fell through. Ranwan had no protectors here. It was the logical thing to do—the feds are always happy if they can nab an offworlder. They hate to deal with the locals—it brings on too many problems."

"So you turned it in."

"We did, boys. It got thought reform and probation."

"Probation! So it's free?"

"No, no—it's in the Tombs, as I said."

"Well, what about the probation?"

"That comes after the thought reform."

"How long does thought reform last?"

"Until the authorities believe it's ready for the probation."

"Well, how long is that—normally?"

"Normally...it's never."

"Never?"

"Nobody is ever released from the Tombs, boys. Nobody."

"What was the charge?"

"Violation of System and Federal regs on offworld data transmission. It's a serious matter—it'll never see the light of day again, that's certain."

"The System, you say. The feds."

"That's right."

"Would the Governor have been brought into it?"

"It'd certainly have been informed of the arrest."

"Who runs the prison?"

"The Director of Reform—Japrad Marsh."

"Does it take money?"

"We all take money, boys."

"Does it, specifically, take money?"

"It's rotten to the core."

"Could someone be bought out of prison?"

"It's an intriguing concept. We don't think it's ever been tried. People with money usually don't go to jail in the first place. Normally, we just split up whatever little is left when the feds grab someone. Does it owe a favor to this Ranwan Lima person?"

"Not exactly. Our employer wishes to speak with it—that's all."

"Its employer is going to a great deal of trouble."

"Tell us—your prison system. Does it use genetic ID to classify the inmates?"

"Genetic ID? Not on the run–of–the–mill inmate. That's expensive. Our prison system is very basic—the records are all manual. We know the feds can do it, but it's not routine."

"Would it be done for an infolink violation?"

"We don't know, boys. Probably not—unless there was some other reason, unless it was suspected of serious interstellar crimes, maybe. We'd help it if we could, boys, but we really don't know the answer to that one."

I glanced over to Dragon. "Outside," I said. He nodded.

"Take five, Biergart. We'll be back."

"Anything else it wants, just ask. Anything, boys! It's got it."

* * *

The view from the patio was magnificent. We looked out over a great, green wilderness. Misty grey clouds sliced through forested hills—the sky was grey and a wet, cool breeze washed gently over us.

"It's a shame about the Originals," Priestess said. "Did you read the history of Katag? They were a wonderful people, living in perfect balance with the forces of nature. Then the Outworlders came. Now the Originals are all drug addicts—and criminals. A dying race. It's a shame." We were leaning against the stone wall that ran the length of the patio.

"It's the System," Dragon said, "that does it. They encourage crime to ensure the population is at each other's throats. That way, nobody thinks."

"How's the driver?" I asked Priestess.

"He's secured," she responded. "What did you find out?"

We told her. Then we discussed it, standing in the teeth of a rising breeze under that cool grey sky. It looked like it might rain. The air was too thin, I decided—not enough oxygen.

"So they may not have done the genetic ID."

"Or they may have—we don't know."

"It's possible the Governor doesn't know who he has."

"It's also possible he does."

"Maybe he doesn't care—money can buy forgiveness."

"Maybe. Maybe not."

"So we go to the prison."

"March right in!"

"All or nothing!"

"Money talks!"

"He might be just waiting for us."

"If we offer enough, the word might never get back to him."

"It's natural for the lowest–ranking person who has the power to release her to take the money and do it."

"Auto–payment to be made upon the successful arrival of all four of us through Customs at any Systie world."

"It's the usual arrangement, according to Tara."

The wind was rising—it was getting cold. "All right, we do it," I said.

"We've got to do Biergart and his driver first," Dragon said.

"I've been thinking about that," I said.

"There's nothing to think about," Dragon countered.

"There's no need to kill them," I said. Dragon looked out at the view, silent.

"We've got that displacement monitor," I insisted, "and we've got contac. We can leave the two of them together in the basement. If they shift position too much, it goes off. We explain it to them—they won't move!"

Dragon said nothing. Neither did Priestess.

"It'll work!" I said. "There's no need to kill them. He's just a nobody—he's scared stiff. He won't give us any trouble."

"He'll turn us in first chance he gets," Dragon said.

"He won't get a chance! He'll be secure in the basement, staring at the displacement monitor."

"It won't work, Thinker," Dragon said flatly. "We don't know if we're under surveillance or not. They could be all over this place the moment we leave. We can't leave them here."

I was starting to sweat, even in that chill breeze. "Look, he's just a sub. He's not important. He's got a family. And the driver is just a spectator. It's not his fault he works for Biergart. We can't just murder them!"

Nobody said anything. It started to rain—a fine mist.

"You want me to do it?" Dragon asked.

"Priestess, what do you think?" I asked. She was my last hope. Surely Priestess would not countenance the cold, brutal murder of two innocents.

Priestess turned her perfect face to mine. It was devoid of emotion. "Our first duty is to our mission, and to ourselves. Your proposal would put us all at risk. You're a soldier of the Legion, Thinker. And it's your op. We'll do as you say. I know you'll do your duty." And she turned away, facing the rain.

I could hardly believe it.

* * *

"Our wallet, boys. It's on the table." Biergart was sweating again. He knew something was up. Dragon and I paused before him. We had earlier dumped his effects on the table, but had not even looked at the wallet.

"We don't want your wallet," I said.

"Just open it, will it?" He was very subdued.

I flipped it open. There was a holo of his family—Biergart, plump and content; a chubby, smiling wife with reddish hair. Two impish children, bright eyes and ruddy gold hair. I closed it quickly.

"They'll miss us, boys. It's not going to kill us, is it?" Sweat, dripping off his nose.

"Relax, Biergart. We're just going to change rooms." I stepped behind him and touched his bonds with my left hand. My right brought the vac gun up to the back of his head. I fired. The echo did not want to end—it seemed to go on forever, bouncing harshly off the walls. We had loaded the vac gun with cenite darts.

Dragon did the driver. He did everything else—I was out of it. I had done my duty, and I never wanted to do it again. I decided that if we got out of this one alive, I was finished with Tara—we had paid our debt, already.

Chapter 15

The Mask

"The Warden will see Cit now." The guard was a bodybuilder, dressed in a dark brown uniform. He had a vac gun at his waist. We were in a small reception room just outside the Warden's office. Right in the heart of the beast. I was not at all happy with the sit, but we had no choice. The door hissed open. I was high on mags and totally unarmed. I knew there was a good chance we might never leave.

Priestess and I followed the bodybuilder into the Warden's office. Dragon waited outside—there were several other heavies to keep him company. A man rose from behind an extra–large desk of wood and marble. There was something strange about him—a fleshmask, I suddenly realized. He was wearing a fleshmask. An attractive girl with straight dark hair stood by with a notecard and a lightpen. Several chairs faced the desk.

"Welcome, Lady Arbell," the man said. "We are Cit Japrad Marsh, Director of Reform and Warden of Tombara Reformary. We are pleased to greet such a distinguished visitor, and we will do what we can to assist Cit. Our secretary will take notes of our conversation, just for our records. Please be seated."

"Our thanks, Excellency," Priestess replied as we found our seats. She was as cold as ice. I was impressed, because my heart was thumping. "We appreciate Cit's taking the time to see us. Our secretary is also here for the record, but in view of the subject to be raised, we ask that formal notes not be taken. It is a delicate matter." She passed the warden her business card.

The warden nodded to his secretary and she closed her notecard. "Very well. How can we assist Lady?"

"We represent a multi–system investment conglomerate—Regulus Octo. We were recently cheated—rather badly—by a professional scam artist with some very good credentials and a fast escape route. This happens occasionally, even when one's security is excellent, and normally in such a situation, we are prepared to quietly accept our losses and learn from our mistakes. In this case, however, the crime was heavily publicized. It therefore became important that we track down the criminal, deal with it on our own, and ensure that its fate is also heavily publicized, to deter others who might have similar ideas."

"A sound plan. Please go on."

"We have tracked the criminal to this world."

"We see."

"It used the proceeds of the crime to attempt to organize a pirate infolink here."

"An infolink."

"The scheme was detected, and the criminal was arrested and imprisoned, here. The criminal's name is Ranwan Lima—a female."

"Ranwan Lima. We see." The warden raised one hand to his mask. "Tell us...this arrest. It was never publicized. How did Lady learn of it?"

"We purchased the information."

"We understand. Riza—the trues. The L's." The secretary got up and pulled a file drawer off a shelf and placed it heavily on the Warden's desk. We watched her as she went through the file cards manually. File cards! What a break—the bureaucracy on this world was more primitive than we had dared imagine.

"Lima, Ranwan," the secretary said, smiling. "Right here." She handed the card to the Warden.

"Four Six Oh Oh Four Oh Four," he said aloud. "Get me the master." The secretary turned to another shelf. The warden smiled at Nine like a hungry bloodcat, revealing yellow teeth. "We've got it all right. We recall the case. Reform and probation. It's a serious matter. It has been tried and convicted in a court of law, and can expect to spend the rest of its life here, doing reform."

"We have been authorized to expend five hundred thousand credits to recover this worthless criminal," Priestess said. "We can put that into its benevolent fund, pass it to any charity Excellency cares to name, or arrange to have it transferred into any bank account Cit may specify." Priestess sounded almost bored. I had not realized she was such a great actress.

"The master, Excellency." The secretary handed the Warden another file card. It had a holo shot on it—was that the extent of their technology? The card appeared to have been handwritten.

"Yes, this is it," the Warden said. There was something wrong with one of his eyes, I realized. One of them was focused on the card. The other stared glassily at the ceiling. "General Detention, Level Eight. It's a serious matter."

"It's a nasty, worthless bitch," Priestess said calmly. "And we're willing to pay—we've told Cit how much—to get ahold of it. Put it on probation, in our custody. We'll guarantee it won't break any more laws—here or anywhere else."

"What would Lady do with it?"

"We would sedate it and take it with us—off–planet. We will, of course, require Excellency's assistance to guarantee it can pass through Katag's exit procedures without delay. The specified amount will be autocredited to Cit's account the instant the four of us pass through Customs on any other System world. Guaranteed by InterStar Credit."

"A sound procedure."

"Can Excellency assist us in this matter?"

Assuming Ranwan Lima's true identity was not known, the Warden should be anxious to cooperate with us without alerting his superiors— otherwise he would have to share the loot. Five hundred thousand System credits was a King's ransom—Tara was obviously fond of her exec.

And if the Warden already knew Ranwan Lima's true identity, we would probably never see the light of day again.

The Warden blinked one eye, and pressed a tab on his desk. A door opened, and a tall, strong blonde girl stepped in, dressed in prison brown.

"Yes, Excellency?"

"Ozette, this inmate has qualified for probation." The Warden handed Whit's master card to the blonde. "Check it out of GD and bring it here. Return the master to us as well. The citizen will accompany you." He motioned to me. Priestess nodded to me as well. I rose and followed the blonde out the door. Now all three of us were split up— we were in the hands of God.

Down into the dark. What a ghastly place. It was a dungeon of stone—layer after layer of rotting, black, wet stone, sunk deep into the bowels of the earth. Great steel grates creaked open for us. Gates of rusted iron bars fell away, then clattered back into place behind us. Icy water dripped down like rain. Lonely pairs of guards huddled in greatcoats peered at us by torchlight.

We paused at a landing lit by a single, madly flickering light panel. A pale bald giant came at us out of the dark, blinking in the light of the big blonde's flash.

"Isn't that thing fixed yet?" Ozette asked.

"We kinda like it." There was someone else hidden in the darkness; I couldn't make him out.

"We've got a probation today, fellows," Ozette said. "But we think it's a problem." She handed the card to the giant.

"Since when is a probation a problem?" the giant rumbled. "We should have a party." A furtive little man with the face of a rat joined him, bright eyes glittering. The big man looked up from the card. "We see what it means."

"Check its files to be sure," the blonde said.

"No need to check—but we'll do it. Four Six Oh Oh Four Oh Four." The giant rummaged in a rusty metal card file on a battered desk.

"Four Oh Four...yes, here it is. It's gone. There hasn't been time to forward the full list to the top."

Ozette took the card and read it, frowning. "Yes, we knew it. But we had to be sure. The Mask wants it for probation. Now we're in for it."

"Four Oh Four," the little man added. "The Sweet Thing, oh yes, it's gone. Gone from our grasp. It's a shame."

"Cit, is it here or not?" I asked abruptly. "What is the situation?"

Ozette turned to me, troubled. "It was here, but it's gone now. It was a work transfer."

"Signed by the Mask," the giant added.

"That's right!" the little one whined. "Approved in its own hand, so it can't blame us!"

"What is a work transfer, Cit?" I asked quietly.

She looked into my eyes, hesitated a moment, then spoke. "Slavers," she said. "Locals. Under a work transfer, inmates are returned when the contract is over. Actually, that never happens, the actual amount never appears on the papers, and no one cares. The slavers make a prison run once a year, and pay top credit. You understand this information is dangerous and highly confidential."

"When did this happen, Cit?"

She glanced at the card. "It was only last week."

"And if we wanted to track it down?"

"First to the slave markets at Ostra Bal. Ask for the Body Shop, then ask for the Sandman. Slaves move fast—so it had better hurry."

"We thank it, Cit. Please accept a small token." I pressed a hundred credmark card into her palm. Her fingers closed over it firmly.

"Our thanks, Cit," she responded quietly. "We were all fond of Four Oh Four. We wish Cit luck."

Chapter 16

The Sandman

Ostra Bal was a vast tent city, a market town, across the river from the capital. Tents stretched as far as we could see, all joined together, held up by wooden poles. Colorful canvas material flapped in the breeze and everything on the planet was for sale beneath. Goods were piled high on either side of the narrow aisles, stinking fish markets and bloody butcher shops and dry goods and canned food and endless rows of clothing. There were shoe stalls and hardware and cutlery and cookingware, commo gear and military equipment and toys, jewelry and furniture and rugs and live animals and birds, office equipment and datacards and restaurants. It seemed the whole population of Katag was there, streaming along the aisles, blinking in the smoke from the cooking fires, fingering the goods, and arguing with the shopkeepers.

It was hot and sweaty and dirty. This was where the lower and middle classes shopped. We parked our aircar in a heavily–fortified lot and made a token down–payment to a gang of savage–looking punks to keep an eye on it.

"They're selling SG's over there!" I exclaimed. The SG was a good weapon. We had not expected it to be available on the open market.

"Well, let's get some!" Dragon replied. "But first we find the Body Shop."

"All right." I stopped and pulled a ten–C credmark out of my wallet and held it up in front of me. A scruffy punk materialized out of nowhere and landed directly in front of me, raising a little cloud of dust. He gave me an elaborate salute.

"Sir!" he shouted. "We are at its service!"

I smiled. These people were fast. "We want the Body Shop," I said. "Please show us."

He gave us a crazy grin, and spun around on his heels. "Follow us!"

* * *

The Body Shop was a world in itself, a vast razorwire cage hidden behind glowing phospho sheets of thick synsilk tenting. It was shaded and cool and clean inside, with carpeted floors. Uniformed guards with vacguns watched us passively as we entered.

"Welcome to the Body Shop." He was a slender young male, dark brown skin, slick wet hair, bright sparkling eyes, dressed in an elegant synsie suit. He was smiling obsequiously. "We are Armil Samot. Please...let us offer refreshments." He motioned off to one side. A wide low table was set for tea, surrounded by pillow seats. Little lovelies appeared out of the shadows bearing trays of hot tea and delicacies. They wore golden slave necklaces, I noticed.

We went with the program, and I touched the tea to my lips but did not swallow any. Armil Samot was as smooth as oil. A real slimer. I wondered how he would look with the top of his head removed.

"How may we help?" Samot asked. "We have a very wide range of talents and prices, everything from household helpers and agricultural workers to topline sexmates and professional fighters. And if we don't have it in stock, we can locate it very quickly."

I put down my tea. "This is the Lady Arbell," I said. "The Lady wishes to speak with the Sandman."

"The Sandman!" The slimer seemed surprised, but recovered quickly. "May we ask the subject to be discussed?"

I looked over to Priestess. She shook her head.

"We must speak with the Sandman directly," I said.

He hesitated a moment, then picked up a comset and rattled off a brief message in an alien tongue. He listened to the response, then put the set away, smiling. "The Sandman will be here shortly. Please...take a look at some of our units while we are waiting." He raised his hands and clapped once. A procession of enchanting girls appeared from a slit in one cloth wall, lovely little things, soft eyes and long hair and slender, supple bodies. They strolled along a little catwalk that ran right through the center of our table, pirouetting like models showing off a new line of clothes. But these girls were all clothed in short, filmy tunics of gossamer silk. They all had golden slave necklaces at their throats and each girl had a number on a little plastic disk pinned to her tunic. They were followed by several youths with oiled skin, handsome and well–muscled, naked but for their jox, also wearing slave necklaces and numbers.

"Sexmates," the slimer was saying. "They are well–trained. Our units are all graduates of the Home Arts Institute of Lucos. And our prices are very competitive."

"How competitive?" Dragon asked. "For one of the girls, for example. How much?"

"Well, which one interests us?" The slimer brightened and stopped the parade, and brought the girls back. They stood behind him patiently, eyes downcast. Precious little dolls. If this slaver knew we were Legion, he would probably shit in his perfectly tailored pants. The Legion's role was to kill slavers, without hesitation or mercy. I was aching to put a laser burst right between his bright, beady eyes. It hurt, sitting there doing nothing while those little, helpless sweeties were standing there, completely in his power.

"We just want an idea of the general price range," Dragon responded. "For example, Number Sixty-five."

The slimer made a quick gesture and Number 65 glided down the catwalk onto the table and pirouetted slowly above us. She was a genuine heart–stopper, slender and willowy, long silky brown hair and exquisite tanned legs and generous breasts and big dark eyes and soft full lips. Dragon had good taste in women.

"An excellent choice," the slimer said. "Quite frankly, Number Sixty-five is one of our more expensive units. It is not truly representative of our mid–line prices. Besides its obvious beauty, it is a medically–certified virgin. There is a big demand for virgins and this drives the price up. Please, look over its stats." He handed over a glossy brochure to Eight, then nodded to the girl.

She touched the tunic and it fell away, leaving her completely nude. She pirouetted once again. She was truly lovely. She was doing things to me, already. I wondered who would end up owning her.

"And the price?" Dragon asked again.

"For a virgin of such exquisite beauty," the slimer said, "We would have to ask one hundred thousand credits, to recover our costs and allow us a modest profit. However as I explained, this one is a special case. The others are less dear."

"Security," Priestess cut in abruptly. "Close your mouth."

"Yes, Lady," Dragon responded meekly.

"Cit Samot," Priestess said, "it may tell the girl to put its clothes back on. We are not interested in purchasing this unit. Our employee has been amusing itself. We have serious business with the Sandman, and it does not concern Number Sixty-five."

"Of course, Lady." The slimer nodded to the slave girl. She picked up her tunic and disappeared. Dragon and I watched her walk away with regret. We were pigs, I suppose. Priestess had every right to be upset.

* * *

The Sandman was a tall, wiry Outworlder with suntanned skin and long blond hair tied behind his head with a black ribbon. He wore stylish, dead–black sungoggles and a weather–burnt field coat and sandboots that had been worn white. He moved with authority, and the slimer faded away when he approached. He had a vac gun at his waist. As he accepted a tea from a slavegirl, his eyes were invisible behind the goggles, but I knew he was checking us out. He took a sip, and slowly put down the cup.

"Lady Arbell—We are Sandman. How may we help?"

Nine took a copy of Whit's master file from the reformary and passed it across the table to the Sandman. He picked it up and examined it carefully. How could he see through those goggles?

"We believe Cit recently purchased this criminal from Tombara Reformary," Priestess said quietly. "We wish to purchase it from Cit. Our reasons are not important. But we will guarantee a higher price than anyone else."

"If we had known this girl had so many friends," the Sandman said with a faint grin, "we would have held onto it. The people from the Reformary were here only an hour ago. Cit's running a little late."

Priestess looked my way. We knew the warden would be doing his damndest to get Whit back, and it probably didn't matter much whether he got to her before we did. The Mask was going to get his money either way, for we needed his help to get off–planet.

"Where is she?" Priestess asked.

The Sandman glanced at his wristcom. "They should be pulling into Chapezi in an hour or two. We sent her on the overland route by groundcar with a shipment for the frontier. It's to be sold in the market at Chapezi. Highest bidder will get it. We've already alerted our people in Chapezi to the Reformary's interest. Shall we mention Cit as well?"

"Please do so. We'll be there as soon as we can get there. How far is Chapezi?"

"What is our mode of transportation, Lady?"

"Aircar."

"It should not take longer than four hours by aircar. Unfortunately, the Reformary people are also going by aircar."

"Have they already left?"

"I do believe so."

"We'd better get moving," Priestess said to me.

* * *

We paused at the weapons tent. It was quite a place. The proprietor was an old bearded brigand, puffing on a narcotic weed, and his three hoodlum sons tossed us the weapons we needed. The shop was a delight, piled high with exotic weaponry from a score of worlds.

The SG's looked new. I knocked one down right away and spread the parts out on a display table.

"Looks good," Dragon said.

"It's new," I confirmed.

"Our weapons are guaranteed," the brigand said, "everything works."

"Where can we test these?" Dragon asked.

"It's a free sky," the pirate said. "See if it can hit an aircar."

I've always liked the SG. It's a tough weapon. We test fired laser and v and x and flame, up into the sky, and made a hell of a racket, and nobody even blinked. The damned things worked perfectly.

"How much?" Dragon asked.

"Five thousand."

"Five hundred."

"You are joking! It is funny! These are brand new, and highly illegal! Boys—get us tea! Now!" His sons scrambled to obey.

"We don't have time for tea," Priestess whispered to me.

"What's the rush?" I asked. "Even if the Mask gets to her first, he's just going to sell her back to us, right?"

"I'd rather get to her first," Priestess said, "Just to be sure."

"We'll give it a thousand each," I told the bandit, "and we buy three."

"All right, four thousand, because you know your weapons. And we'll throw in five fully charged x–packs, each."

"Four thousand for the three?" I asked.

"No, no—oh, it is funny too! No, four thousand each. My bottom price! Here, here—fresh berry tea. Have some lily crush, too—pure crush, it will put Cit into orbit."

His sons were back already, supervising a young female slave who carried a heavy tray stacked high with elaborate silvery, steaming tea kettles, and a delicately carved wooden box full of narcotic cigarettes. Katag was certainly a man's world.

I balanced the SG in one hand. Lord, it felt good to be armed again—really armed. I had been in a black mood because of Biergart, but the SG was whispering to me, chasing Biergart right from my mind. What a sweet, lovely weapon! Hoist an SG, and the odds are even once again. Watch out, world, Thinker is back! Gleaming cenite and armorite, laser sights glowing calm and pale, fully charged and looking for a new owner. Here was a real slave—molded to my hands. And what is an SG really worth? A million credits? Two million? No price would be too much for this lovely girl, a warm companion for a dangerous world, she'd walk with you all day and sleep with you all night. Well, I got a chill every time I touched one of those babies, E or SG, every single time. We were married for life, that much was certain. She was a cruel mistress, but I loved her all the same.

"Please." The slave girl held out a cup of hot berry tea for me.

"Pay him what he wants," I said to Priestess. "The old man deserves it. He's a saint!" Dragon and Priestess looked at me funny. I'll admit I get carried away on occasion.

* * *

"Doesn't look good." I put the aircar in a flat glide to the deck. The dirt road below snaked along the bottom of a steep ravine between two ragged hills. A perfect ambush site. Thick black smoke rose out of the pass, dirtying the sky. As we approached, there were flames up ahead. Two khaki military aircars rose from the gully in swirling clouds of smoke and shot away from the site. There—burning groundcars, bodies littering the ravine. We eased along the road slowly, and I cut the jets and we settled down in a cloud of dust. Katag soldiers stood around, SG's on their hips. I cracked the door and the heat rushed in, dry and dead.

We walked into the tragedy. Six civilian groundcars, big transports, burned fiercely, all shot up. The rocks of the gully were strewn with loot. I looked up to the slopes. It was a harsh land, great slabs of yellow granite baking in the sun. The dead lay where they had fallen—slaver security guards in uniform, stripped of weapons and jackets and boots, frozen in death, just as inanimate as the rocks around them. And slaves, male and female, some of them burnt to death, black crisps hanging out of the groundcars, riddled with holes.

"Scut," I said.

"Tourists?" A Katag officer approached us frowning, dressed in camfax, his SG pointed in our general direction.

"It's all right, Lieutenant. These three are with us." Another man, dressed in dark brown, strode through the dust. I recognized the uniform. "Lady Arbell, we are from Tombara Reformary. Bad news, we're afraid. It was the HLA that hit the convoy. Did a real job on it." He was a pale, intense, slender youth—we had never seen him before.

"Did anyone escape?" Priestess asked.

"Yes—they got six out of twelve groundcars. But according to the overseers, number Four Oh Four is not among the survivors. The other six cars have already arrived in Chapezi, and it's not there."

"Have we found its body?"

"We're still looking. If it's here, we'll find it."

"What is the HLA?" I asked.

"Homelands Liberation Army. It's the Originals. They're getting better and better weaponry. These cars were taken out with xmax. We can't imagine where the Originals are getting weapons like that."

"They probably went shopping in Ostra–Bal," I muttered.

A military aircar glided overhead. The officer was talking into a comset as a couple of troopers unwrapped a plastic photomap. One of the burning cars exploded again, sending streaks of glowing phospho shrapnel into the bright blue sky.

"Damn!"

"Lady Arbell!" It was the Sandman, his black goggles winking sunlight. He wore a sandy camfax cloak, and a camfax turban covered his long hair. "It's good to see Cit again."

"We wish the circumstances were different," Nine replied.

"Indeed," the Sandman said. "This is a dark day for the Body Shop. The HLA is getting way out of line. We've lost half our shipment.

Damn!"

"The unit from the Reformary told us that Ranwan Lima did not arrive in Chapezi. Is it true?"

"Ah yes, Cit's slave. We've already checked the bodies. We have identified everyone. It is not here."

"So where is it?"

"The HLA have it now. It's out there somewhere." He looked around, up to those barren hills. "They took all the slaves that survived the ambush. Up into the hills. They starburst after a hit. So they're wandering around out there right now in little groups of four or five, on their way to some rendezvous deep in the Chetta. The strike force is going after them, but that's not the way to find Originals. We've got to go after them on the ground. We can't read the sign from the air; we can't see them from the air."

"Can Sandman find them?" Priestess blinked as a gust of oily smoke swirled around her face.

"Sandman can track Originals, sure," the Sandman said. "But they've starburst. We can't track them all."

"Understood. Can it read the starburst for us, and tell what it sees?"

Another military aircar rose in a swirling cloud of dust. "We'll have to wait for these folks to clear out," the Sandman said, "and then we'll see."

I kept quiet. I was supposed to be running the show, but all I had done so far was fall apart after shooting Biergart. Priestess was taking her Lady Arbell role seriously. Her ideas were proving better than mine.

* * *

The Sandman signalled us—four fingers, ahead. It was pitch black. A cool breeze gently washed over my face. Clouds covered the stars. Every muscle in my body ached, and my throat was dry and cracked, and I could hardly breathe.

This Sandman was good. We crawled forward like cats on all fours. We had followed the Sandman on a wide circle around the ambush site, that first day, and picked up seven separate trails. The Sandman could read them like a d–screen. Each group had female slaves accompanying their Original captors.

We had a one in seven chance of choosing the right bunch.

At times like that you just go with the Gods, and pray it's right. We chose a group of two Originals and two slave girls. One of the girls was bleeding from bare feet, and we thought perhaps it was Whit, because she had not been in prison long and her feet would still be soft. We couldn't do a genetic ID because we didn't have the equipment. It wasn't much, but it was all we had.

We followed the trail until dark, force–marching on foot over rugged countryside. We brought plenty of water and SG's and mags. We spent a restless night and started early, under dark skies, following the Sandman as he tracked the Originals like a dog. As dawn broke, we found where they had spent the night—no fire, but there were empty foodpaks buried shallowly, and we could see the marks of their SG's in the dirt. The girls had been tied together, and it looked like both had been raped. We pressed on under the rising sun on foot, not even pausing to eat. We chewed Systie rats on the march. We knew we were gaining on them. They were slowed down by the girls. They beat one of the girls viciously at one point—we found blood on the rocks, and a broken, bloody stick. They were heading over rough country, higher and higher into the mountains. We kept going. We marched all day and into the night.

The Sandman was worried at first that we couldn't keep up. We showed him he was wrong. Priestess offered him quite a lot of money to guide us. He accepted, of course, but somehow I did not think the money was his primary motivation.

We found them on the second night. The fools had lit a fire. It was in a deep pit, but we could see the glow. We approached slowly, slithering up like snakes. The Sandman was still wearing those dark goggles. He had a cut–down x gun and we had our SG's. They were drinking liquor from the caravan, two Originals, just black shadows in the faint glow from the fire. Fools—they thought they were safe. They were dead. They laughed and talked as we stalked them.

"Squirmers! Hee hee!"

"You friend taste good. Haw!"

"Where you pants, girl? Ha?"

"Do it hurt? Aw haw haw!"

A sickly sweet stench tickled my nostrils. Scorched flesh—they were cooking something in that fire. I suddenly realized what it was they were cooking. The Sandman held up three fingers. Adrenalin burst through my veins. I could hear a faint moaning. I could barely make it out—another figure, on the ground.

"You hungry, girl? Aw ha!"

"Make it eat! Ha ha ha!"

"Hey girl, you want a breast or leg? Aw haw haw haw!" One of them fell over laughing, drunk and sloppy.

"So we dork her or what?"

"You such a dumb scut. I try to civilize you, but you don't know nothing. I tole you, we got to torture it."

"Yeah, but first we dork her."

"You so stupid, you hopeless. You got to torture it first."

"Why?"

"You member las' night, dummy? This one kick so hard it almos' cripple me. You torture 'em first, then when you ready to dork 'em, they don't fight you."

"Yeah?"

"You so freakin' stupid!"

Another moan from the body on the ground. A faint, cracked voice. "Please...please. Water."

"Water? Aw ha ha! Yeah, you drink my pee!"

"Haw haw! I so dizzy I can't get up!"

"Please...why so cruel? Why?" I could barely hear her.

"Cruel? Cruel?" One of the Originals staggered to his feet. "I show you cruel! You going to eat you friend! You want water? You can drink her blood! You going make us happy, girl, then maybe we kill you, if you lucky."

"Why are you doing this?" It was a hopeless moan.

The Original laughed. "You don't like us because we different. You don't like us! So why we have to treat you nice? Ha? You tell us!"

Priestess stepped out into the campsite suddenly, standing right above the outstretched figure on the ground. She was a chilling phantom in black, faintly illuminated by the red glow from the pit, her SG tucked casually under one arm. The Original gasped, standing there weaving drunkenly, his eyes widening, his savage mouth popping open, trying to comprehend what he was seeing. Priestess fired once on xmin, and the Original's head exploded, blood and bones and brain splattering everywhere. The Original's headless body twitched once, then fell heavily to the ground. The echo of the shot rolled through the night.

The second Original scrambled frantically to his feet, thrashing around desperately in a pile of junk littering the campsite, coming up finally with a long, wicked cold knife. He was almost naked, wild hair and flashing eyes, stumbling over his own feet in a drunken panic. I had him in my sights.

Priestess dropped her SG right onto the ground, deliberately. She walked casually toward the Original and right into my line of fire. I raised my SG. What the hell?

The Original waved his knife around, frantic. Priestess came at him, swinging a right cross. I could hear her first connecting, right onto his face. He went down hard and his knife bounced away into the dark.

Dragon and the Sandman were with me now, looking around the site. There was no sign of any more Originals. Priestess was standing over the only one left.

"Get up," she said.

He was breathing hard, a ragged, rasping wheeze. He scrambled to his feet again, unarmed. Nine came at him again and hit him viciously before he could react, right in the face. He went down with a faint moan. His nose was broken. There was blood all over his face.

"Get up."

I stood over the firepit. They had cooked the other slave girl here, on a spit—Lord! I had to look away.

The Original forced himself up, trembling. Priestess kicked him right in the crotch, a tremendous kick. He squealed and jacknifed back down into the dirt. Nine was weaving, breathing shallowly, walking around him, her face cold and set.

"Get up. Get up, you pig!" She seized him by his long, wild hair and forced him to his knees. He moaned, clutching his stomach. She backed off and kicked him right in the face. It knocked him onto his back. He lay there moaning, writhing like a broken worm, gasping and coughing and spitting blood.

Priestess stood over him. "Get up. You want to die like a dog?" She kicked him again with all her might, raising dust. His ribs snapped. I could only watch, astounded, as my lovely, sweet little Priestess slowly and deliberately kicked that man to death. A cold wave crept over my flesh. What in Deadman's holy name was happening to us on this world? I had slaughtered a defenseless man, tied to a chair. And now

Priestess was deliberately kicking a man to death. Priestess, the ultimate idealist. Priestess, who had joined the Legion solely because she wanted to help.

"Does it hurt?" Priestess asked, kicking him again. He was a broken mound of flesh now, whimpering, twitching in the dirt.

I found the girl and unhooked my canteen. She was naked, on her back, her arms tied behind her. I cupped her head in one hand and touched the canteen to her lips. She sucked at it greedily. She had short blonde hair—it looked as if her head had been shaved not too long ago. Her face was swollen and covered with ugly bruises. They had certainly been beating up on her. She didn't look much like Tara's exec.

"Why..." It was the Original, twitching in the dirt, whimpering, desperate.

"We don't like you," Priestess hissed, "because you're different!" She kicked him again, hard. I turned my eyes away.

"How's the girl?" Dragon asked, approaching us.

"Looks in bad shape. This isn't her, is it?"

"Don't know."

"Damn it!"

"Don't let it drink any more," the Sandman cautioned. "That's enough for now."

"Who is this one?" I asked the Sandman. "Can we ID it?"

The Sandman bent over her. "They took the slave bracelet for the gold," he said. "We don't know who this is. Can it talk?"

Priestess kicked at the Original again, viciously. The Original was not moving any more. I got up and walked over there.

"Priestess...stop it, will you?" She breathed heavily, weaving, her eyes glazed over. I put an arm over her shoulder and led her gently away from the body. "The girl needs its help, Lady."

Priestess knelt by the girl, staring into space, still breathing hard. She was not going to be any help.

The girl's eyes flickered. She breathed shallowly. Dragon knelt by her side.

"It's all right now," I said to the girl. "It's over. Can it hear us?"

Her lips moved, but I heard nothing. "Can we give it more water?" I asked.

"Just a sip," the Sandman said. I touched the canteen to her parched, bleeding lips. She bit at it like a dog, frantic. I pulled it away.

"Please give us its name."

"...wrists." I reached behind her back and slit her bonds with a bootknife. She sighed and her arms twitched. When she brought them around to the front her wrists were bloody. I noticed the bottoms of her feet were shredded.

"Its name?" I asked again.

"Four Oh Four," she replied slowly. "Our name is Four Oh Four. They killed it—they killed Two Six Four. It was our friend—our good friend!"

"It's her, Lady!" I said excitedly. "Lady Arbell—it's her! Ranwan Lima! We've found her!"

Priestess was breathing a little easier now. "Good," she said quietly. She sounded completely exhausted.

"You're bleeding, Nine—you're wounded!" Dragon stared at his hand—it was covered in blood. He had just touched Priestess. Blood ran down the left sleeve of Priestess's field coat. We got her jacket off and examined the wound. A deep slash down her upper arm. I ripped open the civilian medkit we had purchased in Ostra Bal. My hands were shaking. If the Sandman noted Dragon calling Lady Arbell "Nine," he didn't say anything.

"It's nothing," Priestess said wearily. "Don't worry."

"Your employer," the Sandman observed quietly, "is one tough cookie."

"We know," I replied.

Chapter 17

Satan's Spawn

"It should not be much longer, Lady." Our minder from the Ministry of Reform was the same slick young man we had first run into at the site of the aircar ambush. He was not letting us out of his sight. Priestess, Dragon, and I were being held with Maralee Whitney in a VIP lounge in Katag Starport. A young Ministry of Space officer was manning the information desk. He was certainly a security official, and there was no doubt the VIP lounge was a high–class detention facility.

"Our thanks, Cit." Priestess was as cool as ice, but I was nervous and hyper. Whit, previously Ranwan Lima, now Ala–Ka–Sakara, was cruising on mags. She had sultry olive skin and wore dark glasses and a wig of curly black hair. Priestess had repaired most of the bruises on her face. Dragon was silent and moody, pacing like a caged beast. They had taken our bogus ID's and Systie travel permits. They had also confiscated our vac guns, politely but firmly. The Director of Reform, Japrad Marsh, was evidently making a major effort to get us off–world. He had provided Whit with the disguise, an excellent matching ID package and a fully–approved travel permit. However, it now appeared that a struggle was underway for our bodies.

"What do you think, Thinker?" Priestess kept her voice down.

"I think there's nothing further we can do to influence events, Priestess. We've done all we can. Now it's in the hands of the Gods."

"I think Tara's plan is working," Priestess said. "Marsh wants all that money. If we don't leave, he doesn't get it."

"We'll see."

"If they detain us, we go to the next step."

"I hope that won't be necessary." The next step involved revealing our Legion affiliation as a last desperate attempt to frighten the locals into letting us depart quietly. Nobody wanted trouble with the Legion—but we were not on an official mission; it would be sheer bluff and it could backfire badly.

"The shuttle is leaving shortly," Dragon remarked. I glanced at my chron; 1100 hours local. It did not look good.

"If this doesn't work," I told Priestess quietly, "we'll never see the light of day again."

* * *

"Its men are to stand aside, Captain, or we open fire!"

"You have no business here, mister!"

"Our men are under orders to fire if fired upon! Consider the consequences carefully, sir!" The three officers were face to face, snarling at each other. The VIP lounge was swarming with armed goons, Ministry of Space security police dressed in black, Ministry of Reform troops in prison brown, and a third gang in dark blue uniforms, squaring off against the other two groups. The soldiers bristled with arms, SG's and autosubs and vac guns. Everyone was prepped to fire; and if anyone did, it would be a bloody massacre and there would not be many survivors.

"Terrific," Dragon said glumly. The blue shirts had forced their way in first, and demanded to examine our documents. Then the Space and Reform crash teams burst in the door, attempting to eject the blues, and now it looked as if everyone was going to die. We sat in a corner, completely helpless.

"Who are these people, Cit?" I asked our Ministry of Reform minder.

"ICAC," he replied grimly. He had his handgun out and he was pale and sweating. "Independent Commission Against Corruption. They can smell money in the dark, the bastards!"

"We have every right to be here, Captain," the ICAC man was saying. He was a short, stocky man with long, slick dark hair. There was no doubt he was a professional police officer, and as single–minded as a biogen. He didn't look like the type of person who was going to back off. He waved a printout that showed Ranwan Lima, pale delicate face, short straight black hair, and smoky grey eyes. "We wish to examine these two female units! There is a stop order on this one— why so touchy, if there is nothing to hide?"

"You are on our turf, mister—back off!"

"What's the Ministry of Reform doing here anyway? This unit is wanted by the Governor, Captain! It's you who should consider the consequences!"

"That's got to be it, sir!" One of the blue shirts pointed at Whit. "The one with the dark skin—the facial structure is the same!" My adrenalin count was off the scale. I was aching to shoot him right between the eyes, but I was unarmed. Our minder was on his comset.

"It's for Cit, Sir." Our young Ministry of Reform watchdog held out the comset to the ICAC officer, who reached out for the instrument, casually brushing a gunbarrel away from his temple with his other hand. He was as cool as ice.

"This is Major Fifteen Sweet–Teal of the ICAC. Who's calling?"

"Fifteen, this is Japrad Marsh, Director of Reform. We understand there's a little problem at the starport." We could hear the Mask clearly. The VIP room was suddenly dead quiet.

"There's no problem, sir. We've just detained a wanted criminal that your Ministry was attempting to smuggle off–planet. We're just about to notify our superiors."

"Please set the comset to muffled, Major."

"Sure," the Major said. He made the adjustment. "Now, did Cit have anything further? We have a call to make."

We could not hear the response, but it was clear that the Director of Reform did have something further.

* * *

Biergart was on his knees begging for mercy, his arms tied behind him, his face drenched in sweat. I pressed the vac gun to his forehead and fired. Blood and brains splattered all over the wall and the shot was deafening. I awoke screaming, covered in icy sweat, my heart racing.

Priestess was beside me, cool arms suddenly there, a whisper of silken hair on my cheek. "It's all right, Thinker. Was it Biergart again?"

I collapsed back onto the pillow. It was dark and quiet and cool.

"Yes. It was Biergart. I shot him right in the forehead." And his eyes—they had been full of horror.

"We had no choice, Thinker. You shouldn't feel bad."

I thought about that. No, we hadn't any choice—we never had any choice. We did what we had to do. "I suppose you're right," I said. "We're rats, in a maze. It's all a cosmic joke."

"You'll feel better when we get back to Beta."

"I'll feel better when I'm dead."

"We're dead already, Thinker—everyone in the Legion is dead. You told me that yourself, remember?" Priestess was maddeningly calm. She was right, I decided. Immortal, dead—it was the same, in the Legion. We were Satan's spawn.

I hit the lights, and they came on slowly. It was a first–class cabin—the Lady Arbell would settle for nothing less. A cabin of spotless phospho white and pale rose crystal plex. It made me sick to see such waste. We were in the System Ship *Nectar*, bound for Monaro and worlds beyond. Monaro was our first port of call, and as soon as we cleared Customs there, the Mask would get his money. A King's ransom—it appeared that he had cut the anti–corruption boys in for a share of the loot, for we had been hustled onto the starship right after the Mask had spoken with the ICAC officer on the comset.

"We should thank that Warden fellow, don't you think?" Priestess asked.

"The Mask? Why thank him—he's getting a half million credits. He'd have happily popped us into a cell if somebody paid him more."

"I suppose you're right."

"Thank the Sandman, if you want to thank anyone. He found Whit for us."

"He should get the half–million—not the Mask."

"What did you give him?"

"Twenty thousand."

"Maybe Tara can come up with something extra for him."

"Did you make that call?" Priestess asked.

"I sent the message," I replied. "She'll know we're out, and headed for Monaro. Hopefully she can arrange a welcome, just in case the authorities have any reason to harass us."

"I must admit she was right. In the System, money talks."

"That's all that got us out. Tara's money—slave money."

"It's strange how things work," Priestess said sadly.

"All I want is to get back to Beta and have somebody hand me an E and point out the target," I said. "That's all I want. This civilian world is filthy. I feel unclean."

"I feel the same, Thinker. It's too complex out there. Our world is simpler."

"Yes—we're innocents, aren't we? Innocents." Professional killers, I thought, in the service of the unborn.

* * *

Tara didn't even meet us at the door when we finally made it back to her residence on Mica 3. The ape–man Gildron showed us into the sunny study overlooking the pool. Tara was there, poised by a comdesk, totally stunning and totally at ease, warm sunlight glowing off pale brown skin, lustrous auburn hair cascading down to her shoulders, a faint smile playing at her wide mouth, a warm light in her Assidic eyes.

"Well, well," she said calmly. "Welcome back, guys. Is this anyone we know?" Whit was still in her Ala–Ka–Sakara getup, olive skin, curly black hair and dark eyes.

"Hello, Cinta," Whit said timidly.

"That's a new look for Sub, isn't it?"

"We're so glad to see it, Cinta...we thought we'd never see it again."

"You've caused us a lot of trouble, Sub," Tara replied coldly.

"We're sorry, Cinta." Whit was trembling, her eyes blinking rapidly. "Did it...really pay a half million credits to get us back?"

"That will come out of your earnings, Sub. You can depend on that."

"We were foolish not to listen to it, Cinta." Tears, a river of tears, suddenly running down Whit's cheeks.

"The word is stupid. Now get to your quarters and clean up. We can talk later." Tara's face was cold and hard. Whit turned and left the room, crying silently. She looked back once at Cinta, then stumbled away.

"Weren't you a little hard on her, Tara?" I asked. "I thought you wanted her back."

Tara turned her face away from us. "Gildron," she said throatily, "bring dox."

"Are duance," Gildron replied, leaving the room. Tara turned back to face us, bravely, but she was blinking her eyes, and I could see they were wet.

"I wish to thank you all," she said. "You have restored my faith in humanity. I can't tell you how much this means to me. I thought I was completely alone. I asked for help and you came, without question, from across the galaxy. Yes, I wanted her back. When I saw her just now, I wanted to reach out and kiss her. But I don't want her to know

that. I am in your debt, Beta Three. I am in debt to all of you. This kind
of debt can never be repaid. The three of you have a claim on me,
forever. If you ever need help, just call me. I'll come—you can bet your
life on it!" A shudder ran over her slim body.

I was exhausted. Gildron came back with hot dox. My hands
trembled as I opened the top. I could still see Biergart, sweating in the
dark.

* * *

"This is hopeless! There's nothing going there!" I was at the
comdesk in my room, scanning for a fast route back to Veda 6. It was
another hazy golden summer day outside the window for Mica 3.

"There has to be something!" Priestess said. "We've got to get back
to Beta."

"There's a lot of activity out there, but nothing seems to be going
near Veda Six. There's a routine supply run, but that's not for another
two weeks—we can't wait that long!"

"That's a ten," Priestess said.

"Alert, Gang," Dragon said, popping into the doorway. "Check out
the local infonet on Fourteen. Ask for the news."

I hit the tab and the wall screen flashed and revealed a female news
announcer, the background showing a pale, icy green planet girdled
with a series of sparkling silvery rings. It was so utterly lovely and
captivating that the words she was saying did not at first make any
sense.

"First in the news, the Confederation has announced a major new
military offensive against the Omni horde. According to a Starcom
information bulletin released today, strong Legion units have dropped
onto Uldo Four, a System world under Omni attack, to counter the
Omni advance into Systie vac. The ConFree announcement stated that
the Legion offensive was a joint operation in cooperation with Systie
DefCorps units. This is the first joint Legion–DefCorps operation
against the Omni threat, and may mark a significant new chapter in
humanity's response to the alien challenge."

"Deadman!" I was transfixed before the screen.

"That's it," Dragon said from the doorway. "That's the offensive
Snow Leopard was waiting for."

"We've got to get out of here—now!" Priestess stood up.

"Uldo," I said. "You can bet we're bound for Uldo."

"Maybe or maybe not," Dragon said, "but Beta's on Veda Six, and we'd better get our asses back there on antimat drive, or Snow Leopard's going to feed us to the bloodcats."

"What are we going to do, Thinker?" Priestess asked.

* * *

I found Tara that evening outside in the flowerhouse. It was almost midnight, and I hadn't found a ride to Veda 6. The night was soft and warm and the sky was full of stars. The flowerhouse was a wooden pavilion, heavy with exotic blooms, a rich musk saturating the air. Tara was a shadow, alone with the flowers, looking into the dark.

"Hello, Wester." She didn't even look at me, but she knew it was me. She always knew.

"Tara—what are you doing?"

"I'm thinking, Wester."

"You obviously work for a different Legion than I do. We're not encouraged to think. How's Whit doing?"

"She's fine. She'll be all right."

"We're having a little trouble getting transportation back to the Veda System," I said. "You know, our status limits what we can do on our own. I was wondering if you had any Legion contacts who could get us a non–sked to Veda, or anywhere nearby."

Tara didn't answer at first. She just continued gazing out into the night. Finally she spoke. "You know what I was thinking?"

"No—what were you thinking?"

"I was thinking that I have absolutely no control over my own destiny. Do you remember when I was your girl?"

Memories from another world, another time, light–years in the past. I had tried hard to forget her but had never succeeded. "Yes," I said. "I remember."

"We were so innocent, weren't we? We were children, playing at life. None of it was real, was it?"

"Maybe not to you—it seemed pretty real to me."

"Do you love Priestess?"

"Is this some kind of trick question?"

"No, I was just wondering."

"How about you, Tara? Don't you have a lover? You're certainly not alone in this world—I can't imagine that."

She smiled. Still not looking at me. "Sure—I've got Gildron. He's my live–in."

"Gildron! You're not serious. You can't be serious!"

"He's a real man," Tara said dreamily, "and he knows how to treat a woman. I feel so helpless when I'm in his arms."

"You must be insane! You mean you let that ape..."

A little–girl laugh, a squeal of pure delight, and it was the Tara I had known all those years ago. "He fell for it! I always could rattle your cage, couldn't I, Wester? You still believe everything I say!"

"All right, you got me again." I was positively relieved. Gildron! Idiocy.

"My work keeps me very busy, Wester. I have no time for nonsense. But even if it were true about Gildron, who are you to object? You have an alien lover, don't you?"

Tara always took my breath away. I knew she was psychic, but I was always surprised when she demonstrated it. "She's not an alien," I replied quietly. "Moontouch is as human as we are." I was always on the defensive with Tara. Moontouch was an ache in my heart. You can't have lovers in the Legion—they are torn right from your arms.

"And she's had your baby—hasn't she?"

"That's right." I looked around nervously.

"That's a big responsibility, Wester. I'd be disappointed in you if you didn't do what was right."

"It's not always clear what's right."

"On the contrary, I've found that the most important issues are rarely that complicated."

"I'm glad everything is so clear to you. It must be a great comfort when you're delivering a cargo of slaves to some Systie rat–hole."

At first she did not respond. Then she sighed. "We all serve the same master, Wester, according to our abilities. My doubts are long gone. I'm on a mission from God." She sounded deadly serious, but with Tara I never knew.

"Well, could you ask God to get us to Veda Six?"

She turned to look at me, soft liquid eyes and a cascade of silky hair. "Sure." She picked up a starlink and activated it. Only Tara would be contemplating flowers in the night with a starlink by her side. The d–screen flickered and a face appeared. It was her Cyrillian security chief, jet black skin, cold slit eyes and sharpened white teeth.

"Pandaros, how's it going up there?" Tara asked.

"Fine, Commander. All quiet."

"Well, get the *Maiden* warmed up. Recall the crew—now. We're going on a little trip."

"Right away, Commander! When do we leave?"

"Can it get the crew back in four hours?"

"Whatever it says, Commander! We are all anxious to leave!" The *Maiden*'s crew was on the Legion death list, I recalled. A visit to a Legion planet was probably not their idea of a good time.

"All right, do it. We leave in four hours."

"Done!" Tara broke the connection, and the screen faded. A soft, warm breeze washed over us. It was a spectacular night.

"I can't ask you to do that, Tara."

"You didn't ask."

"It's not your ship, Tara—I know that much. You can't just take off on a joy–ride to Veda Six because we want to go there."

"You just watch me."

"But what about your responsibilities? What about that mission from God?"

"Pack your bags. I'm taking you to Veda Six." She stood up, looking past me, somewhere off in space.

"The Legion will have your head."

"They can burn in hell!" Her eyes were blazing.

* * *

"God! This is incredible!" I exclaimed. Stars, wheeling slowly overhead. A frozen night of icy stars, glowing red and golden nebulae, blue hot supernovas crackling a million light years away—an infinity of green gas and silver dust. Starstuff, awesome, magnificent. Meteors, streaking down from the heavens. The music of the stars rumbled away in the background, an awesome symphony, hot young stars screeching in agony, black holes booming out their deadly heartbeats, the voice of the cosmos, popping and snapping and whistling, running over my flesh with a little chill.

"It's beautiful!" Priestess whispered. We were together in the pleasure palace, floating on an airbed in one of Tara's sex cubes, going first class all the way to Veda 6 on the starship *Maiden*. We could do anything we wanted in that cube, but I liked the stars best of all.

The meteor shower continued. It put a chill to my flesh. I was naked, feverish and dizzy. We had been making love for hours. We could not stop. Priestess was so slim and lovely and vulnerable I could not keep my hands off her. She was a sex child, all long legs and arms and tousled dark hair and limpid eyes and yielding lips.

"Will you take off that thing?" I pleaded again. Priestess was naked except for a loose sleeveless top that she refused to remove.

"Kiss me," she whispered. I lost myself again in her sweet mouth. Starstuff, we were starstuff, floating in space.

"Come on, take it off," I insisted, caressing her breasts under the shirt.

"No. It's ugly. I want you to remember me the way I was before." Priestess had been hit on Mongera, point–blank auto x, and almost died. They had rebuilt her breasts, but the scars were extensive.

"I told you, Priestess—it's the mark of the Legion. It shows what you gave for humanity. It's something holy and beautiful. You shouldn't be ashamed to show your wounds. It's a badge of honor."

"No—it's ugly."

"It doesn't bother me! If it bothers you so much, why didn't you have it done back on Atom?"

"There was no time. Beta was off to Veda, and I didn't want to be left behind."

"Then it wasn't that important, was it?"

"Bet you can't make love again."

"Oh yeah? Well, that's up to you."

"To me? Me? Really? What do I have to do?" Another burst of silver meteors, shooting down from a starry sky. It was like a dream—a wonderful dream.

* * *

Veda 6 appeared on screen, a heavenly orb, phospho blue, brilliant polar ice caps glowing white, the filmy skin of atmosphere showing clearly against the black of space. I had to turn my eyes away—it was simply too much. When you saw it from space, it became awesomely clear just how fragile was our position in the universe. We were pond scum, wriggling in a thin sheet of life. Every inhabitable world was precious, as our race exploded into the dark. I knew it could all end in a cosmic instant, unless we were stronger and faster than everything else that was out there.

We contacted Veda Station as soon as we exited stardrive. A very young Legionnaire appeared on the screen as we watched behind Tara and Whit in the command chairs. We had never seen him before.

"This is Veda Station," the kid said. "Repeat your call sign please."

"This is the Personal Ship *Maiden*," I said. "Can you patch us through to Beta One, please."

"Who?"

"Beta One of CAT Two Four, Second of Atom's Road, Twelfth of the Twenty-second. Say, what's the story there? We've got three Beta troopers who want to rejoin their squad."

"Atom's Road! Sorry, guys, your squad is long gone, and so is your ship. Hold on, though, we've got a message for you somewhere."

"A message. Terrific." We were stunned by the news.

"We are in deep fecmat, guys," Dragon said.

"Something wrong?" Whit leaned back over the exec's chair. Her skin was its natural pale color again, and her own blonde hair was starting to grow back. It was still so short she looked like a boy.

"Yeah, I knew it was here. Stand by," the kid said. The screen flashed and Snow Leopard appeared suddenly, his pale face expressionless, his pink eyes focused right on us.

"Nice of you to drop by," he said quietly. "If you're listening to me now, it means you've made it back to Veda Six. That's good, but not as good as it could be. Our new mission is Uldo Four. Beta is understrength and we need you as soon as you can get there. I don't care how you do it—just get there! We'll be waiting. Your mission orders are attached. Beta One signing off."

The mission orders materialized in the doc tray. I called the young Legionnaire right back. "We need fast transportation to Uldo, trooper," I said. "What's available?"

"Sorry, Beta, there's nothing at all. Everything that could move is already on the way there. We're pretty much marooned here until the sit changes. Let's see...there's a supply run due here in two weeks—they're going on to the Meco Sector. That would put you in the general vicinity."

"Thanks—it won't do."

"We could use some extra help down here, guys—it's a bit quiet, but it's honest work."

"We'll let you know." I cut the transmission.

"Do we need another taxi ride?" Whit asked brightly.

Tara turned, and looked back over her shoulder. "We'll set a course for Uldo."

"Wait a frac, Cinta," I said. "We certainly appreciate your help, but you'll lose your ship if you show up at Uldo. A major Legion op is like a black hole—it sucks up everything around it. They'll confiscate the *Maiden*, and you'll be lucky to ever get it back."

"We know all about the Legion," Tara replied. "And we assure you we always know exactly what we're doing."

"Goodness gracious," Whit smiled, "So our guests are staying! That's nice!" She shot a knowing glance at Eight. He gave her a wolfish grin.

Uldo, I thought—we're bound for Uldo. They had mentioned Uldo in Basic, but I couldn't remember what they had said. Something historical—what was it? I knew nothing about Uldo.

"Set course for Uldo," Tara instructed the ship.

Uldo 4, I thought—a System world, under attack by the O's. And the Legion was intervening, with the System's open agreement. That was a first. Hadn't the Legion learned yet that Systies are not to be trusted? They had betrayed us on Mongera!

"This is the big one," Dragon said. "This is where we stop the O's— or they stop us."

A historical mission. The survival, or the end, of humanity. That's what was at stake, I knew, on Uldo. But I didn't care about history any more—I cared only about Beta. How many dead so far? And how many more dead, for Uldo? I felt trapped and doomed and helpless, rushing onward to certain destruction, caught up in a cosmic typhoon, a galactic maelstrom of catastrophic, uncontrollable events. We were just like ants, fighting for our nests. Will it really make any difference to the galaxy, who wins and who loses? No. But it will make a difference to us.

"I heard Uldo Four is already lost," Priestess whispered. "Millions of O's have landed; the locals are being overwhelmed."

"We'll fix that," Dragon replied confidently.

The Omnis—they were a galactic curse. They had appeared as if from nowhere, invincible, merciless alien extremists with a brutal star fleet and seemingly endless resources, psychers with extraordinary powers swarming over world after world, focused only on exterminating human beings. Two billion humans had been killed so far.

We had faced one O on Mongera, and almost perished. We would be facing a whole army of O's on Uldo. I didn't even want to think about it. We're insane, I thought, the Legion is insane. We never beat the O's before; what makes them think we can do it now?

"I'll be right by your side, Thinker," Priestess said. She knew what I was thinking. Yes, we'd be together when we died. With luck, we'd be buried in Uldo's rocky soil, with maybe a Legion cross to mark the spot. Here they lie, two Legion immortals, crossed over to the other side, to fight Heaven's wars.

Immortality and death—that was what the Legion promised, and delivered. My blood was running cold. Uldo! I closed my eyes. My heart was pounding. Let it come. I'm a soldier of the Legion. I'm ready to die. I'm ready for anything! Deadman, do your damndest! I'll follow my orders to the death!

END OF THE BLACK MARCH.
(To be continued in *Slave of the Legion*)

GLOSSARY

ConFree Handbook
313 CGS

Welcome

to the Confederation of Free Worlds (ConFree). The citizens of ConFree greet you in friendship, and wish you a pleasant and productive visit. Your itinerary is designed to familiarize you with ConFree's society, history and government, as well as any specialized subjects in which you have declared an interest. We are proud of our Confederation and welcome information requests from both the System and unaligned worlds.

Your official guide is a ConFree citizen and a Government official. Your guide will answer any questions not covered in this handbook. The handbook covers basic facts regarding ConFree. We suggest you read it prior to commencing your tour. Please try to keep an open mind. You will find that the truth about ConFree is not what you were taught in System or USICOM worlds.

History

ConFree was founded by Outworlder refugees who fled the Inners to escape oppression and slavery under the United System Alliance (the System). They settled in the Crista Cluster on the edge of the Outvac, some 1,400 light years from the Inners. The early Outworlder pioneers were fiercely independent individualists who had personally suffered greatly at the hands of a tyrannical regime, and were deeply suspicious of organized government. They had also been fleeing racial extermination by the System, which viewed Outworlders as a dangerous gene pool fostering political resistance to the System's centralized control. These settlers found scores of habitable worlds in the Crista Cluster and formed independent governments on each world, wanting only to be left alone to live in peace. When the System launched slave raids and attempted to expand its zone of control into the Crista Cluster, however, the settlers quickly organized, forming the Confederation of Free Worlds in Year One, ConFree Galactic Standard (CGS).

ConFree's first act was to draw up a Constitution designed primarily to ensure that the government would never terrorize its citizens (see Constitution). The second act was to form Fleetcom and the ConFree Legion (see Fleetcom, Legion). With these instruments, ConFree was able to eventually repel Starfleet and the DefCorps, with great loss of life on both sides (see 'Conflict with the United System Alliance,' below). Our history reveals our character: we are extremists who worship freedom and independence and despise tyranny, while realizing that only through united resolve and violent action can we guarantee our independence and liberty in a hostile galaxy. Thus came about ConFree's unique blend of personal freedom and personal responsibility. We are proud of our history and our institutions and we apologize to no one.

Constitution

The ConFree Constitution was written in blood by a free people originally representing 21 free and independent Crista Cluster worlds. The Confederation of Free Worlds is a voluntary association from which any member world can withdraw at any time should they lose faith in ConFree leadership. The ConFree Constitution and Bill of Rights guarantees ConFree citizens the right to overthrow a tyrannical government, the right to bear arms, the right to free speech, the right to justice, the right to vote and representation, the right to private property, the right to education, the right and duty to serve the people, and the duty to remain informed. ConFree civilians do not have a right to vote and representation, nor the duties to serve the people or to remain informed, but have all other rights. Citizenship is conferred after six years of community or military service to the people, and all civilians are eligible to volunteer. The ConFree Constitution guarantees member worlds the right to secede at will. None have as yet done so. ConFree's history has demonstrated that eternal vigilance is the price of liberty.

Citizens and Civilians

As noted above, ConFree citizenship is a right which is earned by service to the people of ConFree. All civilians are eligible. Those who volunteer, generally to a term in the ConFree Legion, earn their citizenship by putting their lives on the line to protect the people of ConFree. Those who choose not to do so are guaranteed a prosperous and secure life on a ConFree world, and are not thought less of, but cannot claim a right to shape our future.

Society

ConFree is a largely homogeneous society, consisting of descendants of the original Outworlder race, with healthy infusions of Assidic genes as well. We have a common language, history, beliefs, similar genetic background and vision for the future. The mission of the Outworlder race is to secure a prosperous and secure future for our children. We do not encourage efforts to introduce non-Outworlder peoples into ConFree who do not share our background and beliefs. However, everyone is welcome to volunteer for service in the ConFree Legion and earn ConFree citizenship. We welcome as brothers and sisters all who stand the night watch with us.

Outworlders and Assidics

The Outworlder race is descended from the original pioneers who opened up the outer reaches of what later became the United System Alliance. These Outworlder people fought bravely against Saka the Invincible and the Assidic Empire when it initially expanded into the Inners. As the situation stabilized and the decaying Assidic Empire was replaced by the System slave state, both Outworlders and Assidics found common cause against System oppression. Outworlder-Assidic intermarriage became common on frontier worlds, and a new race slowly evolved. Although still known as 'Outworlders,' a high percentage of our people have Assidic genes, even those who appear to be of 'pure' Outworlder stock. Outworlders and Assidics now have similar beliefs and goals, and a shared opposition to System tyranny.

Government

At the top of our Chain of Command are the citizens of ConFree. ConFree member worlds send representatives to the ConFree Council, which elects an Executive Council. The ConFree Council and the Executive Council are volunteers in service to the people of ConFree. Their decisions must be based solely on the best interests of the people of ConFree. It is a grave responsibility, and all Council members know the penalty for failure is death. At the bottom of the Chain of Command is the Legion trooper, who marches in the mud for the people of ConFree, and dies for them if necessary.

Justice and Law

ConFree is focused on justice, not on laws. The ConFree Constitution is the only law. There are no formal Confederation law statutes. Juries of ConFree citizens are empowered to render decisions on justice, based on local legal statutes and local customs on ConFree member worlds. Local statutes are only guidelines for the jurists, who are concerned with rendering justice, not enforcing laws. All ConFree citizens and civilians are guaranteed justice by the people and government of ConFree. The pursuit of justice is one of our people's most important concerns, and it is driven by our history. We believe it is obscene and immoral to have to expend personal funds to secure justice. Any attempt to purchase favorable judgments is itself a crime in ConFree. Interstellar travelers describing themselves as "lawyers" are detained upon entering ConFree vac, and deported after interrogation.

Crime

Crime is virtually unknown on ConFree worlds, due largely to our homogeneous society and shared heritage and goals. When crime does occur, guilt or innocence is quickly determined by modern mindscans. Punishment is swift and harsh. Juries of ConFree citizens vote on punishment, as there is generally little question about guilt. Those who commit violent crimes are often executed in a manner befitting the crime. Convicted violent criminals who are not executed are often sent into exile, never to return to ConFree. Those found guilty of lesser crimes may be sentences to confinement at hard labor, but generally for not more than two years. ConFree does not warehouse prisoners, nor reward them with free room and board. ConFree guarantees security for both citizens and civilians. It guarantees only instant justice for criminals. Legion military justice is handled by courts martial and is equally harsh on troopers who disobey orders.

Economy and Government Revenue

ConFree's booming economy is based on a private enterprise system that has unleashed the innate productivity of a free people. ConFree's industrial base and scientific creativity has created unparalleled wealth and prosperity for her people, and the highest living standard in history. The ConFree Constitution forbids any form of slavery including Voluntary Servitude and tax slavery. ConFree citizens do not pay taxes on legitimate personal income. We regard taxation of the earnings of one's own nationals as tyranny and slavery. ConFree government revenue originates primarily from tariff charges on interstellar imports into ConFree vac. Access to ConFree's market guarantees high profits for all involved and the tariffs from these interstellar imports assure a healthy yearly budget surplus. ConFree welcomes trading relations with all worlds, including the System. A consumption tax on luxury goods is permitted, as the purchase of luxury goods is voluntary, but the ConFree Constitution limits this tax to one percent of the cost of the item. Any proposal to raise this tax will trigger charges of high treason against the perpetrator. ConFree believes that government financial needs must be met by cutting government expenses, not by penalizing ConFree nationals. ConFree also engages in the mining of precious metals and strategic minerals, and the gold mines of Guarados serve to back Legion Credmarks. ConFree recognizes the historical dangers of high living standards and we remain always vigilant to all threats to our future, both internal and external.

Money and Banking

Outworlders have a historical aversion to fiat plastic and credit money because of financial collapses associated with these failed monetary instruments during generations of System misrule. ConFree mandates a currency backed 100% by precious metals. The current standard is gold. The result has been the strongest currency in the galaxy, and the universal acceptance of Legion Credmarks, even in the System. The ConFree Treasury and banking system is controlled by the government and people of ConFree, not by private bankers. Usury and any form of interest slavery are illegal.

Fleetcom

ConFree's battle-proven Fleetcom has demonstrated strategic superiority over both the System's Starfleet and the Omni Deathfleet. Fleetcom is ConFree's first line of defense against external aggression. Without our Fleetcom warriors and techs manning the frontier of the Outers, ConFree would perish. The people of ConFree recognize this and ensure that Fleetcom has all the resources necessary to ensure continuing galactic supremacy for our star fleet.

The Legion

The ConFree Legion is the ultimate expression of ConFree resolve and is the ultimate guarantor of ConFree independence. The Legion has a long and illustrious history. Anyone, citizen, civilian, or alien, can enlist in the ConFree Legion. ConFree's enemies know that the Legion is a formidable foe, who will fight for victory or death. Legion tradition reminds all troopers of the Eighth Legion, which fought to the death on Uldo against a vastly superior DefCorps army. Although the Legion is a fearsome fighting force, System hateprop regarding the Legion is just that, propaganda. Legion troopers are not biogens, they are not ex-criminals, they do not eat babies, they do not loot, rape or murder civilians, and they do not serve indefinitely. They are all free volunteers, and can leave the Legion upon expiration of their term of enlistment, generally six stellar years. Legion discipline is strong, hardship is common, but criminality in the Legion is rare. We are proud of our troopers.

Immortality

ConFree science has relegated aging and natural death into the pages of the history books. The control of the human body has resulted in the extension of a youthful, productive life virtually forever. All Legion recruits are rendered immortal upon enlistment. Despite this, Legion recruits often have short life spans – immortality does not ward off bullets.

Faith

The Cult of the Deadman thrives in the Legion, and sustains our troopers in their perilous endeavors. Deadman is a symbolic representation of all the Legion troopers who have died for the cause. The Legion Monument to the Dead lists every trooper who died for the Legion, and is reproduced in holo in every Legion chapel.

The Cross of the Legion

When the first Outworlder refugees approached the Outvac fleeing System oppression, the Crista Cluster beckoned them onwards with a view that appeared to form a mystical, starry cross in the vac. The Legion cross was later adopted as the symbol of ConFree. ConFree's ancestors settled those worlds as a free people and vowed in a Constitution written in blood to uphold liberty, justice and freedom, no matter what the cost, and to remain eternally vigilant against all forms of tyranny and slavery. The ConFree Legion was formed to accomplish those objectives. In the above view, the CS Atom's Road cruises the Outvac with her four cruisers escorting her.

Legion Chant

The Legion chant originated during the war of ConFree Independence. It serves as the oath of enlistment for the Legion trooper. System hateprop has distorted the meaning of the chant, especially the phrase 'I believe in Evil.' What it means is that ConFree and the Legion have confronted Evil, and know that it is real. The phrase 'I will deliver us from Evil' reveals our intent.

Battle Chant of the Legion

"I am a Soldier of the Legion.
    I believe in Evil -
    The survival of the strong
    And the death of the weak.
    I am the guardian.
    I am the sword of light
    In the dark of the night.
    I will deliver us from Evil.

"I accept life everlasting
    And the death of my past.
    I will trust no Earther worm
    Nor any mortal man,
    But only the mark of the Legion.
    I have burnt the book of laws
    To serve the Deadman's cause
    As a soldier of the Legion."

"I am the slave of the Future
    At the gateway to the stars,
    Where I can see - Eternity.
    For I walk in the shadow of death
    And yet I fear no Evil
    For I am the light in the dark
    I am the watch on the mark
    I am a soldier of the Legion."

"I will have no talk with Evil.
    The arts of death are the tools of life
    And in the end I will send
    A maxburst to advise
    The O's come by surprise
    And though we kill them where they stand,
    We know it's death's dark land
    For a soldier of the Legion."

Conflict with the United System Alliance

Throughout ConFree's over 300 years of history, interstellar conflict with the System has been a continuing theme. The War of ConFree Independence was followed by the Yellow War, the Popex and the Race Wars, in which ConFree successfully resisted System efforts to populate the Crista Cluster and the Outvac with their surplus population while eradicating the Outworlder race. ConFree has made it clear to the System that any infringements of ConFree sovereignty will result in an immediate response. The System represents the very antithesis of ConFree: slavery vs freedom, totalitarianism vs constitutional rule, empire and expansion vs free association, the dead hand of the past vs the promise of the future. The System makes their children pay for their sins, while we are willing to die to ensure our childrens' future security. We believe history is with us, and that the petrified fossil of the System slave state is in its death throes.

Conflict with the Omnis

The O's are a very real threat and the current hiatus in aggression will surely not last. Our ancestors died by the billions in combating these dangerous alien warriors of immense psychic powers. For 300 years the Legion has served as humanity's trip wire against the encroachment of these alien hordes. During the Plague War, Fleetcom outfought the Omni starships, and forced them into retreat, at a fearsome toll in human lives. When the O's move again ConFree, Fleetcom and the Legion will be there, whether or not the population of the Inners is still taught history.

Slavery

ConFree and the Legion fight tyranny and slavery, without compromise. We regard the System's so-called Voluntary Servitude and taxation slavery as equally as repugnant and odious as involuntary slavery. Any incursions into ConFree vac by slavers are countered immediately by Fleetcom, and result in the immediate execution of the slavers and the freeing of the slaves.

The people of ConFree want only to live in peace, but they will never compromise their independence and will always respond vigorously to any threats to their sovereignty. We hope you enjoy your visit to ConFree.

A Legion trooper died for you today. The Legion needs volunteers for the ConFree Legion. Everyone is welcome. We offer blood, sweat, tears, miserable living conditions, mediocre food, immortality and the best weaponry in the galaxy. Your reward is a chance to shape a better future for your children, and the respect of all ConFree when you become a citizen. Volunteer today, and serve the Deadman's cause as a Soldier of the Legion.

United System Alliance – Ministry of Truth

Date: 1444/01/45
To: All Ports of Entry – Inners, Gulf, Gassies / System, USICOM, All Milzones

Subject: United System Alliance – A Brief Summary for Visitors

Following is for distribution to ALL repeat ALL non-citizen visitors arriving at System Ports of Entry.

The United System Alliance – A Brief Summary

for Visitors

Welcome to the United System Alliance. We hope it had a pleasant journey and we extend fraternal greetings from our State and People. Because of extensive hateprop disseminated by the CrimCon, we find it necessary to assist all visitors in understanding the truth about our thriving galactic society, a showcase for true democracy and equality.

The United System Alliance – a Democratic Empire

The United System Alliance (the System) is a universal, social democratic empire based on Goodlib humanitarian, egalitarian ideals and embracing over half of the inhabited galaxy. All of the Inners and almost all Gulf and Gassies worlds fall under the System's Rule of Law. Only the Outers worlds of the Criminal Conspiracy (CrimCon) still reject democratic ideals. The System represents galactic equality for all, and is the last best hope of everyone who embraces true equality and rejects false doctrines of individuality and greed.

Citizenship – A Mass Democracy

In System social democracy, citizenship is open to all, voting is universal and compulsory, and there are no class distinctions. We proudly contrast our egalitarian ideals to those of the CrimCon, where citizenship is the prerogative of a privileged class, and non-citizens do not even have the right to vote on matters affecting their future. Under the System, everyone votes, without age or other limitations. On Voting Day, the incarcerated, those with mental issues, schoolchildren and alien visitors all participate in choosing our government. The result is a progressive society in which there is a surprising degree of unanimity. Although anyone is free to contest the System, official candidates routinely poll above 98 percent of the vote.

Voluntary Servitude – A Public Duty

Voluntary Servitude (VS) is the foundation of the System and is based on the cooperative, egalitarian spirit that System citizens have always possessed. VS is a decision of the highest Goodlib morality in which the individual voluntarily embraces the interests of the State and the People above selfish personal needs. Through VS, the State is able to accomplish public projects that could never be considered in a society based on individual greed. Those citizens who volunteer for VS are honored by the State for their decision to dedicate their life to serving the State and the People.

Directed Service – Reform and Rehabilitation

As in every society, a handful of malcontents and alien subversives make efforts to wreck and sabotage our smoothly-running democracy. Unlike the CrimCon, we deal humanely with such incorrigibles through Directed Service (DS). After a period of patient psymed reform and rehabilitation (RR), DS units serve the people voluntarily alongside their VS colleagues, helping to strengthen the society they had formerly opposed.

Rule of Law – Equality for All

Under System rule, we are all equal, and any disagreements that arise are settled by the Rule of Law. Whether it is a citizen seeking compensation from another citizen who appears to possess more, or a citizen accused of wealth or elitist thoughtcrime, the Rule of Law will determine the result fairly and redistribute any inequality. Law is our most highly respected profession, the Rule of Law is sacrosanct, and State Lawyers settle all disputes.

Coping with Violence

The System views violence as the inevitable product of the remnants of inequality still present in our society. We do not punish those social victims who resort to violence through frustration, but concentrate our efforts on the targets of the violence. We have found these units are invariably guilty of thoughtcrime, and we detain them for observation and psymed reform when appropriate. As a reminder to visitors, it is highly illegal to resist violence, and when approached by a citizen seeking redistribution, it is mandatory to comply.

Voluntary Contributions – Funding True Equality

No society can function without an efficient Government, and no Government can function without adequate funds to compensate the Administration and constantly redistribute society's wealth to maintain true equality. This is especially true in a universal democratic empire such as the System. Our citizens understand the need for Voluntary Contribution (VC) of funds to the Ministry of Distribution. The current VC rate is 82 percent of income, and it funds a great many important programs demanded by our citizens.

Education – Social Responsibility

In the System, education is mandatory and universal through midschool. The Ministry of Youth focuses on producing good citizens who embrace democratic ideals. The Ministry does not teach the discredited facts-skills-history model but molds young minds to embrace our democratic ideals. Those youth with the highest social consciousness are sponsored into higher education to serve the State.

Health for All

The System is proud of its universal health care, available at no cost to all from the Ministry of Health. Our citizens have repeatedly affirmed their preference for security over individualism, and the State guarantees health and security for all..

Galactic Defense – Resisting the CrimCon

Because of continuing aggression from the CrimCon, based in the Outers, the System is forced to maintain a strong military posture throughout the Inners, the Gulf and the Gassies. Under the Ministry of Peace, our Defense Command (DEFCOM) directs our forces with the cooperation of the United System Interstellar Commission (USICOM) and the United System Defense Alliance (USDA), both representing allied worlds. DEFCOM commands both the Defense Corps (DefCorps) and Starfleet, consisting of our stellar infantry strike forces and our galactic navy. The STRATCOM Information Service is another important element in maintaining galactic peace. Starfleet and the DefCorps have repeatedly defeated the ConFree Legion and the CrimCon's Fleetcom, but the CrimCon continues its reckless and frantic provocations designed to plunge the galaxy into a general war. The System is pledged to resist these piratical attacks. Every System citizen should never forget that the CrimCon betrayed humanity by allying itself with the remnants of the Assidic Empire, and did its best to destroy the System, threatening all humanity at a critical point in galactic development. More recently, while our forces were bravely resisting the onslaught of the Variant hordes, the CrimCon attempted to ally itself with these merciless alien marauders. Although they call themselves the ConFree (Confederation of Free Worlds), the CrimCon is neither a confederation nor is it free. It is a genocidal, dictatorial gang of mercenary anarchists, motivated by loot and greed.

The Ministry of Truth wishes it a pleasant day.

Major ConFree, System and Unaligned Worlds

Name	Sector	Aligned	Society
Alana	Crista	ConFree	Free. CCR. Frontier world
Alphard/Oasis	Inners	System	Slave. AT/LCC/VS/DS/VC. Pacified/enslaved by System.
Alshana	Gassies	System	Uninhabited/proscribed. Pirate haven.
Andrion 2	Outvac	ConFree	Martial law. Legion expeditionary colony 312 CGS.
Andrion 3	Outvac	ConFree	Martial law. Uninhabited volcanic exoseg world.
Angaroth	Gulf	System	Slave. AT/LCC/DS/VC.
Aran	Crista	ConFree	Free. CCR. Frontier world.
Ardoth	Inners	System	Slave. AT/LCC/VS/DS/VC.
Asumara	Gulf	System	Slave. AT/LCC/VS/VC.
Augusta	Crista	ConFree	Free. CCR.
Auraga	Crista	ConFree	Free. CCR. Fleetcom transportation hub.
Berichros	Inners	System	Slave. AT/LCC/VS/DS/VC. Feudal villages of native dwarfs.
Calgoran 2	Inners	System	Slave. AT/LCC/VS/DS/VC.
Camelora 7	Crista	ConFree	Free. CCR.
Capella	Crista	ConFree	Free. CCR. Frontier world.
Chudit/Rima 2	Nulls	N/A	Unsurveyed.
Coldmark/Sista Alpha	Gassies	System	USICOM. AT/LCC/VS/DS/VC. System ward.
Cyrilia	Inners	System	Slave. AT/LCC/DS/VC. Pacified/enslaved by System.
Dardos	Inners	System	Slave. AT/LCC/VS/DS/VC. Loyal System slave world.
Dindabai	Outvac	ConFree	Martial law.
Elidos	Inners	System	Slave. AT/LCC/VS/DS/VC. Loyal System slave world.
Guarados	Crista	ConFree	Free. CCR.
Hell/The Tomb	Crista	ConFree	Martial law. Legion ACT.
Kalalan	Nulls	N/A	See Odura.
Katag 2	Gassies	System	Slave. AT/LCC/VS/DS/VC.
Korkush	Crista	ConFree	Free. CCR.
Kotazh	Gulf	System	Slave. AT/LCC/VS/DS/VC.
Luyten	Inners	System	Slave. AT/LCC/VS/DS/VC.
Magna 4	Crista	ConFree	Free. CCR. Mining of strategic minerals.
Marala 5	Crista	ConFree	Free. CCR.
Mica 3	Crista	ConFree	Free. CCR.
Monaro	Gassies	System	Slave. AT/LCC/VS/DS/VC.
Mongera	Gassies	System	Slave. AT/LCC/VS/DS/VC.
Nimbos	Gulf	System	Slave. AT/LCC/VS/DS/VC.
Odura/Kalalan	Nulls	N/A	Unsurveyed.
Orm	Inners	System	Slave. AT/LCC/VS/DS/VC.
Picos	Inners	System	Slave. AT/LCC/VS/DS/VC.
Pherdos	Gassies	System	USICOM. Sustem ward. AT/LCC/VS/VC.
Pleiades	Inners	System	Slave. AT/LCC/VS/DS/VC. Cluster of System worlds.
Quaba 7	Crista	ConFree	Free. CCR. Hqs Fleetcom.
Rana 2/Torat	Nulls	N/A	Unsurveyed.
Rima 2	Nulls	N/A	See Chudit.
Sagitta Sprial/Sector	Nulls	N/A	Unsurveyed.
Santos	Gulf	System	Slave. AT/LCC/VS/DS/VC.
Sarana	Crista	ConFree	Free. CCR.

Sista Alpha			See Coldmark.
Sirrah	Gulf	System	USICOM. System ward. AT/LCC/VS/DS/VC.
Sol	Inners	System	Slave. AT/LCC/VS/DS/VC. Mankind's origin.
Spartos	Inners	System	Slave. AT/LCC/VS/DS/VC. System capital.
Tanami 7	Gulf	Neutral	Religious settlement.
Uldo 4	Gassies	System	Slave. AT/LCC/VS/DS/VC. Site of the Cauldron.
Veda 6	Outvac	ConFree	Free. CCR. Frontier world. Minos Station.
Veltros/The Womb	Crista	ConFree	Free. CCR. Providence , site of Legion basic training.
Veronica 2	Crista	ConFree	Free. CCR.
Yida	Gulf	System	Slave. AT/LCC/VS/DS/VC.

KEY :

Slave = System rule, Anarcho-Tyranny, government directs people. Insecure, crime-ridden, violent, extreme poverty, lawyers/criminals rule.

Free = ConFree rule, Citizens' Constitutional Republic, people direct government. Secure, crime-free, peaceful, prosperous, lawyers/criminals proscribed.

AT = Anarcho-Tyranny

CCR = Citizens' Constitutional Republic

LCC = Lawyer-Criminal Conspiracy

VS = Voluntary Service

DS = Directed Servitude

VC = Voluntary Contributions

Martial Law = Military rule

USICOM = United System Interstellar Commission (System front).

Printed in the United States
120388LV00003B/212/A

9 781601 451002